# ADDIS ABABA NOIR

## EDITED BY MAAZA MENGISTE

BROOKLYN, NEW YORK

Published by Akashic Books
©2020 Akashic Books

Series concept by Tim McLoughlin and Johnny Temple
Addis Ababa map by Sohrab Habibion

ISBN: 978-1-61775-820-1
Library of Congress Control Number: 2019943614
All rights reserved

First printing

Akashic Books
Brooklyn, New York
Twitter: @AkashicBooks
Facebook: AkashicBooks
E-mail: info@akashicbooks.com
Website: www.akashicbooks.com

# ALSO IN THE AKASHIC NOIR SERIES

MONTANA NOIR, edited by JAMES GRADY
& KEIR GRAFF

MONTREAL NOIR (CANADA), edited by JOHN
McFETRIDGE & JACQUES FILIPPI

MOSCOW NOIR (RUSSIA),
edited by NATALIA SMIRNOVA & JULIA GOUMEN

MUMBAI NOIR (INDIA), edited by ALTAF TYREWALA

NAIROBI NOIR (KENYA), edited by PETER KIMANI

NEW HAVEN NOIR, edited by AMY BLOOM

NEW JERSEY NOIR, edited by JOYCE CAROL OATES

NEW ORLEANS NOIR, edited by JULIE SMITH

NEW ORLEANS NOIR: THE CLASSICS,
edited by JULIE SMITH

OAKLAND NOIR, edited by JERRY THOMPSON
& EDDIE MULLER

ORANGE COUNTY NOIR, edited by GARY PHILLIPS

PARIS NOIR (FRANCE), edited by AURÉLIEN MASSON

PHILADELPHIA NOIR, edited by CARLIN ROMANO

PHOENIX NOIR, edited by PATRICK MILLIKIN

PITTSBURGH NOIR, edited by KATHLEEN GEORGE

PORTLAND NOIR, edited by KEVIN SAMPSELL

PRAGUE NOIR (CZECH REPUBLIC),
edited by PAVEL MANDYS

PRISON NOIR, edited by JOYCE CAROL OATES

PROVIDENCE NOIR, edited by ANN HOOD

QUEENS NOIR, edited by ROBERT KNIGHTLY

RICHMOND NOIR, edited by ANDREW BLOSSOM,
BRIAN CASTLEBERRY & TOM DE HAVEN

RIO NOIR (BRAZIL), edited by TONY BELLOTTO

ROME NOIR (ITALY), edited by CHIARA STANGALINO
& MAXIM JAKUBOWSKI

SAN DIEGO NOIR, edited by MARYELIZABETH HART

SAN FRANCISCO NOIR, edited by PETER MARAVELIS

SAN FRANCISCO NOIR 2: THE CLASSICS,
edited by PETER MARAVELIS

SAN JUAN NOIR (PUERTO RICO),
edited by MAYRA SANTOS-FEBRES

SANTA CRUZ NOIR, edited by SUSIE BRIGHT

SANTA FE NOIR, edited by ARIEL GORE

SÃO PAULO NOIR (BRAZIL),
edited by TONY BELLOTTO

SEATTLE NOIR, edited by CURT COLBERT

SINGAPORE NOIR, edited by CHERYL LU-LIEN TAN

STATEN ISLAND NOIR, edited by PATRICIA SMITH

ST. LOUIS NOIR, edited by SCOTT PHILLIPS

STOCKHOLM NOIR (SWEDEN), edited by
NATHAN LARSON & CARL-MICHAEL EDENBORG

ST. PETERSBURG NOIR (RUSSIA), edited by
NATALIA SMIRNOVA & JULIA GOUMEN

SYDNEY NOIR (AUSTRALIA), edited by JOHN DALE

TAMPA BAY NOIR, edited by COLETTE BANCROFT

TEHRAN NOIR (IRAN), edited by SALAR ABDOH

TEL AVIV NOIR (ISRAEL), edited by ETGAR KERET
& ASSAF GAVRON

TORONTO NOIR (CANADA), edited by JANINE ARMIN
& NATHANIEL G. MOORE

TRINIDAD NOIR (TRINIDAD & TOBAGO), edited by
LISA ALLEN-AGOSTINI & JEANNE MASON

TRINIDAD NOIR: THE CLASSICS
(TRINIDAD & TOBAGO), edited by EARL LOVELACE
& ROBERT ANTONI

TWIN CITIES NOIR, edited by JULIE SCHAPER
& STEVEN HORWITZ

USA NOIR, edited by JOHNNY TEMPLE

VANCOUVER NOIR (CANADA), edited by SAM WIEBE

VENICE NOIR (ITALY), edited by MAXIM JAKUBOWSKI

WALL STREET NOIR, edited by PETER SPIEGELMAN

ZAGREB NOIR (CROATIA), edited by IVAN SRŠEN

# FORTHCOMING

ACCRA NOIR (GHANA),
edited by NANA-AMA DANQUAH

BELGRADE NOIR (SERBIA),
edited by MILORAD IVANOVIC

JERUSALEM NOIR, edited by DROR MISHANI

MIAMI NOIR: THE CLASSICS,
edited by LES STANDIFORD

PALM SPRINGS NOIR,
edited by BARBARA DeMARCO-BARRETT

PARIS NOIR: THE SUBURBS (FRANCE),
edited by HERVÉ DELOUCHE

# ADDIS ABABA

SHIROMEDA

KECHENÉ

FRENCH LEGATION

A3

A4

MERCATO

ABUNE PETROS MEMORIAL

ADDIS ABABA UNIVERSITY

ARAT KILO

ADDIS MERCATO

SHERATON ADDIS

ADDIS ABABA WEST

BEHERAWI THEATER

NATIONAL PALACE

A5

LION OF JUDAH STATUE

MESKEL SQUARE

LIDETA

A1

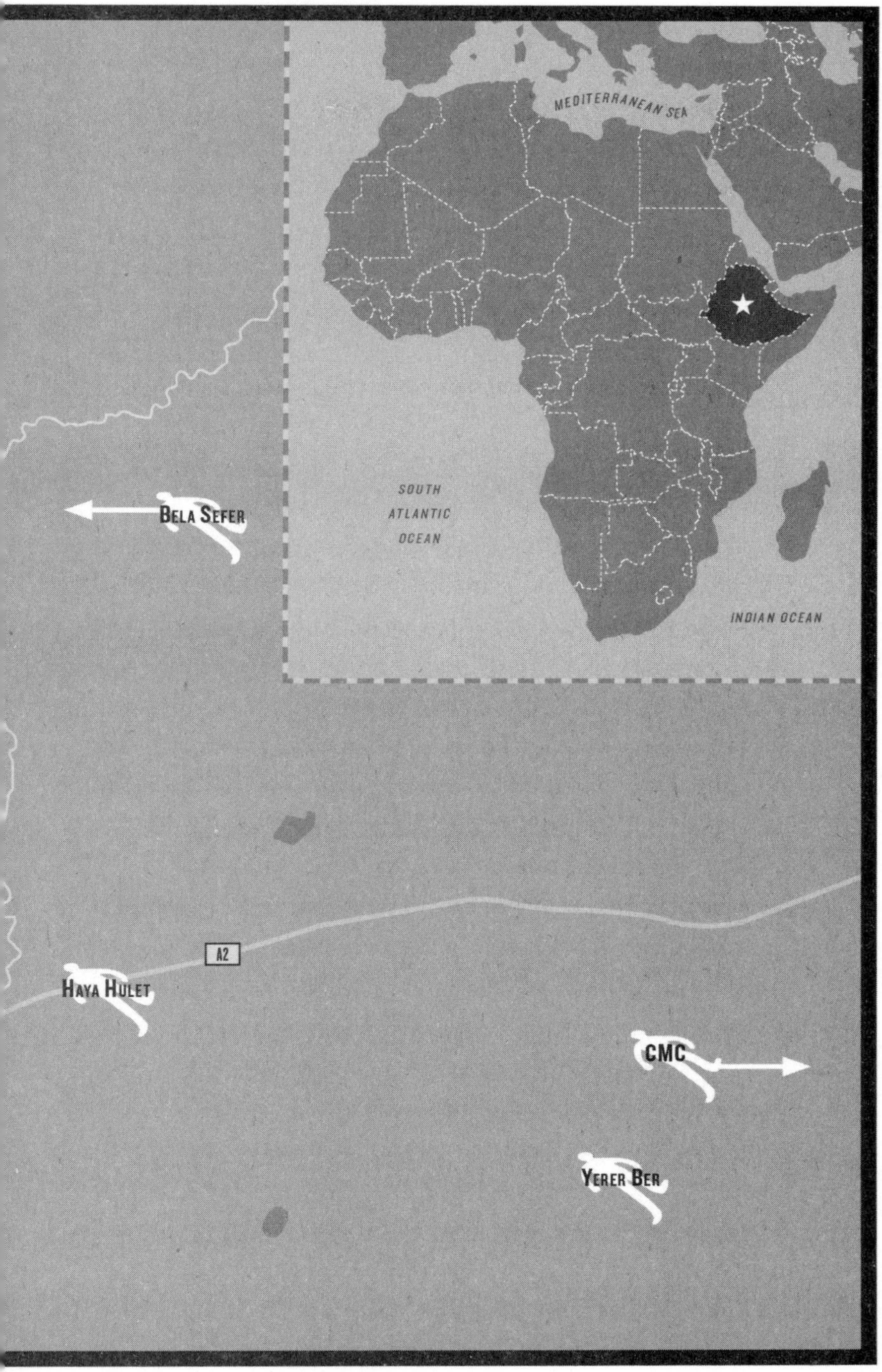

MEDITERRANEAN SEA
SOUTH ATLANTIC OCEAN
INDIAN OCEAN
BELA SEFER
A2
HAYA HULET
CMC
YERER BER

# TABLE OF CONTENTS

## PART III: MADNESS DESCENDS

## PART IV: POLICE AND THIEVES

# INTRODUCTION
## Howling in the Darkness

The faint bedroom light spilled across the floor and slumped against the window. I stood with my ear plastered to the wall, my hands shaking. I heard it again. The growls that darkness could not swallow. I knew what it was. I knew what they were. They were back and there was nothing we could do to stop them. When daylight came, I would walk outside, go down the steps of our veranda, and I would see the hole and the blood and the fur and other discarded parts of the dog that was now missing. I knew where the hyenas came from. I'd been warned to stay away from the forest that began just down the road from our house. The mouth of that forest was a wide cluster of trees intersected by bands of light. The dark patches were large enough to swallow a grown man and make him disappear. And this was another lesson I would learn very soon: that people, too, disappeared.

It was 1974 or it might have been 1975. I was too young to pay attention to years, to understand the sweep of time. I measured days by the nights that fell on us and brought in darker things: revolution and soldiers and curfews and gunfire. Somewhere in between this, the hyenas started coming to eat our dogs. They did this one night at a time. Taking the first and leaving the other two alive to witness their methodical hunger. To froth and whine and jump in mindless fear. They returned soon for the next one, sending the sole survivor into maddened, writhing terror while it waited for the inevitable. They were unstoppable. Every night, as shots rang out between revolutionaries and government forces in those early years of the Ethiopian Revolution, the hyenas clawed beneath the fence my grandfather tried in vain to reinforce. They were diligent. They worked on our fence to get beneath it, then crawled into our compound and found a way into the cage where the dogs were kept and they ate until there were none left.

Let me tell you another story: There are men who live in the mountains of Ethiopia and can turn into hyenas. This fact has always been a part of my knowledge of the world: There are men who can shift bodies and disappear into another form. And as 1974 crept forward and 1975 swept in, as our dog cage remained empty and the revolution ramped up, I began to wonder if all those disappeared people—those I saw one day then did not see again, those whose names adults tried never to speak in my presence—were, in fact, simply changing shape to avoid government forces. Maybe, I used to think, they would eventually find a way back home—but this time, as hyenas. These are some of my early memories of Addis Ababa, but they are not the only things I remember from that time. I had a childhood cushioned by protective parents, loving aunts and grandparents, and neighborhood friends. The brightness of those moments helped to balance the darkness of those other facts of living. What marks life in Addis Ababa, still, are those starkly different realities coexisting in one place. It's a growing city taking shape beneath the fraught weight of history, myth, and memory. It is a heady mix. It can also be disorienting, and it is in this space that the stories of Addis Ababa Noir reside.

Ethiopia is an ancient country with a long and storied history. It has been both a geographic location and an imaginative space for millennia. Herodotus writes of it in his *Histories*, Homer and Virgil reference a region of the same name. Ethiopia and its people can be found in several books in the Bible. It is a country that has reshaped and remolded itself over thousands of years through conquest and conflict, through sheer will and relentlessness. Those who reside within its borders—those relatively new lines of demarcation—are multiethnic and speak over eighty languages and more than two hundred dialects. The present view of Ethiopia is often stunningly narrow when set against its rich historical and cultural heritage. And now imagine that these varied, proud, and robust cultures have wound their way into Addis and made it home. There is a cosmopolitanism that is distinctly national as much as international. To meet someone from Addis Ababa, with its three million–plus inhabitants, may not tell you much about that person. But to meet someone from one of its neighborhoods—Ferensay Legasion or Lideta or Bole or Kechene or Bela Sefer or any of the areas where these stories in *Addis Ababa Noir* are set—may give you a better map leading to more fruitful details. The authors in this anthology extend a hand to you. Let them lead you down their streets and alleyways, into their characters' homes and schools, and show you all the hidden corners, the secrets, and the lapsed realities that hover just above the Addis that everyone else sees.

These are not gentle stories. They cross into forbidden territories and traverse the damaged terrain of the human heart. The characters that reside in these pages are complicated, worthy of our judgment as much as they somehow manage to elude it. The writers have each discovered their own ways to get us to lean in while forcing us to grit our teeth as we draw closer. Sulaiman Addonia, Lelissa Girma, and Hannah Giorgis write compellingly about the visceral and horrifyingly high costs of love and desire. In language that is as supple as it is evocative, Mahtem Shiferraw, Girma T. Fantaye, Mikael Awake, and Adam Reta render mythic worlds that mirror our own with some startling—and often bloody—differences. Solomon Hailemariam, Bewketu Seyoum, and Linda Yohannes focus their perceptive, unflinching gazes on the sometimes humorous, sometimes deadly unpredictability of city life. Teferi Nigussie Tafa explores with stark clarity what happens when ethnic-based tensions and violence are compounded by the onset of the 1974 revolution. This revolution also plays a pivotal role in the haunting stories by Meron Hadero and Rebecca Fisseha. And despite the varied and distinct voices in these pages, no single book can contain all of the wonderful, intriguing, vexing complexities of Addis Ababa. But what you will read are stories by some of Ethiopia's most talented writers living in the country and abroad. Each of them considers the many ways that myth and truth and a country's dark edges come together to create something wholly original—and unsettling.

*Maaza Mengiste*
*Addis Ababa, Ethiopia*

# PART I

*Past Hauntings*

# KIND STRANGER

BY Meron Hadero

*Lideta*

A ddis Ababa was hardly recognizable, a city casting itself into a new mold: taller, more modern, more planned and plotted. I'd gotten used to crossing construction sites with big boulders and chiseled stone, so I was surprised when I tripped. Looking down, I saw a reclining man reaching for me. His head leaned toward his legs, his hands outstretched and clasping. He looked familiar, though it was unlikely that I actually knew him—I lived in the States now, and rarely made it back. It was hard to see him clearly in the long afternoon shadow of the cathedral. I knelt beside him to make sure he was okay.

"Are you hurt?" I asked, and tried to lift his head. I thought about calling for help, but he started talking without any introduction.

"Listen, my child." His voice was barely a whisper so I had to bend down. "One night near the end of the rainy season, I got caught in a storm," he told me.

I reached into my shoulder bag to offer him some water, but he shook off the gesture and kept talking.

"I found myself jumping over the flooded gutters as I ran from the minibus toward home with my jacket over my head to keep myself a little drier, but you know how it is with the rainy season—a losing battle. The whole bus ride, I had to fight for space next to a boy and his damp, smelly goat; that boy showed no respect for his elders standing next to me like that. I was tired, and there was the boy and his soggy little beast, and the rain, and outside there were rows of yellow Mercedes, which I always thought I'd look quite good driving."

I was surprised by this deluge of narrative coming from a stranger, and then tried to do what I thought I should: I felt his forehead, which wasn't hot. I checked his pulse, which didn't race. I rolled up my sleeves and sat down beside him. I tried telling him to take it easy, but he had more to say.

"So that night was—how do they say it in the movies?—a dark and stormy night," he went on in English.

"A dark and stormy night," I repeated. "That's what they say."

"Besides the rain, the power outage made it hard to see except for the bursts of lightning that lit up the street, lit up the homes, lit the acacia trees on the hillside. The lightning flashed just as I was about to take out my keys and open the gate, and that's when I saw her: Marta Kebede standing under a big black umbrella, looking the same as the day she was arrested back in 1980. I hadn't heard of her or seen her since, though I'd thought of her often, of course."

With the words "of course," I knew I had to interrupt, because I thought, *This man has mistaken me for someone else.* He said "of course" like I knew him well, like none of this should come as a surprise to me, and on top of that, the way he leaned his head close and whispered into my ear felt intimate, as did the soft way he grasped my hand. The only thing I could think of worse than unrequited intimacy was mistaken intimacy.

"Sir, I think you have me confused with someone else," I told the man. "Just rest. I think you're hurt. Let me get you a car. I could give you some money." When he declined, I looked again for a wound or sign of injury, but couldn't find any.

He didn't seem moved by my concern and just said, "If you have a minute . . . I just need to rest a minute. If you have a minute, I will take that."

I didn't really have time to spare. This was a short visit to see relatives, and almost every moment was accounted for. Yet I felt like I should stay with him just a little longer.

He didn't wait for my response and simply continued his story: "So I'd just seen Marta, the first time in decades, and there she was, caught in the middle of a storm. The lightning stopped for a moment and I could no longer see her silhouette. I tried to speak into the darkness, but thunder smothered my hello. I jogged toward where she had stood, moving with both excitement and hesitation, for the sight of her made me feel conflicting emotions: elation, dread, and also grief. Isn't that the way it is with grief, though? First we mourn the grief we bear, and then later we mourn the grief we've caused."

As he said these words, the helplessness on his face that I'd taken for kindness seemed to vanish. I thought that this switch was strange, that his emotions could change so easily, so suddenly and completely.

"So that night on that dark street, I called out again to Marta, saying the only words I could think of: 'Let's go for dinner.' It was an awkward thing to say, but once I had said something, I started saying everything. 'It's me, Gedeyon. Don't you remember? We were students in the same class at university—you were getting your degree in pharmacology, and I was studying chemistry. I asked you out on a date the first week, and you said no, and you made fun of my shoes, saying that they were farmer shoes, and that you wouldn't date a boy with farmer shoes because your father would kick you out of the house and your mother would drag you to the priest and drown you in holy water. I saved up a whole half year to buy new shoes, really nice ones, and I asked you out again, and you didn't know who I was. I told you I was going to be a professor and you said you wouldn't go out with me, but this time you didn't bother with a reason. I guess I must have loved you. How else could I explain the lengths I went to get your attention, your approval? I wish it hadn't happened that way, and I still wonder if we would have turned out differently if things happened some other way.' Isn't that a lot to say into the darkness?" Now he gripped my arm and lifted himself onto the boulder to sit upright.

"Yes, it is a lot to say." *In any light*, I thought.

"If she had acknowledged me, if things had gone a little differently between us, maybe I wouldn't have accused her. Did you ever live here during the Derg?" he asked, not giving me much time to consider what he'd just revealed. "I think you didn't. I think you lived somewhere Western, some wealthy country with peace and freedom."

"I know the Derg," I replied. "I was a child of the Derg, born of that era."

Gedeyon shook his head. "Those of you who left here when you were young, without a scratch, and had the luxury of living somewhere else don't know what some of us carry. You know what the Derg *technically* is, but you don't *truly* know. You know the Derg as a definition, a Cold War junta that lasted too long and did too much harm. But those of us who got to truly know the Derg, who knew it as an uninvited guest dropping in on each meal and in every interaction, well . . ."

I felt my face flush, and now it was the grip of guilt that kept me there as he went on.

"I had been tortured by the Derg—that's how I got to

know it. Some of the students avoided school back then to reduce the risk of being arrested and just stayed home. But I was poor. I went to school every day, whether there was a demonstration or the threat of arrest or nothing at all because we got free lunch at the university, and if I didn't go, I didn't eat all day. It was a simple fact of life. So I went to school every day and was arrested, and who knows why back then. Maybe I had a friend or associate who was suspicious, or maybe my hair was too long or too short, or my fingernails were too clean or too dirty. Maybe it was on account of my nice new shoes—who knows? But when the Derg interrogated me, lashing my feet, asking me to name names to get myself free, I gave them Marta's name. She was wealthy, had power, and I thought she could escape, that she'd have a better chance of surviving it than I would. And it's not that I hated her, but she'd stung me. Marta had stung me. Those subtle stings to pride—they're worse than the big ego blows because they're not like some obvious pebble you can remove from your shoe. They are like shards that you know are there but can't find and can't get rid of. Oh, Marta, I wish she'd never made fun of my shoes."

"So did Marta accept your dinner invitation during the thunderstorm?" I asked, trying to keep him awake since I saw his eyelids beginning to droop.

"Well, I kept asking her to dinner, but she didn't say anything. I stood there waiting for another bolt of lightning, and when it came, I saw her far down the street talking to someone, but I didn't know who. The dark, the rain—everything was obscured. I approached her cautiously, ducking behind a tree, waiting for the right moment when I could finally go up to her and try to speak again. After another strike of lightning, she was alone at the minibus stop where I'd just come from.

I walked over and stood next to her tall, illuminated figure. I just stared, hoping she would recognize me and start up a conversation. She eventually turned toward me, even smiled, and said, 'Good evening.' She offered to share her umbrella, so I shifted closer to her. But she didn't seem to know who I was."

"You said you last saw her in 1980? That's a long time ago," I said.

"Not long enough to forget a friend." The way Gedeyon twisted his lips with spite made me think this was a man of impossible expectations. "She should have remembered," he said. "The thing is, she has always been on my mind. I wrapped all this guilt up around Marta, all this significance and longing; so much so that I could recognize her anywhere, even in the middle of a blackout with just a flash of lighting to reveal her face. It never occurred to me that her feelings wouldn't mirror mine, at least a little."

"So what did you do then?" I asked, hoping he'd just wished her luck and walked away, but I already knew him well enough to know that he hadn't. And I couldn't walk away myself because his story now had a hold on me.

He continued: "I responded to Marta, 'Good evening to you as well,' and added, 'Don't I know you?' I thought that maybe she just hadn't given me a proper look yet, but when she turned and looked me up and down with that judgment-filled face, she said, 'No, I do not believe we have met.'

"We began to talk. I didn't say much, just listened. She said she was going to stop by church to give thanks for how life had turned around for her. I realized this was my opportunity to ask about her life—maybe she would have a flash of recollection then. She told me some general details. She said there was a time she'd been in prison during the Derg, but that was then. I told her I had been thrown in prison too, by mistake, and she said, 'What a shame.' She leaned a little closer to me, so I got the courage to ask why she'd been arrested, and she deflected, saying, 'Oh, I don't remember, and besides, does it even matter?' 'Of course it matters,' I said. 'Oh, I don't know,' she replied. 'They'd target you for the most absurd things.' She shrugged as if she didn't want to give it much thought. I imagined exactly what they must have said to her anyway. They'd accused her of being a bourgeois princess, more interested in the state of her closet than the very state in which she lived, skipping rallies to do her hair and dodging speeches to read fashion magazines. That's what they might have said to her because that's what I'd told them. That she was a nonbeliever, a threat to the cause. Those were the words I'd used to trade her freedom for my own. It had to be done."

I didn't know what to say to that.

"I'm sure you'd rather not be here." He stared at me with despair. "You left and avoided these difficult truths. You haven't had to see the heavy weight some of us carry around. Do you think I'm ashamed of having survived the way I did? Why should I be?"

I didn't defend myself; what had I done?

"I never said I'm a good man," he went on. "I was just a regular man, but the Derg, it made me . . . it made me and it unmade me. It took a regular man and then heightened my worst instincts. It gave me the permission to be worse than I was ever meant to be or would have been in another place, another time. It gave my sins a platform, gave them cover, gave them cause. And for whatever reason I still can't explain, I took the Derg up on this opportunity to abandon my good senses and do as I pleased. I believe—really believe—there was good in me once. I guess I don't know that for sure, but I think it's true. I think I was decent once. I could have been a regular kind of man. Maybe I didn't have the courage to be better, or didn't have the luxury to be better. I couldn't avoid the hard choices. I was here, made here, unmade here."

He clasped my hand and held it closer, and the warmth of his breath on my skin began to repulse me. Why did I feel like I owed this stranger something? He seemed frail, and despite his bitterness toward me, I felt like he needed me. I felt his forehead again, which was a bit hot. He put his cheek to my hand, pursing his dry lips.

"So the rain was just pouring down now, and the cars were whizzing by loudly, and Marta was almost shouting, telling me she'd not only survived the experience of prison, but that it also made her more self-reliant and tough. As awful as prison was, she had to invent ways to endure what she thought would be unbearable, what she thought would break her. She said she struggled but eventually created a space to be calm within herself. Gradually she was able to create a space to let joy enter her life as well, even there in prison—they were the most fleeting moments, but they were something. She found a way to make those fleeting moments last. She found a way to forget, which was the hardest accomplishment of her life. And when she learned how to do that, she found a way toward purpose. She hadn't cared about school before because she hadn't cared about much, she said. But she made a choice to get educated, and she was able to do it. The Derg loved to throw intellectuals in jail—the students, the professors, the writers—and the prisons during the Derg were the best schools in the country, as some say. Marta also met her husband there, and when they were both released or escaped or otherwise got free, they fled together to America, swept up in that wave of refugees, and landed safely on a shore called New England where they went back to school and started a family.

She got a good job and didn't look back on that time except to acknowledge that she was lucky in the end."

Gedeyon stopped to catch his breath, and I said, "Well that's about as good an outcome as you could hope for."

"You could say that." He pressed his head to my hand once more. I could feel his fever now. He told me that he'd forgiven himself for the wrongs of the Derg, and damn anyone who judged him for that. "Damn you too, if you're judging," he said. But he hadn't found a way to forgive himself for his other sins, and I saw then that he was making me his confessor.

"Is there someone I can take you to talk to?" I asked him.

"Would you rather me tell this to a friend? A friend who I want to respect and remember me well? Or tell my priest, who I have known all my life and who I respect? My family, who will carry forth my name? My colleagues in whose esteem I hope to remain? Would you rather me call it out from the rooftops and confess to the city? . . . Or should I tell a stranger visiting from halfway across the world who looks like she doesn't make the return trip all that often? And who has managed to be a child of the Derg without carrying the same load, but who should shoulder it as well?"

And he paused, and I saw the evidence I'd been searching for all along, an empty bottle of pills falling from his pocket, and I couldn't tell if these had been to help him or if they were what made him sick. I couldn't even tell if he'd taken them.

When I asked him, he just said, "Listen, child, to my last words."

What could I do but hear him out and share the burden of his secret now? I knew if I said nothing, he'd continue, and he did.

"I asked Marta, 'What was it like, being a refugee?' 'It's not for the faint of heart,' she said, sweeping her short curly hair off her face with her left hand. The strands caught the light and shined, and I thought I'd never seen her look so sophisticated, so strong, so completely out of reach. I was drawn to her, so I pulled in a little closer to listen.

"She told me, 'Not even my mother knew where I'd gone when I fled Ethiopia, not at first, but eventually I was able to send a letter, and then we corresponded as much as we could. When my family finally saw me after thirty-five years, they told me how good I looked for someone who'd come back from the dead.'

"I was gazing at Marta, clenching my fist so tight I felt my fingernails bending back, so I put my hands in my pockets and looked at the beams coming off the car headlights, circling her like she was encased in jewels, her body haloed by the glow of the streetlight behind her. *She is still something*, I thought. *Not just someone who has reclaimed what's lost, but someone somehow ennobled by loss.* I don't know how to explain this, but I looked at her like she was either my proudest creation or my most wretched punishment. I don't exactly know what I felt, but with false pride I told Marta about my own life, the basics: I was a chemistry and math professor, had a wife once, but it didn't last long. No children, my family mostly gone. I lived freely. Mine was what I called a content and unencumbered existence with routines, stability, and modest comforts, which was more than I'd been born with, and so I felt successful, for what was success if not to die with more than what you had coming into the world?

"Marta said I must be proud of all I was able to accomplish despite my time in prison. She added, 'Sometimes, things even out in the end. Karma, justice, and all of that.' 'Like an equation,' I replied. 'That we're always balancing.'

"She said something I couldn't hear over the rain, so I

stepped a little closer, and when she craned her head to see if the minibus was on its way, I fixated again on the light glistening off her hair. I reached out to her by instinct. A car sped by and honked and I pulled myself back, which sent her umbrella out into the darkness, as if a strong gust of wind had caught it. Marta lost her step. She slipped on the muddy curb and fell onto the street, her ankle stuck in the gutter.

"She reached out, and I leaned toward her. She needed me—for once. So I reached for her, my hand nearly touching hers, and Marta whispered, 'Kind stranger.'

"And I froze, because even now, especially now, the Marta of my dreams and nightmares and fantasies, haunting Marta who had scolded me for wearing those old shoes, who had failed to recognize my achievement getting the new pair, who had talked to me for half an hour that very night and still had no idea who I was, now called me a stranger.

"I realized then, as she held her hand out to me, that she hadn't even introduced herself that night, hadn't told me her name, nor asked for mine. I was a stranger and always would be to her. I was frozen and the cars honked their horns, unable to stop, the beams of the headlights closing in, overtaking her, and she lunged desperately for my hand, almost a helping hand, almost a friend.

"When the ambulance came, there was really nothing left to do. I knew I could say with some degree of honesty that it had been an accident—a horn, the umbrella, Marta stumbling, me somehow not being able to get to her in time. I try to make sense of that moment. I thought it was my chance to leave the past behind. But that was not the way, was it?"

He was posing a question, but not to me, whose name he'd never asked, a stranger who was there for him in his moment of need, something he didn't seem to recognize.

"Tell me what you think of my story," he said, and I didn't speak, didn't move as he leaned forward and rubbed the dirt off his shoes, caring for them like they were his salvation.

# A DOUBLE-EDGED INHERITANCE

BY HANNAH GIORGIS

*Shiromeda*

Meskerem didn't believe in fate.

Fate was one of those silly things her Orthodox aunties whispered about in their singsong voices, starry-eyed and full of desperate, ill-advised hope for something, anything. Fate was for people who had abandoned control, the last refuge of the weak and uninspired. Fate was for women who didn't know any better.

So when the call came from back home that the aunt who had named her—the great-aunt who shared her birthday— had died, she felt no grand cosmic realignment, only a churning grief, the kind that empties out your stomach and makes unseasoned mincemeat of its remains.

Almaz had loved Meskerem with a kind of uncommon, unreasonable fervor that bordered on desperation. From the moment she first learned of her youngest niece's pregnancy, the stern woman had softened her heart for the child no one else wanted. This child would be born into blame; this child would need protection.

The whole family had recoiled in performative horror as news of Tigist Negash's pregnancy snaked through their networks. Tigist, the youngest and brightest of seven girls, was the beacon on whom all their hopes had rested. She'd received the highest marks in her class at Kidane Mehret, a future engineer whose first semester at Addis Ababa University had been so impressive that her professors called her mother on several occasions to insist she consider sending Tigist abroad to continue her studies.

It was Tigist who had turned their offers down with a sudden, furious anger. The flash in her eyes was quiet, a lightning-fast break from the pools of warmth with which she normally saw the world. She didn't want to leave—Addis Ababa was home. What could exist beyond it? She hardly left Amist Kilo. Quiet and pious, Tigist spent all her time studying or following her *emaye*.

Until, of course, she met Robel.

Robel Girma smelled like whiskey and freshly printed birr. It was nauseating at first, his scent so strong it knocked Tigist off balance when their shoulders bumped against each other in Shiro Meda one early *kremt* day.

"*Yekirta, ehitey*," he'd whispered through a crooked grin that sent her head spinning. He reached down to help her up, gold rings on three of his calloused fingers. "*Asamemkush? Be shai le'adenish?*"

She'd been shopping for *gabis* that morning, nervous about her first night in university housing. Her oldest sister had moved back home after her husband's disappearance, carrying two children with a bad back and a broken spirit. Tigist's room in their mother's house soon became the children's playground, their constant tugs at her *netela* a consistent interruption to her strict studying regimen. But still, she loved them. And so she planned to spend more time on campus, burrowed in the libraries. That would have to do.

Almaz was a literature professor at her niece's university, a stoic career woman who lived alone in an apartment tucked between Siddist Kilo and embassy row. Sharp and poetic, she prided herself on her pragmatism—even and especially when others told her she didn't behave like an Ethiopian woman should. Almaz wanted Tigist to take her professors' advice and leave; she didn't understand why a bright young girl would want to stay in Addis tending to her family when the world was calling. Almaz had never taken much interest in her nieces and nephews, but she found housing on campus for Tigist the moment she heard the girl insisted on staying in Addis Ababa.

"Don't thank me," Almaz had said, less a demure platitude and more an agitated demand. "Please, *ebakesh*, just meet people who do not live inside your books or your mother's house."

Tigist had been thinking about her aunt's directive as she shopped for *gabis*, pressing them against her face. They smelled strange and dirty, unlike the *gabis* her mother had washed meticulously each season. None of them were soft enough; none of them felt like home.

When Robel Girma bumped into her, Tigist Negash stopped thinking of home.

Girma Woldemariam never wanted his son running around with some common girl in the first place.

Girma was the Ethiopian army's most respected general, and he had a reputation to uphold. Robel could spin lies to these college girls all he wanted, but the oldest Girma son did not have time for romance—and he certainly couldn't be seen walking around Siddist Kilo with his hands intertwined with some girl from a *balager* family no one could name. Robel had business to attend to: his final year of law school was coming to an end, and his father wanted him to spend more time accompanying him to work. His path had been forged for him, and all the ungrateful brat had to do was show up.

All he had to do was stay away from distractions.

When Tigist told Robel she felt sick, fingers fidgeting in her lap as she sat across a table from him at Enrico's, he joked that the cake must have gotten to her. She shouldn't have eaten it during *tsom* anyway, he insisted, before noticing a quick flash in her eyes.

"Are you sure?" he asked quietly, the words hanging in the thick air between them. He didn't bother repeating himself. He knew.

Girma smelled the fear on his son the moment Robel walked into his office the next morning.

"What did you do?" the general barked, pushing Robel into the carvings in the oak door that listed his military honors in Ge'ez.

Robel shrank, his voice cracking as he tried to relay the information. His head spinning, he explained how the girl had come to feel like home. He wanted to do this right, he insisted, eyes trained on the floor.

"I love her," he whispered, his attention suddenly turned to the row of rifles hanging above his father's desk. They shone with a menacing gleam, crafted to be beautiful even in their violent precision. Robel gulped as the last word escaped his lips, a foolhardy attempt at pulling it back into himself.

Girma laughed, a throaty snarl that rose from the pit of his stomach. Spitting at his son's feet, he growled two words, each its own sentence: "Fix. It."

Turning to walk away from the trembling young man before him, the general mumbled something in Amharic through gritted teeth. Reeling from the encounter, Robel could hardly hear what escaped his father's lips, but he didn't need to.

"Or else I will."

\* \* \*

When Tigist woke up in Tikur Anbessa Hospital a week later, her nurse did not address her. Instead, she turned to Almaz, who was reading Baldwin with heavy eyelids in a wooden chair beside her niece's reclining bed.

"She's awake," the nurse announced plainly, meeting neither the woman's eyes nor Tigist's. "Maybe she'll talk now."

Almaz had been sitting in the cold room with her niece for seventeen hours. Each second had felt longer than the last, but she didn't dare sleep. The thin girl lying in the bed looked more fragile than Almaz had ever seen her. She was gaunt, broken. With her body a maze of tubes and plaster, Tigist was lucky to be alive. The doctors had regarded Almaz with concerned eyes when they asked about her niece: Who would want to hurt someone so young, with eyes so warm? What could she have done to earn a beating reserved for prisoners of war?

"*Teseberech*," Almaz heard herself telling Tigist's mother when she could finally access the phone in the hospital's graying lobby. "She fell down the stairs on campus. I am here with her now. The doctors said not to worry."

Before racing back toward Tigist's room, Almaz spun a toothless lie she knew her sister would not question until the girl recovered. "She was racing to class. *Beka*, she missed a step and so she fell. That's all.

"I'll pay for it," she'd added before hanging up abruptly as she caught sight of the clock. Tigist might be awake now, and Almaz had no time to argue with the girl's mother over money she knew her sister did not have. Tigist needed her aunt; everything else could wait.

"Tigist? Can you hear me? Almaz *negn*," she offered tentatively when the girl's eyes first opened. "You . . . you fell, *lijey*. But you will be okay."

The girl tried to move toward her aunt, but the IV yanked her back. Eyes bloodshot and filled with tears, she strained to move a bruised hand toward her stomach. Her breathing quickened, her body tensing. Turning her gaze downward, Tigist whispered: "They can take me, but not my baby."

She couldn't lose this baby, not to the swarm of uniformed men who'd descended upon her. She blinked back tears as images of their terrifying grins played themselves back on an infinite loop.

"*Babiye!*" she'd screamed as the first man pinned her arms back so another could kick her so viciously that she lost consciousness. The word came back to Tigist as a whisper now. "*Babiye.*"

Almaz sighed. "Why didn't you tell me? We could've fixed it. This would never have happened."

Almaz had known her niece was gallivanting around the city with some general's son. She'd warned the girl not to get too close. Powerful men were dangerous, their lust for dominion more potent than any love they might claim to feel for a woman. Powerful men enchanted easily, but their affections waned with all the grace of poison.

By the time Almaz saw the two of them together, waltzing around Shiro Meda in search of a second *gabi* for Robel's room, she knew it was too late. This boy, half teeth and half arrogance, had gotten under her niece's skin.

It did not matter to the girl that the boy's father was a man whom her aunt spoke of only in hushed tones. Almaz had called her that evening, whispering into a pay phone near Meskel Adebabay with fearful contempt: "The only thing that boy's father loves more than his son is his power, Tigist. Do not stand in his way; you will be trampled."

The memory of those words filled the space between Almaz and Tigist for hours, the silence punctuated only by the staccato beeps of the machines attached to the girl's body.

Robel had never defied his father before. Mischievous as he was, the boy had never transgressed beyond disobeying orders regarding his schoolwork or telling white lies about khat.

But when Robel ran up three flights of stairs at Tikur Anbessa and saw the girl he loved fighting for two lives Girma had tried to extinguish, his resolve ossified. He didn't want to walk in his father's footsteps if it meant this.

Breathless and full of youthful indignation, he laid his head in Tigist's lap as she slept. Terrified, Robel had waited behind the hospital until he saw Almaz leave. She'd stormed out of the hospital after Tigist had fallen asleep, presumably to tell her superiors at the university that she would not be teaching class the rest of the week.

In Almaz's absence, Robel cried thick, heavy tears into Tigist's lap. He pressed his head against her stomach, praying for some sign of life as he knelt against the edge of her bed. The girl looked gray now, her skin purple in places where he'd once worshipped its brown richness.

His face a gnarled mess of tears and shame, Robel did not move when he heard Almaz's footsteps approach. He knew she would be enraged at the sight of him. He knew she had a right to be. Still, even the jolt of her heel nearly puncturing his thigh could not match the blunt force of the words Almaz flung at him upon seeing that he'd sneaked his way into Tigist's room.

"How dare you touch her? Her blood is on your hands already!" the woman heaved at him as the girl lay sleeping. "The best thing you can do for her is forget about her. May you and your father carry the shame of your sin until Satan calls you both home!"

Robel whimpered. Wiping tears from his face with scratched, ashen hands, he made a simple plea: "Let me fix it. Let me keep her safe. I will sacrifice my happiness to keep her alive."

When Tigist landed in Washington, DC, she asked the first Ethiopian cabdriver she saw if she could use his cell phone to call Almaz.

The rest of the family had stopped speaking to her, content to pretend the foolish pregnant girl now leaving for America had never existed at all. The days preceding Tigist's flight all seemed like a blur now. Only one thing stood out to her amid the dizzying sequence of packing, pain medication, and rushed goodbyes: Robel had never called.

Dialing Almaz's number as the cabdriver smiled at her for two seconds too long, Tigist wished more than anything that she could apply her family's miraculous power of memory erasure to Robel. If it weren't for Robel, she wouldn't be standing here alone, cold and vulnerable. If it weren't Robel, she would still be home.

When her daughter was born months later, Tigist again called Almaz. "She came early," Tigist said simply, looking down at the child whose eyes already mirrored her own.

The baby had not been due for another four weeks, but Almaz smiled when she got the call in the late-night hours of September 11. "*Meskerem ahnd, ende!*" she'd laughed. "*Ye Meskerem lij naht,*" she mused before the line disconnected. "*Ye Meskerem lij.*"

Exhausted and alone, Tigist resolved then that she'd never tell this dangerous miracle of a child about her father. *Girls are already born into a world of heartbreak*, Tigist reflected. *It's best not to saddle this new life, this new year, with details of the pain that runs through her blood.*

* * *

Meskerem was a brilliant, preternaturally insightful child. As a result of her mother's sacrifices and her great-aunt's blessings, she grew up with the two women raising her from opposite sides of the Atlantic. Their love buoyed her through childhood and adolescence, their faith in her a guiding light.

Meskerem didn't learn that her great-aunt shared her birthday until her sophomore year of college. Tasked with writing about a woman who inspired her, Tigist's only child chose to call Almaz, the woman who had carried them both. Almaz comforted Meskerem when the girl asked why God had let her mother die alone in a car accident while she had been away taking classes earlier that year. Almaz told Meskerem story after story of Tigist's engineering brilliance and the family's hopes for her education. Their calls lasted hours, each one longer than the last. Meskerem delighted in learning more about her family, even if her great-aunt had no answers about the death of her father. It was the only balm she had, the only time she didn't feel alone.

Talking to Almaz made things make sense for the first time in Meskerem's life. The quiet, sullen young woman smiled a little easier. She walked into class feeling more excited than bored. Still, when all her classmates spoke passionately about their aspirations to embody the spirits of women like Eleanor Roosevelt and Susan B. Anthony, Meskerem suppressed the urge to laugh. She had learned of bravery and brilliance that made these women pale in comparison, and she couldn't wait to overshadow their foolhardy presentations.

Standing in the front of the lecture hall wearing only black, except for the yellow Meskel flower pin attached to her combat boots, Meskerem presented the details of her research: a woman named Almaz Gessesse had been born into a poor family in Addis Ababa and became a prominent literature professor; a woman named Almaz Gessesse had found a way for Meskerem's mother to come to America after her husband had died mysteriously (in the war?); a woman named Almaz Gessesse had come all the way to America to hold her after her mother died in a car accident; a woman named Almaz Gessesse had named her after the month in which they were both born.

Meskerem was working on her doctoral thesis when the news came of Almaz's death several years later. Exhausted and angry, she'd yelled at her boyfriend for waking her from a much-needed nap just to answer a phone call.

She saw the +251 pop up on her Viber app and immediately sat up in bed, her whole body an electrical current. Why would someone whose number she didn't have be calling from Ethiopia? She hadn't been back in years—she only spoke to Almaz.

A solemn voice asked for Meskerem Negash, then said simply, "Almaz is gone."

The last time Meskerem had been in Addis Ababa, she'd stayed with Almaz the whole summer. She was young then, a voracious reader about to start high school. She spent weeks cooped up in Almaz's small apartment near Addis Ababa University, reading Baldwin and Fitzgerald and the Brontës. She'd accompanied Almaz to campus and sat in the back of the classroom while the professor taught, eagerly absorbing new phrases in Amharic. After class, Meskerem would beg Almaz to quiz her on the material she'd learned.

The two of them walked through Shiro Meda together for hours, buying whatever they pleased. It had been their first destination the morning after Meskerem's first night in Almaz's apartment, when the visiting child had woken up shivering. Almaz had laughed at the American girl for being so cold in such light *kremt.* "Isn't it freezing in your country?" she'd joked before suggesting the two take a trip to the market to grab another *gabi.* Meskerem had never been so excited to shop.

The chaos of Shiro Meda calmed Meskerem in a way she couldn't explain, even to Almaz. She wanted to lose herself in its alleyways, let herself become anonymous amid a sea of people focused on anything but her. The road felt endless to her, the paths themselves as plentiful as the bounty sold there.

Yet during this trip, Shiro Meda felt like a cage. Even as the sun shone on her shoulders, Meskerem felt cold. She'd walked from Almaz's apartment all the way to Shiro Meda in search of a distraction from the upcoming funeral processions, headphones in her ears. This place wasn't home without Almaz. When she finally reached the market, she was horrified. Where was the charm she'd romanticized all these years? Before she'd seen freedom and excitement, whereas now she saw only the bleak repetition of commerce. Vendors seemed sinister, shoppers selfish to the point of revulsion.

Meskerem walked toward the first seller whose makeshift booth held a selection of *gabis.* Dust and sun in her face, she tried to force a smile on her face when she made eye contact with the vendor. He stared back at her with a mixture of pity and irritation.

"What do you want?" he asked roughly as she stood silent in front of his display. She walked away, unsure if he'd even been asking about merchandise.

With Almaz's favorite songs blaring in her headphones, Meskerem was the last person to notice the general approaching. Shiro Meda had slowed from its usual frenetic pace, shopkeepers and tourists alike pausing to marvel at the tall man with the stunning smile.

"General Girma!" a child squeaked as he raised his hand in salute, running into the middle of the road. His mother scooped him out of the way moments later, and the general looked straight through them both.

General Robel Girma had not been to Shiro Meda in years. Shiro Meda was for poor tourists and even poorer locals, he'd told his son Elias. But today was different. Today he had learned of Almaz Gessesse's death. Today he was thinking of Tigist. Eyes fighting back tears behind his reflective aviators, the general walked down the road with determination.

When all 6'1" of him barreled into a young woman and sent her careening onto the ground, the general didn't apologize. He was not a man who apologized. He simply adjusted his sunglasses and kept walking.

But the girl caught up to him a moment later, pushing his shoulder from behind. The shock prompted him to remove his sunglasses as he spun around to face her, forgetting for a moment that his eyes betrayed the very anguish that had brought him to Shiro Meda that day.

Meskerem opened her mouth to chastise the gruff man who'd knocked into her. She didn't care that he was in uniform. She did not owe some soldier her loyalty; she certainly did not owe him the skin on her knees. He turned to face her, and she was certain in the split second between her push and his pivot that he would hit her.

Robel did not hit the girl who'd pushed him. He grabbed her face with his calloused hand, rings imprinting themselves into her cheek, the second he saw her eyes. They were warm, sad. They went on for days.

They looked so familiar.

\* \* \*

The next time Meskerem went to Shiro Meda, she needed gifts to send back to America.

She'd promised her boyfriend she would return after taking care of Almaz's funeral, but weeks later the thought of leaving her great-aunt's flat caused her anguish. She could hear the irritation bubbling up in John's voice every time he asked why her trip had been extended a week, and then another week, and then another. She missed him, but John would have to wait. She hoped a set of paintings from back home, maybe some jewelry or a *netela* for his mother, would help ease his anxieties. Day after day she went to Shiro Meda, telling herself she'd keep going until she found the perfect gifts to make up for her absence.

Most days, Meskerem just walked to the market. Passing the campus where her mother had studied and her great-aunt had taught became a soothing ritual, a way to bide the time while she delayed her trip back to America. Each day, new people greeted her along the road, but it was the familiar faces who punctuated her path. When she walked past the embassies, important-looking men took stock of her all-black attire and asked who she'd lost. She didn't know where to start, so she'd laugh and tell them, "No one."

One morning, Meskerem sacrificed this curious anonymity for something even more peculiar: a sense of direction The general came to pick her up in his truck, having promised to steer her toward the things she needed to see. In the weeks leading up to Genna, the market was even more busy than usual. Diaspora returnees with stories less tragic than Meskerem's flooded its streets with their fast-paced strutting and their embarrassing Amharigna. A group of them gawked at her as she hopped out of a military truck they'd only seen in movies. Shopkeepers stared as she stood next to the man who'd been driving: she was General Robel Girma's daughter, and she was no longer a secret.

Chickens ran around her ankles, and Meskerem laughed. This wasn't quite home, but it was something like it. The general (she couldn't bring herself to call him "Dad," not after all these years) picked out some housewares and "manly" art for John (*"Habesha aydelem?"* he asked, raising his eyebrows. Meskerem raised hers back; the general wasn't allowed to ask those questions yet). He insisted on paying for the gifts then and later for pastries from Enrico's, and Meskerem protested only once in the grateful, facetious way all Ethiopian children do.

Meskerem walked back into Almaz's apartment that afternoon feeling lighter. She placed John's gifts in a drawer near Almaz's bed, taking care not to upset the balance of the dresser's contents. She wanted to leave before Genna, she decided. She'd already missed Christmas with John in the US, and the prospect of bypassing the awkwardness of the Ethiopian holiday by going back to the States seemed perfect. The general was friendly, but he was not yet family. Leaving would be for the best. It would be like Christmas had never come at all.

She nodded to herself, pacing around the bedroom after grabbing her laptop. Yes, this was right. She would head to the nearest Internet café and buy her ticket now before having dinner at the general's home. It would be easier that way, to let go of all the pleasantries at once. There would be no fight over how long she should stay, no obligatory suggestions that she and his other children get to know each other.

Meskerem had settled into the kitchen easily, cooking herself *shiro* and *kik alicha* almost nightly. The bedroom had taken longer; for the first four nights, she'd slept on the love seat in the living room. When her neck protested violently, she conceded, eventually rummaging through Almaz's closet in search of the outfits that most reminded her of the woman whose spirit still moved through the space. But it had taken weeks for Meskerem to let herself open the door to Almaz's office—the space felt sacred, like the source of her brilliance. She knew it was the space her great-aunt had cherished most.

Meskerem opened the door slowly, like she might still be caught. She walked to the bookshelf instinctively, hands grazing the spines of the books she'd read here as a teenager and the many that had been added in the time since. Pausing to sit at Almaz's desk for a moment and let the scent of their pages wash over her, Meskerem noticed a thick piece of paper sticking out of the same Baldwin novel Almaz read every year. Almaz had treated *Giovanni's Room* with more tenderness than she treated most humans; Meskerem knew she would never shove a random paper into its pages so carelessly.

Pulling it out slowly, Meskerem braced herself for what she immediately sensed would be something she shouldn't see: WE WILL FIND HER THERE. WE WILL FINISH WHAT WE STARTED.

Meskerem stared at the thick, torn sheet. She turned it over, searching for any sign of its origin. The script itself was nondescript, the English letters resembling *fidel* in the way every Ethiopian's handwriting did. Sighing to herself and unsure of what to do, she stuffed the sheet into her pocket and ran out the door.

The general lived in a massive house near the American embassy, the kind that dwarfed all buildings in its immediate area, not for practicality, but to make a statement. When she was younger, Meskerem had walked past these houses and scoffed at the arrogance of the people she'd imagined living inside their walls. What kind of people built monuments to their own grandeur?

Meskerem had been uncertain what to wear for dinner, but she knew nothing she'd packed was right. She had no intention of wearing any color other than black, so she settled for the same black jeans she'd worn earlier that day at Shiro Meda. They still smelled of dust, chickens, and children. She grabbed a top from Almaz's closet, a blouse she'd always loved. It still smelled of Almaz's perfume. Dior.

The family was pleasant enough. The general's wife didn't seem to have a name or many original thoughts. His son, Elias, stared at her from across the table, asking repeatedly why she didn't play video games. He did not call her "Sister," and for that she was eternally grateful.

When the house staff cleared up after dessert and the general's wife retired to her parlor, Meskerem asked to see her father's office.

The two walked the two-kilometer path talking mostly about why she still smelled of the market. She may not have been ready to call him "Father" yet, he insisted, but surely she could at least try to act like a general's daughter. The thought bothered her, but Meskerem tried to laugh anyway. The sound of her ambivalent chuckle reverberated off the trees lining the road.

"I think John will really like the *jebena*," she offered. "I don't make coffee, but he loves it. I told him about it before I came to dinner, and he sounded so happy," she said, unsure of what compelled her to add a lie.

The general was pleased to hear his suggestion would be adored, even if it was by a man he'd never met. He reveled in the feeling of being needed somehow. When he opened the door to his office, he offered Meskerem some whiskey. Turning away from her for a moment, he walked toward his desk to pour from the decanter he saved for special guests.

"Usually this is for diplomats. Or colonels. Sometimes kings even," he said, back still turned. Meskerem stared at him in this environment, suddenly struck by how harsh his consonants sounded when they echoed among all the oak. The door was so heavy, the chairs so tall. She didn't belong here.

As the general moved toward her, Meskerem slipped her hand in the pocket of her jeans and pulled out the piece of paper.

"Do . . . do you know what this means?" she stammered, shoving the sheet toward his face, filled with rage.

The force of her movement caught him off balance, and he fell to the floor. His glass crashed down with him, shards embedding into his palm as the whiskey mixed with his blood. Meskerem screamed at the sight of the blood, then started to crouch toward him until she saw the look in his eyes.

He knew. He had to know. He'd known all this time, and he'd never called after her. He'd known all this time, and he'd never stopped any of it.

Pressing down on his palm to extract the glass, Robel started to choke on his own words. They came tumbling out rapidly, his heaves interspersed with thick tears that only served to intensify Meskerem's anger. She hovered above him as the general told her everything, her body shaking. Robel's blood seeped into the paper as he spoke of his father's threats, and she snatched the sheet out of his hand. Turning toward the door, she noticed Girma's name carved into the oak frame. This had been his office too. This is where he had made the decision. This is where her mother's life had been wagered.

She knew then that they could never coexist, that the general had a debt to pay.

Robel tried to steady himself and stand again, calling after her. "*Babiye*," he whimpered, stumbling as he rested one palm against the desk where his father had drawn up the plans to have Tigist killed.

"*Babiye*," he repeated, finally resting his weight against the desk where he'd begged for her life to be spared, for the baby to live.

"*Benatish*," he whispered, stretching the bloody palm out to touch her shoulder.

She turned to face him quickly, her body moving with an untrained agility more frightening than his own.

Meskerem's eyes were the last thing Robel saw before she reached the last rifle Girma had left him. They were warm, sad.

They looked so familiar.

# OSTRICH

BY REBECCA FISSEHA

*National Palace*


The ostriches are so vivid to me still, as if I had photographed them with my heart. If it weren't for their small bulbous heads and huge round middles, they would have blended in with the iron bars of the palace fence that ran the length of the avenue that my mother drove down daily. They used to observe us, standing in twos and threes, or alone, deep in the tall grass; willowy creatures as mysterious as everything else in the palace compound beyond that fence.

I never noticed them until my mother pointed them out, to help me power through my terror of a rise halfway down the avenue, a speed bump that to six-year-old me was pure torture because on every lead-up to that momentary bounce, I was horrified that my heart would fly out of my mouth. As we approached the drop to that avenue, I would beg my mother to let me get out and walk. She convinced me that the ostriches came and stood near the fence every day just to see if I would be brave once again. It worked. Every time I survived the bump with my heart intact, I would lock eyes with one *segon* and feel all its approval.

But one afternoon during my first year of school, I forgot all about the ostriches because I saw a man sprawled on the ground where I would normally brace for the jolt. After we passed him, I watched him receding through the rear window.

He was lying on his side on the lane closest to the palace side-walk. His legs were bent as if he were running. A newspaper hooked to his shirt, flapping his chest. He was yawning in his sleep and his hands were outstretched. Maybe he had been reaching for something before sleep overtook him, or he was holding that thing in his dream.

My mother usually kept her window down, resting her left elbow on the edge and driving with only her right hand. After passing far enough down the avenue that I could barely see the man on the ground and I began to wonder if he had been there at all, we emerged from the shadows of the trees and into the light, crossing a short bridge over a dirty stream. I turned and saw that my mother had rolled up her window. She held the steering wheel tight with both hands and leaned forward as if there were something written on the hood of the car that she had to read.

Seeing people on the street was nothing new in Addis Ababa, but I had never seen one asleep on the asphalt.

"Why was he sleeping there?" I asked.

My mother braked suddenly and shot out her right hand toward the passenger seat, as if my voice, coming from the back, was an animal that had darted in front of the car. Slowly, she pulled back her hand and picked up speed past the church, racing across Revolution Square without checking for merging cars from five other roads. Overlooking the square was a big poster of three Russian men in profile. We were on our way to pick up my father from work. His office was in the direction of their gaze, but my mother took the road behind them, which leads to the airport.

"I missed seeing my *segon* today," I said.

Realizing her mistake, she turned onto another street. A tear rolled down the side of her face.

"It's okay, I'll see it tomorrow," I said. Her tears multiplied. "Won't I?"

"Sit quiet."

We crossed the square again, this time slowly and carefully, passing under the billboard of the three Russian men who watched us disappear up the road that led to my father's office.

Once there, he stepped into the car and kissed my mother hello where the tears had been. "You're late."

"We took a wrong turn."

"I saw a sleeping man on the road."

Before my father could tell me for the thousandth time not to interrupt adults, my mother said, staring ahead, "Expect us ten minutes later from now on."

My father forgot about me but said what I was thinking. "Why?"

"I'm not driving past the palace anymore. I'll find another way."

"But that would take longer. There's no sense in that, with the gas rations."

She shrugged.

"But that's the quickest way home."

My father waited. I knew that wait. It meant that their conversation was one response away from becoming a fight. All it needed was for her to say words sharper than his. Unlike other adults, my parents never hid their fights from anyone. They believed that disagreeing was normal and good, and always kissed afterward, no matter who won.

But my mother didn't respond that day. She let the silence be. It lingered even after my father rolled down his window to the sound of the city.

\* \* \*

At home, while I was supposed to be playing in the garden until dinner, I hovered outside my parents' bedroom window.

I heard my father say, "In this curfew, every minute is precious—"

"Get yourself home if you're in such a rush."

I smiled. The wait was over. We were still normal.

"Walk? Take public transport? You mean the very risks we should keep to a minimum?"

"Keep pushing me and I'll never drive again," she said tearfully. This threat was real. She was the only one with a driver's license. But my father brushed it off.

"You wouldn't dare."

"Try me. If you think you can get a license with your condition, go ahead."

My mother's crying became muffled. My father must have been embracing her, calming her down—she had won the fight.

Plucking leaves from a bush and staring at the soil below it, I listened, crushed that I might never see my *segon* again.

"The sleeping man?" my mother said. I jumped, thinking I had been discovered eavesdropping, which was just as bad as interrupting them. "The sleeping man your child thinks she saw on the road?"

It was quiet for a while. Then my father said, "He wasn't asleep."

"No."

"None of them are," he said, inhaling deeply. "But love, where can you drive and not see that now? Soon there'll be very few roads without a dead body."

"Then I'll find those roads, no matter the detour."

"And the day you take too long to pick me up, and find me asleep?"

"What do I tell our child? That nowadays people just fall asleep on the streets? She'll understand they are dead people. And then?"

"Remind her to close her eyes and think of her *segon*."

The next afternoon my mother sat me in the front passenger seat on our way to pick up my father. When we neared the bump, I screamed and shut my eyes. She swerved but continued driving. "What's wrong?"

"The man from yesterday is still there."

She looked stunned, like a rock had hit her through the window. She didn't say anything else to me. When we picked up my father, I moved to the backseat.

The following afternoon, I closed my eyes even earlier, because I could already see him.

"My dear, he's not there," my mother said, but she sounded unsure. "The *segon* took him to a better place to sleep."

I kept my eyes closed.

"Open your eyes, it's waiting for you." I only opened them after I felt that we had driven over the little bridge beyond the avenue.

The next afternoon, at the top of the avenue, I begged her to use the two lanes farthest from the palace. She pulled over under the stone lions guarding the first palace gate.

"Do you want to walk? You've always wanted to walk."

I shook my head violently, terrified at the thought of being any nearer to that man.

"Good. Then stop closing your eyes. There's no one on this road. How much the *segonoch* must have missed seeing those pretty eyes!"

From then until we left Ethiopia, we continued to drive down that avenue, on that lane, running over the man. My mother would say, "It's just a bump," pretending that nothing was wrong. I was not afraid of the bump anymore, but I hated it. I had to feel the car crushing the man's head, breaking his hands and feet, flattening his tattered red chest under our tires. I hated it for the squelching sound of the man's flesh and the jab of his splintered bones that vibrated into my body, past the tires and the metal of the car.

Through my tears, I would see my *segon* and it would seem to multiply, as if it had called the rest of its friends from deeper in the compound to come out and watch what a brave girl I was growing into.

At home, my mother began to respond to my father's disagreements with silence, changing from a brief electric lull of the better days to a suspended tension that tinted the rest of my childhood. I stopped listening for the fights outside their bedroom window because listening to silence was exhausting.

I began to see the ostriches everywhere in Addis, no matter what road we drove on, whether I had my eyes open or closed. That avenue cut so deep in my memory that even with a map in front of me, I would have insisted that all Addis roads were teased out of it, that it was the origin and destination of all journeys.

Years later, the memory found me in Toronto, outside the window at my Queen's Park office, where I had a desk with a view of University Avenue that dropped away from an intersection just like the one in front of the palace.

With age, I accepted that what my younger self had kept seeing had been that man's ghost. He faded into the background of my life until my parents died. Then I began thinking of him again. He seemed to be the only other being whose loneliness matched mine. I wondered if he was still there, watched over by the ostriches, unclaimed and alone like me. I hoped for it. If he wasn't, I was truly alone.

"Why have you been brooding out of that window lately?"

The question came from Nick, my colleague with a desk across from mine, a lanky, bearded redhead with big brown eyes and an effortless smile. We'd been hired as clerks on the Justice Policy Committee at the same time—four years earlier—and had stomached the depressing job longer than all who came after us. When my parents died, only he among our colleagues didn't wimp out with, *Call me if you need anything.* Instead, he got into the habit of randomly calling me up just to chat, and one day bought me a coffee mug identical to his. So it didn't occur to me to lie to him.

"University Avenue reminds me of another avenue from my childhood," I said.

"Where in Addis is that?"

"In front of the National Palace."

Of course, he immediately began googling it.

"It cuts the city evenly top to bottom."

He frowned. "Not quite."

"What? I'll have you know my city began on Mount Entoto. Originally, the avenue was just a dirt road for coming down from there."

"It's called Menelik II Avenue."

"Okay."

"And there are hotels and gas stations before it joins with—"

"Revolution Square."

"Meskel Square." He double clicked on the mouse to zoom in. "And before the square there are cafés. A post office. Banks. Even a little . . . bridge? And a church. St. Stephen's. And a big fat street, Jomo Kenyatta."

It was as if a memory wire had been tripped—the bridge over which I'd fleetingly spied slick teens bathing in a muddy, garbage-flecked stream, the church where I had prostrated myself for my sins every Good Friday—all these places sprang into my mind.

I was now looking over Nick's shoulder at the bird's-eye view of Addis, a city I'd mostly known from behind car windows, with its streets labeled and points of interest dotted with icons. There was a roughly rectangular green patch across from the palace, called Africa Park. Nick moved the cursor over the map, graciously not pointing out additional facts about that avenue. Not only did it not go down the dead center of Addis at all, but it was also merely an offshoot of Entoto Street, which itself began timidly somewhere near the base of Mount Entoto in the city's northeast.

I liked that Nick hadn't taken my word about the avenue as truth and hadn't assumed that I would know what I was talking about simply because I was "from" there. I rewarded him with a smile and went back to my desk.

At the end of the day, he caught up with me on my way to the Queen's Park subway station and suggested we walk to the next stop. He adjusted his long strides to match mine, stepping firmly like a man determined that his footprints would be found by archaeologists thousands of years from now.

As we came around the crescent where University Avenue began its drop, he asked, "So, you never explained why lately."

"Why lately what?"

"Why lately you've been looking out the window while thinking of Menelik II Avenue when you should be transcribing witness statements."

"I rode down that avenue every day with my parents."

"But they died awhile ago."

I stopped in my tracks. "According to who?"

"Sorry."

"I guess it's all relative," I said wryly. I started walking again. "I saw something there once, and I wonder if it's still there. I'll look for it when I go back next month." Officially, I was going back to represent the diasporic portion of the bereaved, but more than that I wanted to soothe my ache for a trip to the one place in Addis that might stir my blood.

"What did you see?"

"Okay, we're here," I said, and descended the stairs at the St. Patrick station. I purposely took the train in the opposite direction from the one Nick had to take.

The next time we left the office at the same time, he suggested we walk to the second subway stop beyond Queen's Park, as if more walking was all that was needed to induce an answer out of me.

"You know, if we keep going in this direction we'll eventually get to Ethiopia," he joked.

"You a good swimmer?"

"The best."

Using tactics we both knew well from committee sessions with witnesses, he kept trying to find out more. He was earnest yet gentle, so that I couldn't bring myself to tell him to mind his own business. I began to enjoy our walks, and I did feel an inner loosening. Whenever we found ourselves in front of the elevator at the same time at the end of the day, I felt something I hadn't felt since those rides over the bump: a little jolt of my heart.

Eventually, we walked all the way to Harbourfront. There was nowhere to go other than into the lake, unless we took a ferry to the islands, but it was too early in the season. He invited me to his place.

In his living room, there were many battered *Lonely Planet* books marking his backpacking trips every summer to places like Cambodia, Myanmar, Bosnia and Herzegovina, and Guatemala. When he told me that these locations corresponded to the backgrounds of his ex-girlfriends, all of whom had been asylum seekers, my heartbeat sped up.

"So do you go to the scene of the crime before or after you take the women under your healing wing?" I said. "Let me guess, you first pick a place, go there, and then come back and find a woman whose trauma you can whisper away. Or do you import them with you?"

I waited, just like my father used to do.

He said, "Why not?"

"Fix historic wrongs one girl at a time, huh? Who do you think you are, a one-man Red Cross? Why not start in your own backyard, then? Oh wait, they don't print *Lonely Planet* for reservations."

"Even if they did, a white settler like me shouldn't—"

"Right, right," I said. I tossed *Guatemala* back on the coffee table. We stared at it as if it might get up and do a Mayan dance. "There are stone lions on top of the pillars of the first palace gate in the fence," I continued, "at the intersection where it falls away like University Avenue does."

"Stone lions, eh? Not real ones?"

"Nope."

"Because the emperor used to have a bunch."

"Everyone knows that," I scoffed.

"What's something everyone doesn't know? That only *you* know?"

I got up. "That it's time for me to go home."

"Want company?"

I knew he wasn't talking about my apartment. "What's in it for you?"

"I'd like to see that road for myself." From the way he was looking at me, I could swear he'd somehow found out that whenever he was away from the office for a long period, I would take his mug out of the kitchen cupboard and put it in my desk drawer for safekeeping because I couldn't stand the thought of anybody else's lips on it. "I wouldn't mind," I finally said.

Within weeks I was behind his sofa, peering over his shoulder at a computer screen again. One of the tabs on his browser was open to the Hilton Addis website.

"Is that in your budget?" I asked.

"You see how close it is to Menelik II Avenue."

"Addis didn't used to be a place you go wandering around on foot," I couldn't help objecting. "When I lived there, we always drove on the shortest route possible. On Sundays, cars weren't even allowed on the road. Because of gas rations, only cars with license plates that started with even or odd numbers could be on the road on alternating Sundays."

"Everyone had a car?"

Shit. "We did," I faltered. "But even people on foot kept moving."

"Things have changed."

Clinging to one fact he couldn't debate, I said, "You could only ride downhill on that avenue."

"You mean it's one-way. Otherwise you could as easily be heading up or down, depending on where you were going or coming from."

All I knew is that we were always going down.

* * *

Nick read *Lonely Planet Ethiopia* on and off during most of the fourteen-hour flight there. I couldn't. The very idea of a *Lonely Planet* for Ethiopia bothered me. Worse, it said nothing about the avenue. The guide was already showing signs of wear and tear, and wouldn't stay new or lonely for long. Like all the other used *Lonely Planet* volumes back at Nick's, *Ethiopia* would come to bear the odors and stains of the places we passed through. Its edges would fray and curl in on the sum of our adventures, and its spine would crack.

During the taxi ride from Bole International Airport, Nick kept it in his hand, with his index finger between the pages marking the beginning of the Addis Ababa chapter, a mere twenty-six pages long. He watched the city with the smugness of having done his homework, as if he were taking me to *his* home country.

He pointed out all the pedestrians in the streets, despite the time of night. "That's a lot of people going somewhere with purpose."

They materialized out of the black air in the glare of the headlights, lasting only as long as it took us to pass them. Though it was night, what struck me about Addis was the quality of the light—the trembling glow of single bulbs over produce stands and kiosks; the blinking stammers of festive strings at the doors and windows of humble bars; the exclamations of streetlights and billboards as we neared the center. Together, it was an illuminated murmuring whose message my ears had yet to decipher.

As soon as the taxi crossed Revolution Square, then Jomo Kenyatta and the church, then the little bridge before joining the heavy traffic ascending Menelik II, our stalled debate over the avenue's directionality became moot. It turned out that the avenue was actually a pair of roadways going in opposite directions, separated by Africa Park.

My memory widened out, bringing in sunrise and sunset and the distinct shadows each cast over the palace side of the avenue. Preempting yet another self-satisfied observation from Nick, I said, "In the mornings, it was an uphill drive, and in the late afternoons, near sunset, it was a downhill drive. Of course, I only just remembered the side that runs along the palace."

"Leave it to you to recall only the downhill side."

"The sunset side," I said. It used to be the best the part of the day, when my mother and I went home together.

The next morning, we stood at the intersection before Mene-lik II Avenue. Ahead, cars dipped out of sight as the avenue swallowed them up one by one. Beyond awaited curbstones like bad teeth, grass-fringed sidewalks, the long palace fence with evenly spaced gates, columns of trees, and a glimmer of light that marked the opening to Revolution Square.

From this distance and with so many cars racing across all three lanes, the bump was indiscernible, to say nothing of any ghost that might still be lying on his side, arms outstretched and mouth yawning.

Nick stood with feet planted apart, arms akimbo, like an old-time hunter-explorer striking a pose beside his kill, taking it all in when even the stone lions, still perched atop the gate pillars, preferred to look away.

"I was thinking we'd start here, going downhill, then continue on to wherever these four well-performing legs of ours take us," he said. "And hopefully at some point you'll find what you used to see and let me in on it."

Morning light illuminated the half of the avenue not

shadowed by a row of old trees that stood along the palace fence like sentinels. The pressure from their roots made the sidewalk look like a bunched-up carpet, begging for someone to grab it by the corners and snap it flat.

We began to walk single file down the broken sidewalk: Nick behind me, *Lonely Planet* straining the left pocket of his long shorts, crisp American fifties for emergencies stuffed into the right, camera tucked up his sleeve, the strap around his wrist.

I marched briskly, feeling small and vulnerable in this vast airy tunnel where there was nothing to grab onto other than a palace fence that was off-limits and the abrasive trunks of ancient trees teetering as if they were ready to collapse at the gentlest kiss of wind. Pedestrians ambled by, leaning into each other, more concerned with the uneven ground than the cacophonous rattle of cars speeding past. I kept my eyes on the ground too. All I could think of was the approaching rise, torn between wanting to see that man and not.

Nick mused pleasantly on the benefits of walking, how you discover details you never could from inside a vehicle. There were wrought-iron gates at every interval of the fence, and in the center of each were elaborate designs of shields, crowns, crossed spears, and Ethiopic alphabet characters. Predictably, he stopped at the first set of gates.

"Is this a coat of arms?" He traced his finger along a character that resembled a jigsaw puzzle piece. "How do you say this?"

"*Ha*," I said.

"As in *happy?*"

"And that one," I said, pointing at a three-pronged fork with a handle that dropped from its left side and bent slightly outward at the tip, "is *se*. As in *since.*"

"Happy since . . . infinity?" he said. He touched a character at the center of the design. It did resemble a horizontal infinity symbol, with a vertical line through its twist.

"That is *keh*," I said. "*Keh*, as in . . ." But the snap of the *k*, like a breaking branch, would be impossible for him to sound out. "Never mind. You'll never get it right."

My voice had come out with edge. He flinched but kept a straight face, like my mother during those aborted fights with my father.

"What's *ha-se-keh*?"

"The last emperor's initials. First name, last name, title," I explained, touching the corresponding characters.

"Out of sequence? Shouldn't it be *keh-ha-se*?"

"Visually it works better, as you can see."

Nick retraced the unifying but to him unpronounceable, not to mention misplaced, **Φ**'s twisted loop. He gazed up beyond the treetops, his shoulders slouched like a child in awe. He shook the camera loose from his sleeve and dropped into his palm. He backed away from the gate, almost onto the road.

"Careful," I said under my breath. He didn't hear me.

I started walking again and glanced toward what—other than the coat of arms—he was most likely capturing: details of the fence segments with eighteen red spears joined by stars ringed with silver orbits, stone pillars between the spears. I returned my gaze to the sidewalk, itself geometrically beautiful: six concrete tiles in a row, six inches square, each tile containing a diamond. Between the tiles were gaps of earth filled with knots of parched grass.

In the slight upward bend of the ground, I sensed the incline of the upcoming bump. I lifted my eyes toward the passing cars, then forced myself to behold the rise.

Nothing. Even through the constant blur of tires and

metal, I could see that it was empty, neither the man nor his ghost lying there. The ostriches really had taken him away to rest elsewhere, like my mother had insisted. The past, having passed, was even lonelier than me. Up close, the bump looked insignificant. I felt silly to have been so frightened of it, sorry to have caused my mother so much distress.

I pried off a shoe and, like a swimmer testing the water temperature, skimmed my foot on the asphalt where it met the sidewalk. Other than the vibrations of traffic, my flesh detected no presence. I put my shoe back on. At the fence, I strained for a view of my long-forgotten friends, those elegant ostriches, in the overgrowth of the garden. There was nothing but the ancient trees, the tall grass.

The percussive bursts of Nick's camera reached me before he did. I pointed into the compound like a shy kid at a zoo. He looked in that direction, expecting to see something worth a snapshot.

"There used to be ostriches in there."

"That's what you saw?"

"They saw me too," I said. "But they're dead now."

He stuck his face through the bars. "Who knows how long they can live in the wild."

"That's not the wild. It's a palace compound."

"Could've fooled me. Maybe *ha-keh-se*'s lions snacked on them."

"One forward kick from an ostrich can put a lion out for the count."

He continued to take pictures, my eyes following the direction of his aim. On top of pillars: stone spheres. On fronts of pillars: iron-framed glass-shaded lamps. Or glass jagged. Or glass gone. Inside the frame was a white fluorescent bulb, naked like bone. Etched on stone pillars: warriors, statesmen, and statements. Lions above their heads. Lions on bellies, legs tucked, claws poised over edge.

"Can I have the camera?" I asked as he walked past me. I wanted to preserve only one part of this area: the bump. He handed me the camera and kept walking.

I stepped to the edge of the sidewalk and aimed the camera at the rise in the asphalt. The passengers couldn't help dipping their heads as their cars bounced over it, as if in homage to its power. When there was a gap between the moving cars, I took the shot. The screen blinked, then reverted to showing the road and the blurred lower halves of cars.

As I turned to catch up to Nick, I saw in my peripheral vision a mass of earth rising from the deep bush of the palace compound. I stopped. The mound became a tall, slim figure with a small head. It lifted its long legs and stepped over the dry brush and shrubbery, onto the palace driveway. Steady, graceful like a thin gray bird, it advanced to the fence, gaining speed, one bony leg hurtling forward on the heels of the other. But instead of grand flapping wings, an enraged human voice shouted, "No photo!"

Not an ostrich, but an armed soldier sprinting toward us, chest puffed, in blue fatigues. The soles of his dark boots were jagged and his body bottom-heavy with a rifle and belt of bullets. His finger was on the raised beak of the trigger, ready to bite.

Nick ran back and stood between the fence and me. He put one hand out behind him to keep me back. "No photo!" he echoed urgently. With his other hand, he reached into his pocket. He extended a fifty-dollar bill through the fence just as the soldier reached us on the other side. The soldier slapped Nick's hand away. The money sailed to the ground on the soldier's side.

"We are sorry," Nick pleaded.

"Memory!"

"We are very, *very* sorry."

"Memory! Memory!" The soldier held out his open palm, the blank space between the head, heart, and fate lines hungry for the camera's memory card.

As they screeched back and forth, I extracted myself from Nick's extended arm. With a trembling finger, I pressed the *display* button on the camera.

There he was. The rise I had photographed, which had ensconced the sleeping man inside its bulge, had offered him up. My friend as I remembered him. No, worse—pulverized to almost nothing from twenty years of being forgotten, driven over by people hurrying on with their lives.

Still facing the solider, Nick made a blind grab for the camera like a driver clamoring for something in the backseat. I tightened my hold with both hands. Nick tugged at it, but not hard. He didn't take my resistance seriously. Only when I yanked it close to my body did he turn around. In his eyes was that old terror of mine, translated by this lethal moment into absolute hatred.

"Are you fucking insane? Let go of it!" he snapped.

"No! He's mine!"

"We'll get another card!"

"No!"

"Let go of it *now*!"

The soldier echoed Nick: "Let go! Let go!"

"Here is what I was remembering!" I said. "Don't you want to see?"

"You can just tell me. Don't get us killed!"

"You have to see!"

I doubled over the camera, using all my strength, wishing

I was an ostrich with a neck so long I could spot danger days away and gallop like the wind. The top of my head pushing against Nick's torso, we shuffled in a primitive dance until we'd switched places, and Nick's back was to the traffic and mine to the solider who hadn't ceased his "No memory! No memory!" refrain.

The soldier grabbed my shoulder and slammed my back against the fence. The camera blasted out of my hand and fell at my feet. Nick, betrayed by the energy he had put into pulling the strap, toppled backward into oncoming traffic and got hit by a car before it swerved onto the sidewalk. Drivers stopped, got out, rushed with their hands on their heads to his broken body on the ground.

I was free of the solider. I could hear his boots slap-crunching gravel as he escaped into the bush, but I stayed plastered to the fence. By the weak flailing of his hands, I knew Nick was alive. Bit by bit, the crowd around his body grew layers like the rings of a tree trunk, and I lost sight of him. But he was still alive—that, I knew. I felt ashamed. He was the end to my loneliness, not some ghost, and I had almost turned him into the very thing he'd tried so hard to pry out of me—a dead man.

On the camera display, one body part at a time, the sleeping man faded, leaving a simple snapshot of a bare rise of gray cracked asphalt.

# DUST, ASH, FLIGHT

BY MAAZA MENGISTE

*Mercato*

## I

They would begin digging for bones tomorrow. Alfonso stood next to the jail staring at the flat landscape of the Addis Ababa military base. He'd come today because he wanted to see the site before Lara and the other forensic scientists started, wanted to quietly rest his photographer's eye on the grounds they would soon be shoveling. He wondered if he'd be able to identify a femur from a humerus or distinguish what made one set of human bones young and another old. The Argentine scientists were in Ethiopia looking for the remains of prisoners who had been taken from their families and never heard from again. He came to photograph those remains, to trap between shutter and aperture fragments of prisoners like those he'd been forced to photograph in Argentina. Alfonso adjusted his camera to zoom in on a pick leaning against a wooden fence. Would there be anything in this drab compound that would remind him of the grassy land behind the Navy Petty-Officers School of Mechanics in Buenos Aires?

*It's not what you're used to,* Lara had said the day she finally agreed to let him join the team traveling to Ethiopia. *Your subjects won't be alive,* she said, her light-brown eyes sharp as she took in his stiff suit jacket and scratched cuff links. *There's no art in this,* she added, disgust evident in the smile she let settle on his camera equipment and unopened portfolio. She was a woman shaped out of angles, her bones delicate. She'd kept a notebook with her during the interview but had written nothing while he talked, had chosen instead to pin her unflinching gaze on him. She'd looked tired, her eyes sunken, as if they would bend light if they could and bask only in shadows. *You must know who I am,* he'd wanted to remind her. *I was the last face so many saw before they disappeared. Who better than me to photograph what remains?*

*The others might ask you about a relative who'd been jailed at the Navy Mechanics School when you were there,* she'd said at the end as they stood at the door of her lab, interview over, his hand extended but ignored. *It's better to discuss those things after this job is done, don't mix the two.* She'd nodded and walked back to her desk.

Alfonso opened his lens wide to take in the dry, cracked earth. He saw two Ethiopian men watching him intently from a short distance. Each of them held a photograph to their chest, the image facing his direction. Alfonso felt his stomach tighten. He knew this ritual, recognized the hopes they were trying to place in his hands. He'd seen this same gesture in Argentina. Strangers would stop him in the streets and ask, *Aren't you the one the newspapers talked about? The photographer jailed at the Navy School who took those pictures?* Then, out of nowhere, a photo. *This is my mother, my sister, my father, my aunt, my grandson.* So many. A procession of faces and bodies both candid and posed, staring at him, waiting to be found, to be taken out of the land of the disappeared and reclaimed.

Alfonso lowered the camera and held up both hands to the approaching Ethiopians. He walked backward, shaking his head. *Yekerta,* he repeated again and again, silently thanking the guide for teaching the scientists and him what would be the most important word on this trip, in this country full of people still waiting to properly mourn their dead. *Sorry. I'm sorry.*

It was Lara's idea to go to the dusty *tej bet* near the hotel that night before the first dig. The rest of the team, tired from a day of meetings and briefings, had excused themselves to sleep, and only Alfonso remained.

"I drink one beer the night before we start working at a new place," she said to him on the way there. "Everything will taste like dirt by tomorrow."

The bar was a tiny, dim building made of what looked like adobe. It was painted blue with a pale-green door that swung limply on rusted hinges. A scratched-up slab of wood made up the counter and, behind it, a strikingly pretty waitress with clothes that clung to her soft body smiled and pushed two beers toward them as they sat down.

They drank in silence, Alfonso trying to feign disinterest in the envelope Lara had taken out of her purse and held gingerly at the edges.

It was then that Gideon walked in. Lara shifted her attention to the door and watched the old man with interest as he stopped and stared at them, momentarily startled, before taking a seat at the end of the counter.

She stared as if she were scrutinizing a document. When she spoke, it seemed directed to no one. "He's lost someone," she said. Her black wavy hair fell over her face and she pushed it back and took a drink of beer.

He stole another look at Lara. Despite what she'd told him at the interview, the other scientists had plied him with questions about those they knew who'd also been jailed at the Navy School. She was the only one who'd never asked.

They set their beers on the counter and watched Gideon as the waitress started talking to him, animated and tender-voiced. Gideon sat straight, alert and expressionless. He seemed to refuse to look their way; he simply pressed himself deeper into his seat and wrapped his fingers around his beer, nodding to the waitress's chatter. It was the way he stared at his hands that made Alfonso look at his own. What was he doing in Addis Ababa?

It was hard to tell his age. Gideon looked sixty; he carried a weariness twice those years. In the soft light that outlined his straight nose and papery skin, Gideon resembled a worn prophet, a man who should have been illuminated by nothing but dying candles.

*Tenastilign.* Alfonso tried to repeat the greeting again. He'd never learn the hard consonants of Amharic, the lilt of the language. He dipped his head for a quick bow and waited for Gideon to return the greeting. He smiled, understanding after only four days in Addis Ababa the reserve of Ethiopians.

Gideon took a long, deep drink of his beer and turned away.

After another failed attempt at conversation the pretty waitress with dewy eyes told Alfonso that Gideon didn't talk. "He sings," she said in her thick English. "Famous. A long time ago. Now . . ." She wrapped a hand around her throat and squeezed. Her bright-red nail polish clashed with the soft glow of the light hanging over her head.

"He can't talk?" Lara asked, leaning into the counter, suddenly interested. "How come?"

The girl shook her head. "He just stopped. He drinks one beer every night." There was an awkward pause as if there was more she wanted to say but didn't know how.

Alfonso caught her staring at him, curious about their

presence in this bar that was far off the tourist maps. He smiled at her and she turned quickly to drop a cassette tape into the dilapidated stereo. A mournful voice held a note above a jazz trumpet climbing down the scale in slow steps.

The change in Gideon was immediate, but maybe only he could see it. Maybe only a man who'd witnessed so many moments of terror would have been able to recognize it. Gideon folded into himself and became just another man caving into his chest until his back could bend no more, became just another body in a long line of bodies that Alfonso was ordered to photograph, became just another face filled with fear staring starkly into his lens, pleading without words for a salvation both subject and photographer knew would not come.

"*Dónde?*" Alfonso asked the commander, knowing where the brightest patch of sunlight streamed into the window of the small room in the Navy School of Mechanics. "*Aquí?*" He swallowed hard and pointed, disgusted by his impulse to photograph in the best light. "Here is good."

The prisoner shuffled against the blank white wall and stood in the gentle sunbeam. He was a young man with a long face and wild curly hair now matted to his head. He shook in his chains, his thin arms cut and bruised, his eyes nearly swollen shut.

"*Señor.*" Alfonso spoke softly to prevent the sudden jerk that raising his camera usually elicited. *Lo siento*, he said with his eyes. "Raise your chin and look at the camera," he said with his mouth. The young man stared at him instead, as they always did, and curved his chest as if to dodge a blow to the heart. Alfonso heard a soft whimper, saw the trembling lips, then forced himself to meet the young man's gaze. He saw that moment when disbelief gave way to naked terror. *I'm sorry*, he wanted to say, but the commander was standing just behind him with his thick breaths and sweat, mumbling, "*Bueno. Bueno,* the *generalissimo* will like this one for his collection. You'll take one of me next week for a new passport." The commander winked. "You'll make me look like a new man, *sí?*"

He was on the fourth floor of the Navy School. He'd been picked up in San Isidro just outside of Buenos Aires three months ago. He'd been stopped at gunpoint in his car. He'd had his camera on the seat next to him, the windows down, enjoying the bit of wind that cut through the moist evening heat. There had been three soldiers and they gave no reason for dragging him out of his car. It was Argentina in 1978, General Jorge Videla was in charge, thousands were being disappeared. Maybe those were reasons enough. But what he thought of, in the dark backseat of an unmarked car speeding down Avenida del Libertador, were all those years he'd turned away from his mother, a woman so hungry for affection that Alfonso was sure it was her heart that killed her, not her asthma.

The music was dying. The waitress hummed, her voice wavering over the last notes before fading in a soft breath. Her expression was earnest, her eyes tender. He could have watched her for another hour, could have held her under the steady gaze of his lens until her body swayed just so, until she was simply a figure dissected by a thick band of shadow and a wilting strip of light.

She lifted her eyes to him. "'Tizita.' A famous song," she said, turning the stereo off with a careful press of a button then tilting toward him so her arms rested next to his on the counter. "It means memory. A good song to hear in Ethiopia." She stole a shy glance at him through her lashes, avoiding

Lara, who had removed a carefully folded newspaper article from the envelope.

Alfonso cleared his throat and smiled uncertainly. "*Birra.*" He pointed at himself and Lara and then to Gideon. "What's that?" he finally asked Laura, gesturing to the article.

"No more, thank you." Lara waved the new beer aside. She slid the news clipping toward him. "So you understand what we'll be doing tomorrow."

Alfonso looked at the article. There had been a massacre of an entire village of men, women, and children in a place called El Mozote in the mountains of Morazán in El Salvador. Hundreds of corpses had been found, ranging from newborn to elderly. Villagers in the surrounding area reported a ghost had begun to roam above the mountains after the *matanza* by the Salvadoran army. Naked and wild-haired, she could be seen crouched near the river under the moonlight, wailing for her dead children with a dying fish flopping in her hand. Argentine scientists had arrived to exhume the site of the massacre and had been cautioned by villagers and the military about the ghost.

He closely examined the image of Lara and four colleagues standing next to a roped-off area, pointing at three tiny crushed skulls.

"How long ago?" he asked. "You look much younger."

"It doesn't matter," she said. She took the clipping from him and folded it precisely and slipped it back into the envelope. "The ghost the people claimed they saw," she said, turning to face him. "There was no ghost. There's no such thing." She had leaned close to him, her back to the waitress and Gideon.

Alfonso nodded, confused. "People make up these stories."

Lara shook her head. She spoke urgently. "There was no

ghost because even though the army killed infants and children and weak women, even though they burned men alive, even though they retraced their steps to make sure they'd gotten everyone—there was one survivor. More than a thousand killed but one lived. She hid in bushes then ran into the mountains. I met her while we were there digging. She came down from the mountain when she saw us with the bones. She wanted to find her children." Lara paused, her eyes on the envelope. "She lived. She's still living."

The waitress held the new beer toward Alfonso, who shook his head. He waited, uncertain what to say to Lara. This was the most she had said about anything not relating to their work in Ethiopia.

"Just because someone is missing," she continued, her gaze direct, "it doesn't mean we'll find them. You don't know anything unless you have proof." She was focused on his camera. "If you can't see something, you have nothing."

Alfonso expected her to get up and walk out after that, the silence drawing thick between them. But she didn't. Instead, she stared at his camera for so long, Alfonso raised it to his eyes. And when she didn't do anything, he took off the lens cap and adjusted the meter. He suddenly felt he could see her better this way, framed in the small box that shut out everything except those deep-set eyes and hollow cheeks, the rapid blinking and slow shake of the head. The slender, frail fingers reaching up to wipe an eye and dropping to reveal once again the stern flatness of her gaze. He aimed.

"No," she said firmly. He flinched at the way Lara frowned and her hands flew up to cover her face.

"No, no—no photo," the waitress said, reaching out as if to take the camera from Alfonso. "No."

It was then that Alfonso noticed that Gideon had stood

up and covered his head with one arm. The waitress had also moved to stand in front of Gideon, her body becoming rigid and stiff, straight-backed and strong. All pleasantness had gone from her face.

Gideon turned his back to them and walked out quickly. The door creaked on its hinge before coming to a rest. Lara slid out of her seat.

"We'll be starting early," she said. Then, with a thank you to the waitress, she too left the bar.

The waitress relaxed once they were alone. "He's a nice man, he's my friend," she said, pointing to Gideon's empty seat. "But in Qey Shibir . . ." She snapped her fingers looking for the right word. "Red Terror. The revolution in 1974. He was not good. He was famous, many photographs of him in Addis Zemen."

Alfonso nodded. He was familiar with the Red Terror, the intense period of violence heaped on the people of Ethiopia by an iron-fisted dictator.

She pointed to Gideon's empty seat again. "He was a singer."

"For a band?" Alfonso asked, remembering a small brochure at the Ghion Hotel that recounted the history of the popular hotel band. "Which one?"

The waitress's face clouded and she brought that second beer back over to Alfonso. "For funerals."

"The families liked him, then?" Alfonso asked. "Like Alberto Cortez in my country."

The waitress scrubbed the inside of a glass dry and held it up to the weak light for inspection. She set it down softly. "He was a Derg singer." She continued when Alfonso shook his head as if he didn't understand. "He sang to celebrate deaths of the Derg enemies. The families hate him. Even now, some people never forget." She peered over his shoulder at the door, a faraway look in her eyes. "How could you forget? His voice was beautiful." She fluttered the fingers of one hand gracefully.

The beers were giving the room soft edges; he'd been drinking on an empty stomach. The flimsy wooden door, which couldn't prevent Addis Ababa's smells from seeping into the bar, began to pulse in slow rhythm to a new song spinning out of the old, worn stereo. Exhaust fumes, manure, smoke, *berbere*, and, beneath it all, the sweet pungency of myrrh mingled with the sharp smells that were coming from either the waitress or the plastic jug of *tej* that he hadn't been brave enough to sample, choosing bottled Ethiopian beer over the homemade honey wine.

"You are visiting Addis Ababa?" the waitress asked, her hard smile and knowing eyes forcing his gaze from her hips to her face.

He didn't know when the horror had ebbed and he'd begun to pose his subjects, straighten their clothes, and use shadow to hide bruises. The impulse had grown slowly, between f-stops and focal points. The slight shift to include the whole face in the frame turned into attention to composition and expression. He'd never ask anyone to smile, he'd tell himself, but for the prettiest prisoners, the ones whose cuts started below the necklines of their gowns, he found himself unable to resist. *A small curve in your mouth, señorita, to soften your face,* he'd whisper. *Just for me, ignore the soldiers.* The look they gave tipped into helplessness.

At some point, after hundreds of photos of hundreds of prisoners who had walked out of frame and into an interrogation room or the line of fire, Alfonso began to hide a few damning rolls of film from the commander. He'd dreamed about his mother and her distaste for his photography, for his bourgeois skills in a working-class family. *It will turn you into something else,* she'd once said to him, *and you won't be my son anymore.* In his dream, she'd become the bird that tapped ceaselessly on the window of the fourth floor of the Navy School; she'd tapped a hole into the room, flying onto his camera and perching on the flash. Her wide-eyed stare, first at the sheet he'd pinned to the wall, then back at him, had forced him awake with a hand swinging at empty air.

"I'll keep these for you, Commander," Alfonso had said the next day to the heavy-breathing man who sweated profusely, a damp handkerchief constantly in his grip. "You don't need to hold these, they're a bother." He put a used roll of film in the pocket of the same filthy trousers he'd worn since his arrest. He tucked the exposed rolls into his front pockets, then his back pockets, and then into the pocket of his shirt—and when there was no more room, he smiled widely, innocently, and slid a few into his socks.

Whenever he could, he would hide a few rolls inside his cell, a square cold box of a room that held a rotating group of twenty prisoners. Raul, a baby-faced university student with an unflagging spirit, dug a small hole into one wall for the film, then stood or slept in front of it until one day he too was called to pose for Alfonso. Alfonso scratched an R into the film canister of the roll that held Raul's forgiving smile. Four years later, when the junta fell and he was released from prison, it was the first one he took out and slipped into his shirt pocket.

If there was such a thing as redemption, he reasoned, he would give the families of these prisoners proof that, once upon a time, there had been a man who looked into the face of their loved one and saw a life worth remembering. That he did nothing to save them the indignity of a photograph just before death, he hoped no one would ever point out.

"You're a tourist, visiting?" the waitress asked again.

"I'm working," he told her, patting his camera.

"Journalist?" she asked, her face suddenly curious and interested. "For the trial of the Derg officers?" She spat out the words, her features contorting into a scowl. "Let them die for what they did to us. They kill us, they leave the bodies on the streets. My sister . . ." She stopped and took a deep breath. "It's good you are here," she said simply, then turned away as if embarrassed.

After a revolution dethroned Emperor Haile Selassie in 1974, the Derg regime had reigned until just three years ago, 1991. The Red Terror had been declared by Mengistu Haile Mariam to eliminate all opposition, meaning a population that Alfonso was all too familiar with: young, educated, idealistic, innocent except for the crime of hope. The Red Terror had nearly stripped Ethiopia of an entire generation, kept her in the firm clutches of violent and bloody chaos from 1977 to 1978. But the violence had started earlier, and it had never completely stopped until Mengistu fled. Many had not been allowed to properly mourn for their dead. Others had never found the bodies of the disappeared. When a new government came to power, the first steps toward bringing Derg officials to trial began. But courts needed evidence, proof.

The team of forensic scientists had come from Argentina with skills honed in their own land, among the bones of their own people. They had come to excavate mass graves in Addis Ababa and prove what former Derg officials tried to deny. The team had been to other places—Kurdistan, the Balkans, El Mozote, and Croatia—before Ethiopia, they understood the power that the dead still hold. They worked under the belief that witnesses, documents, even photographs could deceive, but a restored skull, a bone fragment, a skeleton dug up from a hole filled with the remains of dozens of others, spoke a kind of truth for which there was no defense.

And Alfonso, he'd come to Ethiopia because he wanted to stand in front of these remains and pretend the bones could substitute for the Argentine prisoners who understood what they were really looking at when they turned to face his camera. "I know how to photograph the dead," he'd said to Lara during the interview. "We know each other." She had finally relented.

"What is the singer's name?" he asked the waitress now, blinking rapidly to keep the tears back. It still surprised him how easily he cried since his release from prison. He pointed to the door behind him as if the man were standing there.

"Gideon," the waitress said. "Once, he had a son." She shook her head sadly.

## II

Walking back to his home near the crowded Mercato, Gideon didn't know what to make of the *ferenjoch* sitting in his favorite bar talking to Konjit. Seeing these foreigners had startled him so much he'd drunk his beer in three gulps. Maybe Konjit had put on the music for the tourists' benefit. Maybe it was her way of asking why he hadn't come to visit her in a week. Maybe it was her way of punishing him. So many people in Addis Ababa found small ways to make him pay for what he'd done in the past. Jabbing him with a sharp elbow in a crowd. Kicking him in the leg. Shrinking away from him as if he were a leper. He understood the language spoken in these moments. Expected it. Some days, when he thought of his son, wished for it. But the song, "Tizita," had come like a sharp, bitter slap; the unexpectedness of Tilahun Gessesse's soaring voice in the dark *tej bet* had been like a fist to his chest. It had been his own closing song whenever he had performed at the palace in the days before the Derg.

*Samson*, he would have called out if he'd had a voice—the shock of hearing that song had been that strong. He would have called out his son's name, and in the country where he still had his voice, he would have still had his son and his son would have come running. *Samson, my son*.

*Abbaba*.

A muezzin's voice rose from Anwar Mosque in the wind, light and vibrant. As he did every day when he heard the call to prayer, though he'd abandoned any religion long ago, Gideon touched his throat and cursed his gift, willed it to stay trapped where he'd shut it long ago. He walked by a small café near one of the overcrowded shops in the area and saw a group of men hunched over newspapers, frowning. A young newspaper vendor ran to him in dusty sandals and waved a paper in his face.

"Digging has started at the military compound," the boy said, the corners of his dried lips stained from chewing the numbing khat leaves. There was a glazed look in his eyes, an out-of-focus stare that Gideon had once envied and even thought he'd needed.

He tried to wave the boy aside to let him pass when the boy reached into his pocket and pulled out a small bundle of khat. "And this?" he asked.

Gideon had tried the leaf for the first time soon after Samson disappeared, had wanted something to ease the loneliness that felt like a knife in his side. He'd chewed alone, in a dark corner of his modest home where Samson's bed still lay unmade, just as he'd left it weeks ago. It was 1978. He was no longer a singer with a popular band loved by Emperor Haile Selassie. The emperor was dead. Hundreds had fled the country. Soviets and Cubans seemed to have appeared from nowhere. Soldiers were everywhere.

Two policemen had come at five a.m. to take his son for questioning. They'd promised to bring him back. Gideon knew of this familiar lie meant to quiet parents into submission. He'd grabbed his son with both arms around the waist and dropped to his knees. One of the policemen had taken his rifle and hit the back of his head again and again until he finally let go of his son. He'd gone immediately to the jail and was told to come back the next day. He'd spent the night on the jail steps, and when he'd gone back to the counter with his son's picture, the weary officer had pointed him toward the hospital morgue. *Try there,* he said. *They were all taken there last night.*

When he hadn't found Samson and two weeks had passed, Gideon went to a small kiosk in Mercato and asked the owner for khat.

"Gideon," the owner said, "this isn't like you. Wait instead, go to church, your son will come back." But the owner hadn't been able to look him in the eye and in the end he'd slid the tiny bundle of leaves toward him and refused Gideon's money.

All the leaf did to him was make his sorrow take shape and come alive. It settled inside his chest, grew fur and teeth, and gnawed against his rib cage. His chest had felt as tight as a drum. The voice calling out for his son sounded like his wife's, but when he turned, he found nothing but his own hand groping clumsily in the air for the woman who'd taught him how to love, then died in childbirth.

"Digging has begun," the newspaper boy repeated, shoving the paper in his face. "Read about it. They're working over there." He pointed toward rolling hills where a military base sat. "If you lost someone in Qey Shibir, you should read this."

Gideon paid for the paper and examined the front page. Standing at the end of a row of serious men and one woman was the tourist from Konjit's bar.

He pointed to the photo and gave the newspaper boy a quizzical look.

"You don't know?" the boy said. "There are graves in the military base. These people," he pointed to the picture in the newspaper, "they came to dig up the bodies. They know how to do it."

Gideon's hand shook. His son had been taken to that jail; he'd followed the truck for as long as he could on foot then hailed a taxi to the gate. He'd memorized the license plate and seen the same truck, empty, in the jail parking lot. Gideon clutched the paper to his chest and leaned so hard on his good leg he almost tipped into the boy, the memory of the days searching for his only son pressing down like a heavy hand.

The soldiers had stared at him at the counter, his son's photo pushed toward them with shaking fingers. They refused to respond to his questions. They tried to ignore him. They turned their backs and let him run his voice hoarse asking them where they took his son. They let him stand at the counter and weep for Samson. Then they began to tire of his never-ending sorrow. One of them threatened him. Another pleaded with him to go home. When he stayed, with that tilted stance that forced him to lean one elbow on the counter, they beat him back with fists and kicks. They swung their rifles into his short leg and watched him fall. They insulted his father's name, his band, his dead wife. Still, Gideon woke the next morning and walked back to the jail, Samson's photo in hand.

It was on the fourth visit that one of the soldiers had pulled out a small sheet of paper, then pointed to Gideon and said, "Maybe he's the one the general's looking for."

He didn't protest when they took him to another building next to the jail, because they knew where his son was and that was all that mattered. The soldiers shoved him in front of a large wooden desk where a man as thin as a dried stick coughed in his seat as he gripped his stomach. The man inspected him, beginning at his feet, his mouth curling as he glanced from one leg to the other, then broke into a wide smile when he got to Gideon's face.

"The Great Voice of Ethiopia, with talent only worthy of an emperor, is here in my office volunteering to sing for our cause?" the man had asked. "How did we get so lucky?"

On his way home, Gideon remembered a story he learned in school. Once upon a time, there was a goat who believed he was king. He was caught by a peasant who mistook the king for a goat. *Just sing,* he told himself. *Nothing changes just because it is called something else. A song is only a song, but a son,* he reminded himself again and again, *a son . . .* And he stopped and sighed at all a son could be.

His first funeral was for the only son of a couple who could not stop shaking their heads at the sight of their child's grave. "Is this real, is this him, is this my son?" the mother moaned into the chest of the grieving father. Gideon cursed his voice, his throat, the air he breathed. He kept his mouth clamped shut until he felt the soldier's rifle in his side. He started softly, a mournful song of longing and loss, but the soldiers raised their guns and pronounced the corpse an enemy and made him sing of Chairman Mengistu's valor. Then the soldiers pointed their weapons at the mother and said, "Dance, Emama, we do not weep for those we hate."

Every day for a week, Gideon went to Konjit's bar and waited for the two *ferenjoch*. He'd put on his only suit from his days in the band. It was pin-striped with broad lapels and a blue handkerchief sewn into the jacket pocket. In his shirt pocket was Samson's photo. He ordered one beer and sipped it slowly, sparingly. Then he waited, ignoring Konjit's questioning look and her attempts to talk to him.

During the second week, one night near closing time, the man came in alone just as Konjit was trying to make Gideon go home. Gideon felt his mouth go dry, even though he'd just taken a drink of beer. He spun around, his mouth open, and for the first time in years, he regretted swallowing his voice and making it disappear.

The man had dark circles under his eyes. There was a fine sheen of dust covering him, and the weight of the camera slung over his shoulder seemed to tip him to one side. He didn't look at Gideon or Konjit, lost instead in the Amharic letters on a beer bottle sitting on the bar. He breathed with his mouth open in soft gusts. Gideon couldn't tell if he was near tears or simply at the point of exhaustion.

"*Birra?*" Konjit asked, holding out a fresh bottle to him. "You are tired?" She smiled, then let the smile fade when the man didn't return her gaze. She set the beer in front of him and turned to stack clean glasses on a shelf.

Gideon felt for Samson's photo. Its edges pressed against his shirt and burned into his bare skin. His heart hammered against the photo, beating his son's name into his chest then up to his throat. His mouth opened and closed over silent words.

The man waved aside the beer and began to breathe normally. He laid his hands flat on the countertop and stared at them intensely. He began to unload his camera and his lips quivered as he took the roll of film and slid it into his shirt pocket. Then he wiped his eyes with the back of his hand.

Gideon slid Samson's photo out of his pocket and laid it gently on the counter in front of the man. He tapped the man on the shoulder, keeping his hand there to comfort him, then he led the man's gaze to the photo, then back to himself. He did it again: Samson, then him. Samson's face, then his face.

Konjit shook her head with mournful eyes. The man turned away. He put both hands over his face as if to shield himself from a bright light.

"Please," he said, one of the few English words Gideon could understand. "Please. No more." He shook his head back and forth and said something quietly to Konjit, his eyes glued to the counter, focused on his hands gripping his beer as if the bottle were the only thing keeping him in place.

"Leave him alone," Konjit said to Gideon, her concentration on the man's mouth. "He is saying that too many families came today."

Gideon shook his head and pushed the photo closer to the man. He tapped his shoulder and pointed to the picture again. *Samson*, he mouthed desperately. *Samson*. He faced the man and waited.

The man spoke in English to Konjit then nodded in his direction.

Konjit took a deep breath and spoke gently: "There are nothing but bones now, Gideon. There is no way to identify by a photo."

*But isn't every bone different?* Gideon wanted to ask. *Isn't the shape of my son's face unlike any other? Look at his jaw, its strength and strong lines. Who else but my Samson has that? Look at him!* Gideon wanted to shout. *There is no other like him, even after all flesh has gone the way of dust, even after all has turned to ash. There is him.*

### III

Gideon has come every day for a week to watch us dig. He crouches beneath a tree and sits quietly, holding a photograph in front of his heart. He's dressed in an old suit that's neatly ironed. His shoes are polished to military standards and I notice even from this distance that one has a thicker heel than the other. Alfonso sits with him when the sun goes down and we've turned on our lights to continue to dig. They do not talk, but I see them sitting so close, one could be leaning on the other. He doesn't leave until we pack our equipment and drive away. Alfonso stays until Gideon gets up to go home, helping him to his feet and saying words I can't hear from where I crouch, documenting pieces of what were once whole men.

I'd refused Alfonso's request to travel with us to Ethiopia. *Added weight and cost,* I'd said, trying to make my denial sound professional. Diego pulled me aside and whispered, *Lara, don't you remember him in the news? They kept him for years. The things they did to him. Let him come. Besides, he gave my family the last photo of my brother.*

I don't want to ask if he remembers my sister. I have no courage. Alicia ran away from the police the night they tried to arrest her. She was always the fastest in her school, she could outrun the boys. She ran out of Buenos Aires toward the sea then floated away to a new place. She'll come back when we have finished with all these bones.

We are nearing the end. The bones have been dug up and

laid on metal tables into the semblance of a human frame. We've packaged and labeled the clothes, jewelry, ID cards. All the bodies have been identified. Now the mourning can truly begin. Our job is done. Soon we leave for Argentina, until we are called back or called to another place full of unclaimed sorrow.

I have separated my information about Ethiopia between what we know and what we do not. Between fact and assumption. There is no room for the disappeared. There is no section in my report that will include the hopes of all who have heard of Lazarus and believed. All that we have is what we can dig out of the earth, hold up to the light, then return back to dirt.

This is what we know from this latest dig: forty adult male prisoners were taken to a wooded corner of the military base and strangled with a nylon rope. Some also suffered blunt force to the skull, nasal fractures, broken bones in their hands and feet. Each piece of rope was cut exactly 159 centimeters and the ends were heated to fuse frayed strands. The exe-cutioners (could just one have the strength to kill forty who want to live?) tied simple knots at each end to allow for a bet-ter grip. The killers then looped the cords around the necks of the prisoners.

This is what we can assume: some of the prisoners strug-gled, but not all. It was a futile fight. They all died from liga-ture strangulation. I wonder which of the prisoners lived the longest, and if every breath of life was worth the struggle.

They were buried under meters of heavy stones and lime. We found them under those stones, and ash. They were clothed. All but one had a blanket around him; the night was cold. All but that same one had the cinched nylon rope tied around his neck. That prisoner who died without a blanket, with his rope flung far from his body, what new story could he tell us about that night that his bones choose to hold secret? I ask myself this question as I copy data onto paper, record it so that the next time we must dig for bones, we have the stories of these to guide us forward.

I am writing the last of my notes, leaning against a tree just beyond the site, when Alfonso and Gideon walk over to me. They seem to hesitate as I look up.

"Sí? Can I help you?" I ask Alfonso, not wanting to be rude, trying to respect what he must have seen and endured in the Navy School. I realize that the tormented look I first noticed when he came to us has not changed. It is permanent, like a scar.

"Gideon. He has something to show you." He points to Gideon, who takes a picture from his suit pocket and holds it out to me, cupping it like an injured bird. "This is his son, Samson," Alfonso says. "He disappeared years ago, he was jailed here."

I shake my head, already knowing the question. "We've found everyone. There's no one else here. Tell him I'm sorry." And I have to wonder at a man who wants the bones of his son, who chooses not to believe in escape and flight.

"Please look," Alfonso says. He pauses. "For his sake, just look at the picture. Then tell him."

I see a young man, a boy really, with eager eyes and a wide smile. I see his father's strong jaw and high cheekbones, a chipped front tooth and sloping forehead. He is flesh and blood, this boy, so alive. We dig only the dead.

"No," I say. "He isn't here."

# PART II

TRANSLATIONS OF GRIEF

# FATHER BREAD

BY MIKAEL AWAKE

*Kechené*

They nicknamed him Abba Dabo for the bread he offered the poor each Sunday. Devout as dawn itself, he would rise, say a prayer, iron one of his two good shirts, and climb the steep hill to Guardian of the World Church. He nodded kindly at the white-shawled women who sold candles along the road, while two of his little orphans struggled to keep pace behind him, lugging a golden loaf the size and weight of a table.

*Abba*: Father. *Dabo*: Bread.

The drunkards in the tavern, still up from their endless night, would feel a rare sweet lump of sorrow in their throats as they watched them pass.

"There goes a good man," one would say.

"You mean a *smart* man," came the reply.

"What's the difference?" another would say.

"If you don't know, you must be a good man."

Back and forth they would jest until the warmth of a new day covered their mouths with sleep.

Waves of progress were crashing over the city, but washed along the gates of Guardian of the World Church was what the tide had left behind: legless old men dragging themselves through the dirt, blind girls nursing howling babies, listless boys from the country, all begging for spare change from the sweet-smelling churchgoers who had come to pray away their sins. Every week, Abba Dabo would stand before the hungry and unveil the loaf from its muslin cloth. It drew them in like iron filings to a magnet. They would tear eager handfuls so quickly that the taste almost immediately became a memory.

"Come with me," Abba Dabo would tell the children. "We will feed you like this. We will love you as one of God's chosen, and we will find you an earthly home." A cloud of wispy white hair ringed his shiny pate.

"Like the halo of an angel," said the churchgoers, who bowed and blessed him as they passed.

The children who returned with Abba Dabo to his orphanage had traveled from the parched villages of Arsi and the flooded farms of Gurage. They came from the fertile Omo Valley where foreign investment had bared its teeth. Most would only stay a few weeks before they were lured away by the promise of the sprawling city below, never to be seen again. Only the most desperate stayed with him long enough to find homes elsewhere in the wealthier parts of town or with families abroad. Of course, many of the children were suspicious of his generosity, casting wary glances at Abba Dabo and quietly leaning against the crumbling stone wall of the church to finish their bread.

"He can keep his love," they'd say, "but I'll eat the bread."

The day he arrived at the orphanage door, the boy was alone, barefoot, eyes laden with shame, fatigue, and grief. His body was smaller than it should have been. A tattered shirt with the Converse logo went below his knees. Abba Dabo thought he recognized the boy from the church gates, one of those usually shoved aside in the line for bread. *He must have followed us home,* Abba Dabo thought, then summoned the girl who worked in the kitchen to bring him some bread.

"My child, eat," he said, offering the boy a plate of injera. "Where are your parents, my child?"

The boy stood staring at the plate balanced in his tiny hands, afraid to look away for fear it might disappear. His ashen head was fully shaved but for a small strip of tight black curls near his forehead, which he shook from side to side.

Abba Dabo uttered a mournful sound from the back of his throat and made the sign of the cross over himself. "My little lamb," he said, "did the crops fail?"

The boy shook his head.

"Did the well dry?"

Again, the boy shook his head.

Abba Dabo made the usual guesses—flooding, violence, eviction—but each time in reply, the boy simply shook his head. This struck him as unusual. *There must be something wrong with him*, Abba Dabo thought. In the past, he'd made the mistake of caring for badly damaged children and knew the costs outweighed the benefits. "May God bless you," he said, laying a gentle hand of farewell on the boy's head. "May God protect you."

Just then, the boy lifted his eyes and muttered, in the softest voice anyone had ever heard, "Hyenas."

The boy was from Toglet, a remote valley deep in Amhara, a place as quiet and unknowable as the afterlife, whose people were stoic and meek but had a reputation for vengefulness. For centuries, the lush vale was crisscrossed by narrow footpaths and only accessible by mule, but recently Chinese contractors had built a paved road leading to town. They say that a woman carrying kindling was walking along the Chinese road when she stumbled upon him. Those early morning hours were so thick with fog that she didn't see the boy until her damp feet tripped over his.

She recognized him as the youngest son of a landowning farmer, a man of some stature. The boy appeared as she'd always seen him, wearing an oversize flannel shirt hung like a dress over a tattered pair of shorts. But today his clothes were damp and discolored.

"Have you been hurt?" the kindling woman asked.

The boy shook his head and pointed with his thumb at the fields behind him, where his father and all fathers had ever worked and lived since the childhood of man. The woman followed his thumb—it was clubbed, with blood under the sliver of nail—to a lonely, fenced *gojo* in the middle of the field.

The boy would not answer her, not lifting his eyes from the ground. The woman dropped her pile of bound wood on the road with a sigh and took his hand in hers. She passed this way regularly on her way to town, but you did not trespass a man's land without good reason. She was curious, but she was cautious. They walked in silence toward the lonely homestead. All was still. A rooster strutted into the front yard, hiccuping. The sheep were agitated in their pens. No other noises came from within. The boy's hand in hers was small and soft as the tendril of a fern, and they were slick with a sticky kind of dew that she would only later know was blood.

If you ever go to Toglet and find yourself up at dawn, hold your breath for a minute and sit in complete silence. They say that if you do this, you can still hear the kindling woman's whooping screams echo through the valley.

The birds alighted from the trees and did not return for six months. The roosters went silent for a year. The bravest hunters of the valley disappeared for weeks on end, slaughtering everything on four legs that had the misfortune of crossing their warpath. Since that morning and to this day, no one in Toglet has ever slept peacefully through the night. And how could you after the carnage they found that morning in that house? The heap of bones, entrails, heads, eyes, hands, feet, hearts, and brains which had once been the farmer and his family. Every part in its wrong place, sliding out onto the kindling woman's feet in a tide of warm black blood.

"And God spared you," said Abba Dabo, voice quivering with emotion. "Eat your bread, child. Eat."

Every night they would sit near the fire, still and silent, as his mother added wood and the servant girl stirred the *wat*. The boy, his two older brothers, and his father crouched on low stools around the glowing pit, transfixed by the red tongues of flame lapping the pot. By this time of day, all were light-headed with fatigue and hunger from their endless work on the land. His father spent the daylight hours supervising his two older brothers while they navigated a plow through the soil, stumbling in their black rubber boots as they whipped and insulted the annoyed oxen, who dragged the heavy steel blade through the furrows. His mother tended to the homestead with the servant girl, sorting grain, plucking garden herbs, milling, churning, butchering, and sweeping. The boy, because he was so young, had the relatively easy task of herding the sheep. All morning and into the hottest part of the afternoon, he ranged across the hills with expert footing up and down the ravines, in search of grassy swaths and clear streams and only a walking stick twice his height to keep him safe. He was not old enough to do much else. When the flock grazed, he often sat under the shade of a tree, making up little songs in his head.

Steam from the simmering pot of *shiro wat* was dizzying. It rose into the rafters of the *gojo*, enveloping them. Pools of excitement formed in the backs of their mouths. The boy watched the servant girl pour a pitcher of crystalline well water over his father's hands, gnarled and brown and tough as wood. Most in the valley could not afford the extra food and space that came with hiring a servant girl, but his father was not like most in the valley. He nodded to the girl that he was finished, and she moved on to his oldest son, then his second oldest, then his wife, and finally the boy, who was last in all things.

At the start of every meal, his father would lead them in the same prayer and instruct them to begin eating, but they knew to wait until he had taken his first bite to follow suit. As the boy began to nibble politely on a second helping of *shiro wat*, a serving just as humble as the first, the rumble of his father's voice broke the placid silence.

"Did I tell you to begin eating?"

The boy stopped chewing. He was confused and scared. His father had a quick temper and had punished him for odd things before. Not fully closing his eyes over prayer, taking injera with his left hand, chewing with his mouth open, chewing with his mouth closed too tight. The boy knew to keep quiet, knew that to say anything out loud, to mention the unfairness of it, would only make matters worse. If he protested, his father would punish him more severely for having done so.

"Get up," said his father, glaring. "Sleep outside tonight."

The boy had food in his mouth still, but he was too upset to keep chewing. He felt like spitting it out, but he knew the waste of it would only bring a lashing with the ox whip. He kept the unchewed food in his cheeks and stepped from the warmth of the firelit room into the cold echoing chamber of night.

On the dirt floor of the shed behind the house, he lay awake beside the ox plow, unswallowed food fermenting in his cheeks like the bad feelings in his chest. This was supposed to teach him a lesson. But what was the lesson? It never came. His punishment never *meant* anything. He could never predict or understand it. The lesson that night was supposed to be about self-restraint, as it often was. So the boy silently scolded himself for his selfishness. He had a reputation, after all, for not knowing how to control his urges, for being greedy. He grew self-conscious about his desires, ashamed of his wants, his longings. He no longer knew what he desired. He no longer ate food without being told to eat. His father's lessons taught him nothing but shame as he sat in the ox-plow shed. The air in there was stuffy, and the smell of rust, manure, and soil was pervasive. The hoot of owls, the distant growl of mountain lions, and the hiss of other unseen nocturnal creatures prowling the land slipped easily through the shed's porous metal walls. The boy never slept well in the shed, but he knew that his pain was the point.

"He hasn't known a day of hardship!" he heard his father bellow. "He is not grateful. I will make him grateful." And come morning, with bits of injera still rotting in his cheeks, the boy would be grateful, but not in the way his father could have imagined.

That was the night the hyenas came.

Not long after, an American couple became very serious about adopting the boy. When Abba Dabo told them how the boy's family had died, the wife began to weep uncontrollably.

"Well," said the husband, trying to lighten the mood, "it looks like we have no choice." They were in their forties and had attempted to use nature and science to have children of their own, but with no luck. A terrifying absence had opened inside their lives that only a child could fill.

Abba Dabo nodded gravely and warned them about how

long the adoption process in Ethiopia could take. Four, five years sometimes. He shrugged and sighed out words like "corruption," "bureaucracy," and "red tape." But Abba Dabo knew it was too late. They were already using a recent photo of the boy as the background for their laptop screens. The absence in their hearts was already filling. They would not be happy again until the boy was theirs. Abba Dabo was a master at telling orphan tragedies to the foreign families who came to him. The boy's bus ride to the city from Debre Birhan, where he had stayed with distant relatives, became a weeks-long odyssey on foot. He conveniently skipped the part about the farmer, the whore, and the part about the abuse the boy had endured at his father's hand. Foreigners often balked at the first whiff of narrative complexity. So he kept it simple, kept all the orphans and their families as innocent. They were just the victims of bad luck and cruel circumstance. In Abba Dabo's version, the hyenas had spared the boy because they had glutted themselves on his five other family members. (The servant girl had become a sister.) When Abba Dabo quoted them an estimate for how long it might take and how very expensive it might be to process the boy's paperwork, the wife blew her nose and said, almost embarrassed, "Is there anything we can do to help speed the process?"

It took effort for Abba Dabo to keep from smiling. Oh, Americans. When they have their hearts set on something, they want it right then and there. He tried to look surprised, but of course this was precisely the response he'd been hoping for.

"It is possible," he said. "But it won't be free."

*Praise God*, Abba Dabo said to himself once he'd crawled into bed that night. There were repairs he needed to make around the place. The cranky baker who delivered the bread was threatening to stop if he failed to pay him again. There were still wheels to grease, officials to keep happy, and important people to make look the other way. It had never been easy running a place like this.

And he hadn't even begun to think of his own needs. Yes, he'd been able to buy some new shirts after the Dutch couple paid him a little extra to expedite the adoption of the deaf girl. But what about all the other children who did not get adopted, who needed food and medical care and shelter and clothes and tutors? The overhead was unimaginable, the pressure constantly overwhelming. Was it a crime to daydream about a new pair of dress shoes? Or a new suit? Was it wrong to go online some nights and browse airfares to Thailand? Where was the harm in that?

"You must miss having a family."

"They were not my family," said the boy, wiping crumbs from his lips. "That's what they always told me."

Abba Dabo crossed himself. "Poor thing," he said. "But you must forgive them in your heart. We must remember the dead with kindness and move forward with life."

They were sitting in the sunlit courtyard of the orphanage, sharing a midmorning plate of bread that was marbled here and there with spicy red veins of *berbere*. It had been two months that the boy had been living with Abba Dabo. He no longer waited for permission to eat. His body was free of lice and ringworm spots. He wore a clean white cotton shirt, a smaller version of the one Abba Dabo always wore. They had burned the clothes he arrived in. The boy's limbs no longer looked like fragile twigs. Now they were sturdy branches.

"You are my family," said the boy, as he watched his friends Aida and Omar laugh wildly over a game of cards. There was no sound more beautiful than the laughter of other children. "This is my home."

"This is no one's home," said Abba Dabo, patting the boy on the knee and rising to his feet with effort. That was another thing he could do once the funds from the Americans came through: finally see someone about his back.

Four months. That's all it took. It must have been some kind of world record. That's what Abba Dabo said when he told the Americans that their application had been expedited.

"The fastest ever," he lied.

"Really?"

"Really," said Abba Dabo. He watched their happiness flare brighter with the thrill of overachievement, and squirmed at the sight of them kissing, averting his eyes awkwardly.

After they had thanked Abba Dabo no less than a dozen times—another world record, he thought—the husband cleared his throat. "We were just wondering," he said, "if maybe now, you know, because of the process, you were right, we shouldn't get our hopes up, but—"

His wife cut in, curtly: "Can we say hi now?"

"Now that it's official," the husband added.

For the past several weeks, Abba Dabo had been dodging their request to speak to the boy. After they had wired the funds, the wife asked repeatedly, and Abba Dabo always told her that it wasn't wise to meet him and grow attached until after the process was officially complete. They had him trapped. He watched himself squirm in the tiny square at the bottom of the screen. Abba Dabo couldn't blame it on the process anymore. Now, he was forced to make up something new.

"The boy is very shy," Abba Dabo lied. And this time, he could tell the wife wasn't buying it, so he went on: "We are working to bring him out of his shell. He has been through a lot. Sometimes this happens with children."

"I imagine he's still dealing with some PTSD," the husband offered, though even he had a new furrow of suspicion forming on his brow.

"Yes," said Abba Dabo. "Very PTSD."

When he ended the call, Abba Dabo found that he had sweated through his dress shirt. Dark stains spread at his underarms. It was a blessing that one could not smell others over the computer.

The problem was simple: the boy did not want to be adopted and did not want to leave the orphanage. For a while, Abba Dabo thought he was just being stubborn, that he could convince the boy over time to embrace the idea of a new life with a new family. But the boy had refused every call with the Americans, even turning down a pair of sneakers Abba Dabo had tried to bribe him with earlier that week.

Abba Dabo's worry suddenly transformed into rage. He stormed out of his office and found the boy where he had left him on his bed in the main sleeping quarters, staring absently, unblinking, at the ceiling.

"What's wrong with you!" he shouted. No one had ever heard him this angry. The outburst so startled the other children that everyone in the room immediately filed outside, nervous, distraught. Abba Dabo tried to calm himself. He began pacing at the foot of the boy's bed.

"Don't you want a family who will provide for you? Who will love you?"

"I am happy here," said the boy.

"Anyone would kill to live in America!"

"I don't want to."

"You think it matters what you want?" An incredulous

smile spread over Abba Dabo's face. "It's already finished!"

"No."

"What do you mean, *no?*" Abba Dabo was livid. He had never in his life dealt with such arrogance. "Shall I send you back to where you came from to let the animals finish the job?"

Tears instantly poured from the boy's eyes and his body began to shake with sobs. It was the cruelest thing Abba Dabo had ever said to anyone—man, woman, or child. But he had never encountered such amazing stupidity in the face of such wild generosity. He had already spent a good portion of the Americans' money fixing the plumbing.

"You will thank me one day," said Abba Dabo, resting a tender, apologetic hand on the boy's arm. "When you graduate from university and you get a good job and a big house full of food and nice things and you have the freedom to do whatever you want with no bother from anyone watching over you, then you'll say to yourself, *Thank you, Abba Dabo, for giving me a better life.* That is what I do. It's what I've always tried to do for all of you."

Later that night, Abba Dabo woke to the sound of a small voice singing softly near his bed. The voice threaded through his sleeping thoughts, wove dream into reality, as his eyes parted to take in the surroundings of his darkened quarters. In the corner, he saw the silhouette of the boy, his small body crouched against the closed door.

"*There once was a boy from far away,*" sang the boy, barely above a whisper, "*who all the children called Moritay. They said at night he turned to a beast. And on those who had wronged him, he would feast . . .*"

"*Ayzow,*" grunted Abba Dabo, well versed in the night terrors of orphans. "Go back to your room. Drink some water."

But the boy went on in a kind of trance: "*A farmer said God had cursed his mother's womb. Now the farmer lies silent in his tomb. Then the boy met a man made of bread, who gave him clean clothes and a nice warm bed. This man would soon rue the day he tried to sell off poor Moritay . . .*"

"Why are you disturbing me at this hour?" Abba Dabo sat up and switched on the lamp by his bed to better glower at the boy.

"I didn't do anything wrong," the boy replied, then chuckled as though remembering a joke.

"What has happened?"

The boy paced the room in tight, quick circles, and then he started to laugh. It was a strange laugh. Humorless, breathy, high-pitched. It was like laughter in a different language, one that came from an unusual place in the body. The air in the room grew thick with a sour, feral odor, and Abba Dabo's heart seized with terror as he watched the transformation in utter disbelief. The boy began to mutate, placing his hands on the floor, the little spine drooping backward into the hips. Fur spread like fire wherever there was skin, from his back to his tiny hands, tiny hands which now tightened into knots of bone and claw that clacked against the floorboards.

"Nothing will ever happen to me," said the hyena.

The following Sunday, for the first time in anyone's memory, Abba Dabo failed to appear at the front gates of Guardian of the World Church to give bread to the poor. The children waited and waited, but as it got later and services began, they resigned themselves to begging churchgoers for food or change or whatever they could spare, just as they did every other day of the week, every week of the year.

As with all untimely deaths in Ethiopia, the specific details and circumstances of Abba Dabo's demise were shrouded in mystery and fiercely debated on street corners, in church pews, at markets, and outside taverns. Ethiopians visiting from the diaspora laughed aloud, slightly embarrassed at such a superstitious tale being told so earnestly in the twenty-first century.

"A boy who turns into a *jib?*" they said. Give them a break.

Others worried about the story's ethnically charged interpretations, while a few told the sensitive ones to lighten up. It was just a story, after all.

Most simply swatted the story away as one would a fly. "I'm too busy to be bothered by such gossip," they said.

But the young unemployed men who sit around the kiosks all day still whisper unsavory rumors about gambling debts and dangerous friends who had turned on Abba Dabo. They lifted eyebrows and said, "We know what really goes on."

No one was punished in the end. The Americans are still in court trying to retrieve their dollars. The boy disappeared, like so many others, back into the madness of Addis. No one ever saw him again: not outside the church, not prowling the streets near the orphanage, not anywhere. Though he had vanished, he was not forgotten. Back in his village, a proverb was born. All knew its hidden meaning. *The hyena does not laugh because it is happy.*

Abba Dabo became a saint and an omen. He was remembered as an angel, which is how even the worst of the dead are remembered. He was memorialized as a symbol of good crushed by a cruel world. The city demolished the orphanage. They say there are plans underway to build a hotel there. The trucks have already started coming, filling their steel jaws with rubble as silent people watch them feast.

# THE BLUE SHADOW

BY MAHTEM SHIFERRAW

*Yerer Ber*

When she spoke, the room filled with yellow. Her tone could paint the whole house in one stroke, walls suddenly blooming with perennials and *adey abeba*, floors caked in branches of *tsid*, and corners sprouting with the blue of *kiremt* rain. The air would become thick and creamy, and if anyone happened to listen to her voice at that specific moment, they would be in awe, as they were most of the time in her presence. It was not what she said that fascinated them, but the way she said things with such elegance, such poise.

Weyzero Fantish did not know this, of course, but she did know a lot of things she ought not to, which was perhaps the most obvious reason for her untimely death. When she was found, the big black eyes of her teenage son Amare were resting on her limp body. She could see a blood clot forming around his neck, and though tears did not rush to his eyes, his fists were clenched as if he were ready to explode and spread himself thinly around the room. Weyzero Fantish saw this and observed the rest of the room: it was still as spotless as she'd left it, but drawers had been opened and closed in a hurry, and the walls no longer resembled the blue of the lake where she was born. Instead, they were sagging with a somber deep green. That was when she knew she would not be coming back.

Weyzero Fantish peered into the boy's eyes. She could tell he had aged so quickly, so quietly. She had seen this before, the way grief appears suddenly and claws its way into the insides of people without their knowing. It was happening again right in front of her, and this time, she was the cause for such sorrow.

When she looked up, he had found the handgun that was clenched in her left palm; he knew who it belonged to, but she didn't know yet. Amare released the weapon from her grip and was caught by surprise—his mother's body was still warm. Weyzero Fantish stood next to him, and for a moment, he turned to her as if he saw her, but she quickly realized he was staring through her, to the walls. He sensed the change in colors too: the blooming buds must have shrunken themselves back into dry seeds. He found the Bible right beside her body. He split the pages open and read the first thing that caught his eye—something about a valley of dry bones. He closed it quickly, grief leaving him and replaced with a shadow that inhabited the hollow sockets of his eyes.

Weyzero Fantish followed him out. Her lean body still fit elegantly into the white dress, her head still wrapped in *netela*, hands resting on her belly as if she were observing something she had never seen before. Her black eyes darted quickly, right to left to right, long lashes flickering with the rain. It was only midday, and a light drizzle was turning the neighborhood into a grim gray.

For the first time, Weyzero Fantish regarded her son as if he were a stranger. She followed him from behind and noticed the ampleness of his shoulders, marveling at how long his back was. If uncovered, Weyzero Fantish knew she could find entire continents worth of pain on his shoulders alone—the invisible scars of siblings from different families, the bigger scar left from his own father. Amare walked briskly and did not respond to passersby greeting him. They noticed the blue shadow behind him but could not see Weyzero Fantish fluttering in her white dress, walking as quickly as she could, careful not to stain her dress in the viscous mud.

Amare went straight to the house of Weyzero Asnaku, their neighbor and his mother's close friend. He aimed the gun at the woman, who was staring at him with a horrified look on her face. She demanded to know what he was doing there, and if he had gone crazy. *She is arrogant even in her fear,* Weyzero Fantish thought.

Amare turned the gun away. He didn't need to say what they all knew: the gun belonged to Weyzero Asnaku's husband.

"My husband is not home," she said.

"Your husband is never home," Amare replied bitterly. He was referring to the man's multiple affairs with the women of Yerer Ber, including his mother, Weyzero Fantish.

Weyzero Asnaku insisted that her husband was at work. She told Amare to come back later to get the answers he needed, and suggested that he leave the gun with her, for safety.

Amare was not listening to her. He was looking past her, to the room behind her where the bed was still unmade, and suddenly he smelled it: the scent of a man, reeking of sweat, like a body that has stayed in the sun for too long or got caught in the rain and brought all the elements of the *kiremt* weather with him into the house. He could smell the colors too: vivid purples and fuchsias, mixed with freshly brewed coffee in an old *jebena*.

He knew then: Weyzero Asnaku was involved in her own love affair.

Amare put the gun down. Weyzero Fantish left him momentarily to check the bedroom: hiding under the bed she discovered the short figure of *Ato* Belayneh, the detective. She whispered something in his ear and though he didn't hear her, he was startled and bumped his head, his breathing suddenly quickening; Weyzero Fantish already knew how much he would lie later to keep his affair a secret.

When she left the detective and returned to the living room, Amare was gone.

Sorrow was her profession. Her voice would come like a waterfall at first, her tone gurgling like deep riverbeds, her eyes wet as algae, an ocean of words fluttering from her mouth with such grace, such harmony, one couldn't tell how deeply she was actually mourning. Her face too was a poised landscape: eyes as deep as wells, spitting fat tears, cheeks marked with the old razor scars, lips as dry as the earth in mid-*bega*. She covered her hair in an all-black *netela*, her arms swinging from her sides as if they did not belong to the same body. Her fingers were lean and nails sharp, and she would later sink them deep into her chest, skin coming undone to reveal her deepest pain, flat palms hitting her own bosom in rhythm. It was a masterpiece in the making; not the woman, but the unbearable sorrow, the art of grief so eloquently and selflessly executed.

When she was wailing, the space she inhabited turned completely white—the absence of life colorless, blinding, enveloping her without warning. Her voice would start out melodious and honeyed, especially when she talked about the life of the dead. But it would gradually become a cry, then a wail, then simply a hiss, a whisper of sorrow, and by then she would have stirred waves of tender blue-black into the ears of the mourners, and it would take them hours before they would let her paint them with yellow again.

Although Weyzero Fantish was a woman afflicted by many sorrows, she also loved life deeply. Mourning was what she did best, and she wanted to do it because everyone deserved to be mourned for, to be longed for, and the seed of sorrow she planted in her mourners' hearts always loomed larger and more intricate, and would come back to her in the shape of kindness and kinship.

As she caught up with Amare again, Weyzero Fantish realized he hadn't yet told anyone of her death. She passed through him and quickly walked three steps ahead of him. He was headed back to their house and his face was black with anger, something she hadn't seen in him in a while. He summoned the maid and lashed out at her about random things: she had not cleaned the house yet, lunch was not yet ready, and had she heard from his mother today? He was too irascible to notice the tears on the maid's sullen face. Behind her was an ocean of tears, the somber faces of neighboring women outside already dressed in black, their *netelas* turned upside down to mourn his mother.

He still seemed to not understand.

The maid did not respond, but nodded quietly at his requests.

"You will clean the house!" he shouted. "For lunch, you will cook *misir wot*," which his mother loved, "and you will brew some *buna* before early evening!"

He was not to be disturbed, and nobody was to enter his mother's bedroom.

The women looked at him without uttering a word, though they were whispering among themselves, and he failed to see it then too: the brownish stain of pity, leaking slowly through their bodies and attaching itself onto his. It was nauseating.

He walked into his mother's room and shut the door. He didn't realize it would be this difficult to breathe, and the air surrounding him seemed to grow thicker and creamier, and the terrifying feeling of someone choking him arrested his whole body and sent it into convulsions. The shaking became stronger, and only then did he see the colors: a pale burgundy, a spongy yellow, and something of a purple blemish, all spiraling toward him with the force of *Nehase* winds, taking over his body quickly. It entered his limbs at first, then nested in his abdomen, filling his chest with multiple explosions, and finally sputtered from the sides of his mouth into a snowy foam. His eyes dimmed as he fell onto the ground, and though the thump was loud and clear, the women had been instructed to stay away from him, so he was left alone—alone with his spiraling clouds.

The husky corn plants of Yerer Ber painted a sea of blue-green in the early morning and dark gray at night. Their corpulent arms were constantly in motion, as if breathing heavily at the smallest hush of wind. The neighborhood was at its busiest in the evening; the local *tella* and *tej bet* were just opening, the corner *suk* was filled with children buying bread and sparkling water, and people were walking quickly through the mud back into their homes. But the fields were at their quietest: there was no sun shining on their glowing skin, no forceful wind breathing on their hairy necks. The moon was not bright enough to expose their flesh, and their fruit was stolen by schoolchildren. The hyenas were not yet hiding their hunchbacked bodies in the corners of the field, and shepherds had not found shelter underneath their frocks. In that moment, everything was still in the fields, a peaceful moment before the night descended unhurriedly.

Weyzero Fantish followed the detective to a local *tella bet*, but she didn't dare cross the threshold of the establishment, mostly because she did not want to see or hear the lustful conversations of men inebriated with sweet honey and in the company of *masinko* music from *azmari*. She waited for him outside, but was quickly distracted by the chatter of two women on a side street; one was selling fire-roasted corn, the other vegetables arranged in small bundles.

They talked rapidly, as if they'd already rehearsed the conversation. Their gossip was sweet, like the aroma of boiled eucalyptus, yet venomous, like a pint of *senafich* accidentally inhaled through the nose. Nonetheless, Weyzero Fantish realized she already missed this, this unhealthy camaraderie between townspeople. There was something ignoble yet necessary about these kinds of hushed-up conversations, mostly because they brought embarrassment to the subjects of the chatter, and an unyielding sense of belonging to the gossipers—Weyzero Fantish used to be one of them.

The women spoke swiftly, selling their merchandise to passersby, unbothered in their exchange. It took awhile for Weyzero Fantish to realize they were actually talking about her, something about poison and a neighboring lover.

"And the gun?" one of the women said.

The other shrugged her shoulders.

"*Igziabher bicia new yemiyawkew.* God only knows what the gun is for. Her son found her in her sleep. It was already past midday, and he was up and running."

"Poor boy, what did he do?"

"Nothing. He didn't do anything, he didn't even cry."

"*Endet? Malkes 'ema yighebawal.* He must cry. He must."

That stuck with her more than the poison. She did not know the truth yet but found herself longing for the boy already, the son she hadn't even realized she had lost until the women brought it up. Weyzero Fantish walked back to her home slowly, her shadow making its way through the wet mud, as a light drizzle started to pour unceremoniously on the neighborhood. She saw everything: the eyes of men wandering to women who were not their own, the *listero*, the shoe shiners stealing from customers, the *suk* owners raising prices on small items such as gum and soap, the taxi drivers heading back home, hunchbacked and starved. She saw this, and yet she saw nothing.

Her house was drenched in heavy orange, as if engulfed entirely in flame, its roof spiking into a razor ice-blue. She did not want to enter, but a thin sliver of grayness removed itself from its walls and rested beneath her shadow, her tall figure succumbing to grief. She followed it inside: women were busying themselves, their chatter buzzing in her ears. They were quick and efficient in their actions because they had done this many times before. They cooked, cleaned, and tended to guests dropping by to pay their respects, mostly people of the neighborhood speaking of Weyzero Fantish in dewy and sugary voices.

Weyzero Fantish looked at no one in particular and left them, her shadow now moist with a cobalt veil. She entered her bedroom and sat beside her body. Her oak dresser was still in its place, her *barciuma* just as she'd left it in the corner, her four pairs of shoes aligned neatly by the doorway. That was when she saw him: his arms limp, his head tilted to the side, his body dried up like a fig.

Before the horror settled in, she wondered whether they were both made of the same shade of blue, but she knew they were not. Amare was made of steel blue, and his shadow had already left the room and lodged itself between the corn plants—free, out in the fields of Yerer Ber.

Then it came: the scream she screamed only to herself, a wound gashing so deeply into her shadow, she did not know how to swallow it, how to collect herself together into a colorless being. She rushed back to the living room, where the guests were gathered for her mourning. She screamed at them, wailed, threatened to reveal their secrets, cried, implored them—but nothing. That very moment, that was what it felt like to be a shadow: it was an achromatic world without sound, without a soul to hear her thoughts, a world where a mother dies and grieves for her son soon after.

Weyzero Fantish's shadow was now filled with streaks of a cavernous burgundy. She did not know it, but that was the thing that lit her fire into being again. That was what brought her back to Yerer Ber.

On a stormy night, her body would have been dragged under the buttery shadow of a split-cheek moon and taken three or four kilometers away to Mebrat Haile or Gurd Shola. It would have been loaded into a *wiyiyit* taxi, the lump of it resting where a passenger's feet would have otherwise been. The ride would not have been smooth, but it would have been slow and steady because her lover was a patient man with an impeccable driving record. Then the corpse would have been discarded in an open field, as if it were a sack of *teff* in the middle of the night, when there was no one else to watch it happen, no one around to witness its last doom. But this was neither a stormy nor ordinary night, and though Weyzero Fantish may have left her body, her blue shadow was still refusing to leave, itself having now undergone a transformation: the head turquoise, the chest flattened with cobalt veins, arms now long blocks of lapis lazuli, feet sprawling in cyan grass, her mouth spewing flames of a cerulean gray.

She was finally coming to terms with her death.

Weyzero Fantish was standing too close to her body, which was now claimed by women with grim eyes in black dresses. The women busied themselves with delicate gestures, washing, clothing, and preparing the body for burial. Weyzero Fantish watched them for a moment, her gaze lost between them and the priests who came to perform her last rites. For the first time since she departed, Weyzero Fantish felt cold, as though ice had been injected deep into her body and her bloodstream was filled with hail and sorrow. Her eyes were searching for her son, but he wasn't in the house. The place looked so small now with fifty or so mourners inside, and more outside waiting to be seated to pay their respects.

Weyzero Fantish approached a group of women quietly chatting by the doorway and overheard that Amare was in fact alive and well—he'd simply had one of his attacks.

"It must have been difficult to see her like that," one said. "Where is he now?"

"Tending to affairs. He must have gone with the boys."

The other women seemed puzzled.

"Why isn't he acting like someone in his situation normally would: grieving, staying in the house, and waiting for the townspeople to come and offer their condolences?"

"Maybe he was afraid he was going to have another attack?"

They shook their heads.

"But he didn't have to go with the boys to work. He must not even realize his mother is gone."

Amare walked quietly with the strongest boys. They were called in on days like these, when death disembarked unexpectedly in Yerer Ber. They were called from all corners of the neighborhood, and they came obediently in pairs, dragging their little brothers with them toward the *hazen bet*, the home of sorrow. They were fast, diligent, and efficient in their work because they had done this many times before. They were sent in small groups of five or six, and they walked briskly through unpaved streets into the residence of the *idirtegna*, where they would fetch auburn tents, folding chairs, pots and pans, and other utensils to bring back to the house of the mourners. Though the boys were often jovial in their work, this time silence swallowed their bodies whole and sewed their mouths shut. They walked as if they were part of a small army, all to the same rhythm. The afternoon rain had created a softer and more viscous mud around the neighborhood, and the green sea of cornfields was now turning emerald-quartz, prepared to be enveloped by a thin fog. They knew whose mother had died; what they didn't understand was why Amare was working with them as if nothing had happened. Or worse: why did he seem so normal, so unaffected by her death? But it was not their job to question such things, so they did not.

Weyzero Fantish stared at him from a distance, relieved to glimpse him alive. She had seen him sick many times before, but she never actually witnessed one of his attacks, at least not like this.

By the time Amare had uttered a few words, the tents were already up outside, chairs aligned for mourners, and the food steaming hot. No one addressed him directly or called him by his name, and from this he knew how people must be looking at him then, a steel cloud still hanging beneath his eyes. He bit his tongue sharply to swallow the tears that came rushing like river water. His tongue went numb, and so did his limbs, but the numbness protected him from the bloodless sorrow that would have split him in half.

When the food was blessed and the men stood in their

dark suits, the women were still laboring, their clothes smelling of sautéed onions and *berbere*. Amare clutched his abdomen, trying to contain a scream that lodged itself between the bones of his rib cage, small explosions already starting to bloom in his chest.

His breath was heavy, his saliva sour.

Before he had a chance to collect himself, two strong hands grabbed him and directed him to his mother's bedroom. Her body was still there, along with a priest, the maid, and Weyzero Asnaku, their neighbor. Amare was told to sit on his mother's *barciuma*, and he did so obediently. The detective's hands were used to these kinds of situations, and his words fluttered out quickly from his mouth, his spit landing onto Amare's face. It was a somber evening, and it would be a long night of sorrow.

The *aslekash*'s long arms flapped heavily when she hit her own chest, thumping rhythmically as if the seamless sound of a lost song was trapped inside her body. Though her eyes were dry, her mouth was moist with fresh saliva; each phrase she spoke was followed by a whirring sound, her head swiveling, back bent then thrust forward into the tumultuous dance of grief. This was not mourning: this was storytelling in its finest form. Her inquiries about the deceased were always detailed and poignant, but since she had actually known Weyzero Fantish, her grief was more personal, more detailed. She was not interested in death itself, but rather in the life Weyzero Fantish would have spent if she hadn't died so soon: how many New Years she would have celebrated with her family, how much joy she would've brought to her neighbors and friends, how happy she would have been to see her teenage son marry, how much she had longed to hold a grandchild, and so on.

By the time the storytelling began, the *aslekash* had already done her job; words spurted out of her mouth quickly, as if Weyzero Fantish was someone she loved and treasured deeply, as if she was the person most affected by the tragedy of it all, as if she had never experienced death before, and the pain was too great, too much to bear in her lonely heart. And the best part came after that when the crowd roared all at once, as if it was awakened from a deep sleep. It was an incoherent wailing, crying, and screaming that caught them by surprise, enveloping them in a black cloud of grief they didn't know they had birthed in their souls, filling their tents, all the rooms. Their voices lifted up to the mountains, past the tops of eucalyptus trees, deep into the night, flowing into the next morning. Every passerby who heard the *aslekash* would be touched, because grieving was communal in Yerer Ber, as was everything else. By the time the funeral was announced for the next day, it would look like the grief had quieted down, but in fact it would have only just begun to sink its deep claws into tired eyes and beaten chests.

The detective's head was as big as a moon, his neck almost completely absent, eyes almost out of their sockets when his hands shook Amare into reality. Something about the larger purpose of death, or the purpose of all things, hung heavy in the air. Something else about the gun also whispered softly under his breath, the hairs of his mustache flickering rhythmically.

But Amare was not in the room, he was not present with the men in dark suits hovering over him like menacing shadows, not there mourning with the women, not there helping the boys or the girl. He was not there when the neighbors collapsed on themselves stricken with grief, when long-lost siblings came back and greeted him with tears. He was not there because the images ran quickly by him, and he instead caught a glimpse of his past self on a rainy day, wearing a gray sweater and washed-out jeans, hunched over the poisonous herb, snatching it with quick gestures and stuffing it inside a thin coral *festal*.

*That is not me*, he assured himself. It was a different boy, a different man, who did not understand the woes of his mother, who was tired of the neighborhood's gossip surrounding their home, threatening their lives, who was angry at any man who had ever touched his mother's big brown body, every woman who had betrayed her confidence, every stranger who found it necessary to intrude in their lives. That was a boy who was tired of living in such a small neighborhood, who couldn't stand the cold, or the rain, or *kiremt* for that matter. That boy would go home, light candles, and brew some *shai*.

The pot was steaming, hot black tea and herbs mixed in a spewing lava, and he poured it in a cup slowly, and he thought, *This is it, this will slow her down, this will tire her, exhaust her from being herself, even if just for a little while.*

But the boy poured the tea and found his mother in a white dress and as a blue shadow, and the sorrow was too great, the guilt even greater, so the only thing he could do was barricade himself behind a thick shroud, fluctuating between a sharp indigo and the honey of wet eucalyptus leaves, and as he was readying himself to tell the truth, the whorl approached, porous gold and amorous red, quick, quiet, and efficient, and when it choked his throat it was not coarse or stinging; it did not awaken his entire body, nor did it stop his eyes from reversing, his tongue from folding onto itself, and though the detective and other men were screaming and trying to help him, he did not hear a thing, because the colors

lulled him slowly to sleep, and there was only a blue shadow
to keep him company.

# A NIGHT IN BELA SEFER

BY SULAIMAN ADDONIA

*Bela Sefer*

I spotted the ad about a night job in Bela Sefer at an Internet café in Mercato:

> *Looking for a young man with feminine traits.*
> *A good listener. Sexual nature involved.*
> *Should not be circumcised.*
> *Earn up to $500.*

Although I knew I qualified for all the criteria, the sexual element of the job kept me from sleeping well for days prior to calling the agency. The "earn up to $500" was persuasive. After all, I thought, this would be a one-off job. Take the money and leave.

But there was another reason that I repeated to myself on the way to the agency. I observed my city through the window of the bus, the city I had hoped to never have to leave even if buried inside me was a part of myself I was scared to show the light of day.

*Looking for a young man with feminine traits.* Perhaps then, in my Addis Ababa, I could be my full self. Even if for just one night.

*Hayat stood outside her shack in Bela Sefer, waiting for the man she'd hired for the night. The idea had come to her in the forest of*

*Bela Sefer, where she had buried her clitoris, the piece of flesh her family had removed when she was fifteen, because she had kissed her sweetheart, Negus. "Now, she will never ensnare another man," said her aunt, her circumciser.*

*Hayat returned to the forest every night, to pay homage to the part of her that was gone, to try to find something else on her body that could give her pleasure. But no matter where she touched herself, how hard, long, and deep she explored her body, nothing stirred her. She feared her aunt was right, that all her past desires had turned into thorns with the passage of time. But if that was the case, why, as she held a pair of scissors and leaned between his thighs, did warm fluid escape her vagina without touching it?*

I reached the agency in Mercato. For a moment, I stood with my back to the iron door, facing the street and the way back home to my parents. Back there, I continued to hide that thing inside me that I feared to let out publicly, just like how my father refrained from speaking about his political beliefs for fear of the secret police.

I turned and knocked. Frantically.

"Okay, okay, I can't fly," said a voice on the other side of the door.

"Good afternoon. Are you with the agency?" I said to a man wearing a dark-blue V-neck cashmere sweater and sarong.

He turned his head left and right, following the wail of a siren. When the sound faded, he sighed. "Yes, yes, I am." He lowered his glasses from his forehead and examined me in silence. "You must be here for the night job." I could see khat leaves stuck to the inside wall of his mouth.

I nodded.

"Let's go to my office," he said, looking over my shoulders

again. He spat out the leaves, pulled me inside, and closed the door.

I saw three large boxes lined up against the wall in the hallway. *For female pleasure*, read the red stickers on the sides.

Next to the boxes, books were stacked from floor to ceiling. I paused to read some of the titles. There were books on poetry, capitalism, Marxism, and some on the ever-complicated relationship between Eritrea and Ethiopia, countries that like me stood torn, full of hate and love. One cover with a long title grabbed my attention—*Intercourse, an Outdated Concept: Alternative Sex.*

I leaned over and checked the author's name. *Hayat*, it said. There was no surname.

"Come on now, let's go upstairs."

I followed him up the squeaky wooden stairway. He huffed as he threw himself into a leather chair behind a table. I glanced around his gray office. On one side of his desk, a bunch of khat leaves were scattered around a half-empty glass of tea. On the other side sat his telephone.

He opened a drawer and took out pen and paper. "You are Brhan, right?"

"Yes."

"I remember your name," he said. "We only had a few responses."

"I can understand why."

His eyes crinkled at the corners as he ticked a box. "Perceptive," he mumbled. His attention returned to my face and he continued to mumble as he jotted down: *glowing face, groomed and arched eyebrows, a mole under his left eye, would have been sexier under his lower lip.* "No one is perfect, ah, Brhan," he said.

I bowed my head.

"Brhan, correct me if I am wrong, but your slender body and feminine face suggest to me you are from the northwest of the country?"

"Yes," I whispered.

"I can't hear you. Please look up as you talk."

"Yes, you guessed right," I said. For the first time in my life, I didn't object to this comment about my appearance.

"Good, now pull down your pants and whatever you are wearing underneath," he said.

When I did as he asked, he stood up with his piece of paper and directed his attention below my hips. He smiled. "Brhan, I must say you fit every single criteria. We will take you on. If you do the job well, then you will get five hundred dollars—not birr. My client deals in Western currency." He chuckled. His face shook like brown jelly as he stood up to hand me the address of my client and the directions to her shack.

"Shack?"

"Yes, it is in Bela Sefer."

*Isn't this sort of job for a rich place like Mekanisa?* I thought as I glanced at the address again.

"She will be happy to meet you," he said.

"She?"

*Bela Sefer was built by the poor who came to Addis from small villages. But since they couldn't afford to live in the city, they made their homes here, at the foot of the forest. Hence, these temporary buildings have quickly erected walls and makeshift roofs. Wind shakes them; a storm could rip all the shacks off the ground in a second. At times, when the forest rages, things fly around. If you were to walk in the woods, you could notice trees dressed up in* shammas, zuris, *and torn pages of holy books.*

*Negus was the most stable fixture in Hayat's life.*

*They lived on the same street, their shacks opposite each other. A dusty and sloping alleyway separated them. Her desire for him was sown at night, when they used to bring their beds outside to allow their parents privacy in the small shacks. Because the pathway was narrow, their beds touched. She heard his dreams, just as she felt his warm breath. She first masturbated after he went to sleep on one of those nights and she feasted her eyes on his body, stretched taut and translucent in the moonlight. She climbed into his bed. The next morning, her aunt, Negus's mother, who doubled as a circumciser, came to her shack with the news of her licentiousness.*

It was early in the evening when I arrived outside the church in Bela Sefer on the day of the job, as instructed by the agency. When I got out of the taxi, I stepped on something with my foot. Red juice splattered over the dusty ground. Someone had dropped a tomato.

I trembled as I unfolded the directions, a series of Bela Sefer landmarks dotted on the yellow piece of paper: a church, a sex worker known for strangling her customers to exorcise evil as she brought them to orgasm, a Somali kiosk, a café, the only compound with a TV.

Just then a scream erupted behind me. I turned. This was the path that led to the sex worker's shack. I was sweating. I took off my blazer and continued on my way to find the client.

Farther ahead, a group of women emerged from a bar. A quick dance competition exploded in the middle of the street and drew in a crowd. As the winner hugged her ten-birr note, the loser high-fived me. Her touch invigorating, I strode away, shaking my shoulders until I came across men in turbans with *gabis* draped around their shoulders, huddling in front of a café. They talked in whispers. *We are a land of laughter and preaching except when it comes to sex and politics,* I thought as I turned left and counted a hundred steps. In this stone-paved lane, I paused.

"Why am I doing this?" I mumbled. I had come all the way here without a thought about the risk. I had known an activist cousin and her friends who were kidnapped by the police. I had seen a woman surrounded by armed men because she had taken in a lover the same way her husband did.

I tried to remember if I had said or done anything political or controversial that could have led to me being lured to a secret place from which I would never return. I couldn't recall an occasion of me being outspoken on any issue. I took my risks quietly, like staying up all night long to bring the woman in me to life, in the dark, when everybody around me was asleep.

But here I was, on my way to give my body to an Ethiopian woman who wanted me as I was, an Ethiopian man, with both my femininity and masculinity. I quickened my pace.

*Hayat worked at a studio in Bela Sefer assisting an old photographer. In his darkroom, she learned that everyone had a dark side.*

*But she no longer wanted to conceal her dark side. Instead, she cultivated it until it became as visible as all of her other sides. Every evening, she would go to the forest that had become not only her place of solitude and reflection, but also the laboratory where she continued to experiment with her own body.*

*Months had passed since the celebration of Hayat's cleanliness. One night, she was sitting under a tree in the forest, watching another man run down to Bela Sefer, his shadow darting on the moonlit leaves. The man tripped and fell in a hole she had dug to trap animals. She heard his scream and the deafening, maniacal laughter of hyenas.*

She leaned back on the straw rug, the same one upon which she had been laid when her aunt carried out the operation on her, and when she turned on her side, her silhouette against the wild bush aroused her. She raised her legs, her toes dangling under the stars, the screams continuing in the background. That night, as she touched her anus, a burning sensation invaded her.

Dawn. Alive.

She climbed the tallest tree in the forest and looked toward Addis, where the buildings were so big that she didn't know whether the clouds hung low or the city had stepped up. The billboards of shopping malls promising Western happiness appeared like a mirage against the hills. The cars on the bridge looked as if they were flying over the city. This was a change she didn't feel a part of. She had once been called the future of Ethiopia. The future, though, had arrived without her.

Dazed, she lost her balance. What saved her from falling wasn't herself. Rather, it was a subconscious thing, this residual resilience that the poor built over the years. Her arms grasped a branch and she swung from the tree.

She returned to a deserted Bela Sefer, breathless, dripping with sweat. She picked up a pair of scissors from her shack and returned to the passageway. Negus had gotten married earlier that day. She heard a moan coming out of his place. The moan of a virgin. Awhile later, he walked out and went to the back of his shack to relieve himself, where Hayat was standing with her scissors.

"Hayat, what are you doing here?" he whispered as she sat in front of him. She could smell sex on his penis, which quickly became erect when she took it in her hand. Memories came to her of the first time they'd both unveiled themselves to each other, of the dream that they would make endless love, before he told his mother about their kiss.

The trees of the forest rammed against each other. This blinding *violence found itself to her veins. Hayat took the scissors to Negus's thighs.*

*Clouds of smoke gathered above Bela Sefer. The forest where she used to get lost, hide, shower in the rain that dripped from the tree, that large, dense forest where she'd met Negus and they opened their eyes to each other's naked skin, where she buried his foreskin next to her clitoris, this place now smelling like their sexes.*

A mustached man in a three-piece suit preached to passersby from a high chair, holding leaflets in his gold-ringed hand. "I will teach you ten ways to overcome poverty and get rich," he said in a bad American accent. "Places are limited. Grab this information pack and book fast to avoid disappointment."

I took a leaflet with an American flag printed on it, the symbol of a place where God and money could coexist. But I wanted neither. I unbuttoned my shirt, as if to air out that thing caged inside me. *It isn't only governments that imprison,* I thought. *We are just as capable of doing that to our own selves.*

I was deep in my thoughts when I saw the preacher strut to a nearby Mercedes. Girls surrounded the car, some with babies strapped to their backs, while others carried firewood or buckets.

My eyes moved from the girls to a group of boys forming a circle around two youngsters who stood back-to-back, the beginning of a duel. The fighters turned their hands into the shapes of guns and paced away from each other. When they turned sharply, it was as if their shots missed each other and instead made the sky bleed. Dusk arrived to Bela Sefer with a splotch of red seeping through the thick clouds.

I checked my client's address once again. She lived along the last row of the shantytown at the bottom of the forest.

Following the hastily written sign pointing to the forest

of Bela Sefer, I turned left. The ground became darker and steeper, and the water in the potholes rippled in the breeze. I caught the reflection of a boy standing on a barrel, urinating, and I shuffled past. Finally, I spotted the cluster of corrugated tin shacks: some roofless, others covered with wooden planks or fabric. My spirits sank. *Is this a hoax?* I wondered. *How is it possible for someone living here to pay this kind of money, and what could "sexual nature involved" mean in this place?*

I pondered whether to turn back, when I remembered the girl in my school who had changed my voice.

"Your voice is too high, like a girl," she'd said to me one day at recess. "Here, this will help you to deepen it."

She'd placed a handful of herbal leaves in my hand that I put in water overnight and drank every morning before I came to school. And every morning, she would take me aside and test the depth of my voice. The day she was satisfied, she introduced me to her friends as her new boyfriend.

But it was more than a defect in vocal cords—it was the voice of someone else. The other me I couldn't name back then, but now could feel and would soon present to a Habesha woman. The very thought of being able to openly express myself alleviated my doubts and set me forth on my way to my client's shack, illuminating the path ahead of me.

I passed through several alleyways with the damp air sticking to my face and arrived on a bright street. Although there were no lamps, light still emanated from furnaces and stovetop fires. I ducked under the clothes hanging on ropes tied between two shacks. Water dripped on my head and the scent of Imperial Leather soap made me light-headed.

A woman with her hair set in rollers emerged from a shack and wiped her child's bum, then walked toward a group of women sitting in a circle around an open furnace. Murmurs broke out. I moved closer and listened to the crackling fire, watching their faces glow from the embers, their eyes squinting as the smoke curled in front of them. Above their braided heads, a flash of lightning struck as they recollected men lost to wars and women isolated in opulent homes across the Red Sea.

*The moonlight broke through clouds. Hayat lit a cigarette and glanced at her watch. Brhan, a light, was bound to arrive in her life. She had sold her mother's wedding jewelry to hire him. She went inside the shack, leaving behind her a cloud of smoke.*

I arrived on a street lit by a single dim bulb. The noise of a generator spilled out from a compound. I peered over the stone wall and saw men watching a Bruce Lee film under a rhododendron tree.

As I approached my client's home, Ethiopian jazz emanated from her shack. I leaned against the wall and my shoulders slumped. It had been a long time since I'd had a girlfriend. I always told myself it was because women couldn't understand me, but it was only here, in this darkness, that reality began to reveal itself.

I had never had an orgasm before. My last girlfriend left me, like the others did, because she thought I was impotent. I would always grow still around women's naked bodies, forgetting that I was meant to drive them to some memorable destination. But I couldn't live up to their expectations, nor did I want to do the driving. When I reached my client's door, I realized that I could only satisfy a woman who wanted to take charge and knew her desires.

The music stopped. I peeked through the window and slipped inside the shack. The flame of an oil lamp licked the turquoise-painted tin wall, and a horsehair flyswatter hung on the wall next to an empty picture frame. I studied the space but could see nothing else besides shoes on the bare ground and some clothes scattered on a bloodied straw rug.

I was about to turn away from the window when I noticed soapy water trickling onto the floor in rivulets. I assumed a shower room was adjacent to her shack. I heard a door opening somewhere inside, but I couldn't angle my head enough to get a good look. I then saw her silhouette on the wall, the shadow of her head and chest fitting perfectly within the empty picture frame. I stared at the scene, the live painting changing as she twisted her hair into a bun. My eyes lingered across her collarbone as she placed a cigarette in her mouth. As she inhaled, the glow of her cigarette illuminated her dark nipple on the turquoise wall.

Breathless, I knocked. A few moments passed before she opened.

She wore a long, wide dress, a *gabi* around her shoulders. "Are you Brhan?"

I looked at her in silence.

"Are you Brhan? Yes or no?"

"Yes, I am."

"Well, don't just stand there."

She smelled of alcohol, but she walked in solid steps.

I followed her through a curtain in the middle of her shack to a small adjacent room. I could see a bed, a black box, and an old typewriter next to a pile of papers.

"Take off your clothes," she said. "All of them."

I didn't. I leaned against the door, my arms crossed over my chest.

"Surely I don't need to remind you that you are here to satisfy me," she said. "And it starts by listening to me."

After a moment of staring down at my feet, I turned around to undress.

She chuckled. "Actually, I am not after your penis. But it seems you instinctively know what I want." She ran her hand over my buttocks. I felt a squeeze on my wrist. "Now turn around."

I did as she asked. She took off her clothes. When I noticed a tattoo in the shape of Africa between her breasts, I realized this was a woman who loved our continent and perhaps nothing else.

"The lights of Bela Sefer will go out soon, so allow your eyes to feast," she said. "I want my body fixed at the front of your mind like a mural sparkling in the dark."

I followed her with my eyes as she strutted to the other side of the room. Sitting on her bed, she asked me to come toward her. "But slowly," she said. "We have all the time in the world."

I had never felt so exposed, so inspected. Yet it was what I had always dreamed of; not so much to be owned, but to be released from the shackles that tied me to an idea of manhood I couldn't fulfill. I wanted to create my own definition of what it was to be a man: I could take the role of a woman with a woman if I wished, or take the role of a silent lover. When I realized that all of the rage that had accumulated inside me was because I was trying to be someone I was not, I moved slowly toward her. When I arrived to her side, I decided to let go and surrender to the unknown, thinking that this was the key to my freedom.

She wrapped her arms around my thighs and inhaled. She breathed out. "I love that scent," she said. "Come and sit next to me."

We sat in silence for a long time.

She then leaned over the black box and took out a pair of cuffs and pushed me onto the bed.

"Hey!"

When I attempted to stand up, she put her hands on my chest. "Trust me." The pen holding her bun up fell out and her hair covered her face. It was quiet outside. "Now lie down and relax."

She cuffed my arms and legs, and when she pulled a scarf over my mouth and gagged me, I closed my eyes.

"I asked for a good listener because I am going to tell you a story first," she said. "It's about an Ethiopian girl who was born to love, and on the way, she was forced to discover a different path to happiness . . ."

She must have talked all night long. I could hear the birds chirping, the muezzin calling, and the church bells ringing. Bela Sefer was rising, starting another day, another attempt at hope at the crack of dawn.

"They say I am a jinni. I will possess you. Your voice will become mine."

I thought she laughed, but perhaps she just smiled. Her tin shack amplified every noise, as if the only way to live here was to double up its thrills.

But she didn't possess me. She freed me. As I began talking, I heard my high-pitched voice again, the feminine sound that earned me ridicule at school, which some said was because an evil spirit had possessed me and I'd suppressed it for all these years. Yes, I could hear my old voice, the voice of a woman inside me, the voice I had buried under the pretense and deceptions of manhood. I closed my eyes and listened to the echoes of my own voice.

I could no longer distinguish between Hayat's voice and mine. *We are one. We are one.*

She left the room, reappearing moments later with a lit candle in her left hand and a razor in her right. When I parted my legs, she walked over to the book that was sitting on a bedside table—*Intercourse, an Outdated Concept: Alternative Sex.*

As her right hand swooped between my legs, I remembered how my mother had thrown herself over me in defense when my father wanted the local woman to circumcise me.

A howl went through the forest, Hayat, and me.

*A howl went through the forest, Brhan, and me.*

# PART III
*MADNESS DESCENDS*

# INSOMNIA

BY Lelissa Girma

*Haya Hulet*

6:15 p.m.

He was sitting at the Terrace Café somewhere in Haya Hulet and watching the people going up and down the road. The day had been long, and the setting sun seemed to promise an even longer evening. His body was tired, but his mind continued to churn with a nagging persistence. It had been more than fifty hours since he last slept. He feared if he went home he would not be able to fall asleep and would have to walk through the streets again. Based on how he was feeling now, he was unsure if he would ever sleep again.

The street was bustling with cars and people on their phones. Across the street, there was a private hospital with visitors pouring in and out and tires squealing when they pulled into the parking lot. As he ordered, he remembered that coffee had caffeine, then realized the caffeine would have no purpose since his body had stopped responding to stimulants.

The girl who served him gazed intently at his face as she gently set down the cup. She was expecting him to recognize her, but he was too tired to recognize anyone, and focused his attention on the oily-looking liquid in front of him. When the girl started to walk away, however, he began to notice her, especially how her pants fit her so well that day. Her body almost seemed malleable, taking the shape of the clothes she wore. He stirred the coffee, thinking about how the fabric looked so rigid that it must be abrasive.

When he turned his head toward the street, he sensed that the rhythm of pedestrians and cars had quickened, and his heart began to pick up its pace as if to match the commotion outside. He pressed his hands to his temples and felt them throbbing. *I must get some sleep today*, he promised himself. The noise was making him more and more tense. Amid the traffic, taxis stopped and lured people with their honks, and people were running around with seemingly no sense of direction. The laughter, the whispers, the woman pulling along her children with runny noses, parking attendants writing on tickets, tacking them under wipers—all of this brought up an urge in him that he had to fight against. He could visualize this so clearly, the bottle of Baro's dry gin just at his fingertips. While he was fighting the urge, the madness of the street seemed to settle down. He eased into a daydream, thinking of the woman with her lipstick-smudged matchbox and her laughter. He caught himself getting lost in the wheels of memory, and returned his attention to the street.

He saw a group of girls all in the same clothes and walking in perfect sync. He studied them closely, wanting to register them in his catalog of beauty. Then he counted more than a dozen men who had shaved heads—the local skinheads with their shiny scalps. Looking at them from where he sat, he imagined how cold they must be and began to worry because he believed their heads were made of something soft like the shell of a boiled egg.

*6:27 p.m.*

He finished his coffee. He heard a voice in his head say, *Go home and sleep. Stop thinking, go to sleep.* He wondered if somebody could hypnotize him. A part of Yannis's piano routine rang in head.

*He heard the laughter of a girl. That spontaneous laugh that would start casually then extend like she was imagining another layer to the joke, or she was combining all of the laughter she'd had throughout her life in that one moment. Once she began to laugh, it would go on and on until everyone laughed alongside her, contracting her glee. She would get worried in the middle of her laughter that it was going to die suddenly, and would refresh it by extending it with sounds that had nothing to do with laughter.*

6:28 p.m.

He shook his head and turned his attention back to the street.

A man got out of a taxi and walked toward the private hospital. He was holding a construction helmet, which he placed over his head once he reached the entrance.

He thought that he had made it up—it made no sense that a man would wear a helmet to enter a hospital to visit a patient. *If what I did see was real*, he thought, *then those skinheads should learn from him and protect their soft heads.*

He waited for the man to come out. When he didn't, he called for the waitress and paid. This time he smiled and she smiled back. She had teeth like the tines of a fork. When she turned, clanking his cup on the tray, he studied her from behind, and continued to do so even after she was gone.

6:49 p.m.

As he stood up, the urge came to him again. This time he knew he couldn't fight it. His body was tired, he had a headache, and he was having memories that made it feel like something outside of him was ordering him about. His body begged for sleep and though he would have gladly granted it, he had forgotten how. If he went to a bar and spent another night without sleep, he knew he was going to damage his brain. He began to sweat. He didn't want to go home anymore. He knew that if he went and couldn't sleep, he would probably go mad and take rat poison, or do something else very unpleasant.

*He vaguely remembered the other boy they told him about: how the boy took an extra dose of rat poison before running away from home, how they searched for and found him two days later and he wasn't dead. They took him to a hospital and admitted him into the psychiatric ward, and he began covering his face with his shirt after that to hide from people . . .*

*Another time, everybody laughed in a taxi when a friend was telling him how, in his old neighborhood, they had brought back a man who had stepped on a land mine on the battlefield. Everybody laughed when he explained how they had taken him home in a bucket because he'd been blown to pieces. They brought him home because he loved his mother and refused to die without seeing her. He was dead serious when he told the story and was trying to make a point that the debt of death must only be paid when one is ready and not when it is due.*

7:30 p.m.

He wanted to call somebody but he had nobody that he could call. Everyone he wanted to call was either dead or from his imagination. Now the memories were becoming vivid, like he was watching a movie made especially for him without a beginning or an end, a movie intended to drive him wild with regret. It played inside the deep recesses of his soul, with scenes powerful enough to remove him from reality. It was a movie he couldn't choose to walk out of, and the movie's score was Rachel's terrific laughter.

He decided they were in love. Rachel knew all the sounds that ought to exist, and it was those sounds, that voice, that would not let him be. They kept lingering even after she was gone, and prevented him from sleeping.

*Henock could never sleep. He had gotten a desk job at some office as a clerk. Mornings were horrible for him, but he got there on time and slept while working in snatches. After lunch he chewed khat and would be like Lazarus, resurrected back from the dead.*

*Even as a kid he'd never slept as soundly as he should have. He almost never slept without a nightmare. There was always something picking up his bed or dropping him into a bottomless pit, or hairy spiders chasing him or cold hands holding his feet, sliding him down through the grills of the bed.*

He wanted to be his old self again and be with the girl, wanting to hear her laugh. He also wanted to rinse his mouth with a gulp of gin that stung on the tongue and ate away his brains when it was supposed to make his memories go away. He wanted to forget. He knew that once he could forget, he could get some sleep.

*8:50 p.m.*

In the bar while he waited for sleep to come, he had to drink quickly to slow down the movement of the people around him. His nose cleared suddenly, sharply, making the air he breathed in feel like acid, bringing tears to his eye. *There is no single reality*, something inside him thought, *as there is no single truth, or meaning to life or love or God.*

"Why can't I yawn?" he said aloud to himself. He feared he

had forgotten how to do that as well. He remembered his grand-mother's meek voice, her humming the gospel ringing in his ear. To drown the voice out he clanked the ashtray with a glass, but it didn't work. The waiter came and he ordered another drink.

*His stepfather's mother was of a different sort. She was always in constant motion: visiting people, helping around funeral homes, comforting mourners. She was a sociable old woman, but that wouldn't thoroughly describe her. She was known for doing things that seemed to completely contradict each other but would be normal in her eyes. She once helped some people move their fences over to their rich neighbor's lawn so that they could have more space. When the neighbor returned and wanted to know who was behind the debacle, she helped him by telling the truth and even went to court to testify against herself and the others. After they were fined and her neighbors deemed her as untrustworthy and two-faced, she still went on being their friend and would go out for coffee with them. Or, in another case, she would always say that she hated Henock's blind grandfather. Yet she would spend hours after hours in his company and would prepare his meals. Once, she gave him his food on a plastic pan that children would sit on before learning how to use the toilet. When Henock asked her why she would do such a thing, she said that it was because the pan had never been used, and besides, a blind man could never tell the difference.*

9:00 p.m.

He wanted to be his old self again, playing the role of a younger and better Henock. *Perhaps if I play the part well enough*, he thought, *some of it might actually rub off*. He would clench his jaw, grind his teeth, and force his bad habits to go away, but he knew he had neither the will nor the anger to do it. He would never get his old self back.

*10:07 p.m.*

He was getting drunk now. He felt a yawn coming but sneezed instead. He left the table and went to the toilet. There was a mirror on one side of the wall where he saw his reflection. His heart skipped a beat—he didn't realize that he had let his health decline this much. He felt the drunkenness leave him and he was stone-cold sober and alone—very much alone.

*It was late when they left that night. Rachel was drunk and happy. Henock thought she was pleasant when she was drunk—it was the first time he had seen her drink. They reached his house and found more to drink. They were talking nonsense the entire time, blabbering and laughing about things requiring no real intelligence. Then they quarreled. She raised her voice to a crescendo and he dragged her to the bedroom, locking the door so that they wouldn't disturb the neighbors. He expected her to cry but instead she made a lot of weird noises and rammed against the door, so he let her out. He begged, trying to cool her down, but she continued to sound like a trapped animal hammering its head against a crate. He was stu-pefied.* I shouldn't have made her drink, *he thought. She started talking about how he was beginning to neglect her and how she thought he might have women on the side. He calmed her down after a lot of pleading, but when he got her to sit on the bed, she started all over again. She ran to the door and demanded to be let out. He thought of throwing a cup of cold tap water on her. When she picked up the bottle he wasn't sure what she was going to do, but then she flung it and hit him on the head. It bounced against him like a billiard ball. He stood for a moment as though he didn't know where he was, leaned against the wall, then advanced toward her. Rachel tried to evade him but he held her by the hair, twirled her, and knocked her against the wall. Rachel slid to the ground* and started convulsing. He kept on kicking her while she lay writhing on the floor, a pitiable mess. He massaged the spot where the broken bottle had hit. She got up from the floor and dragged herself onto the bed, sobbing silently as she took off her clothes. When he called her to him, she sullenly obeyed; her hands and legs were like tendrils that were made to cling to him. She stopped crying when he started to respond to her. The bed was soft and submerged their bodies, and she whispered Jesus Christ into his ear every time she felt him coming closer to her. Once the seat had dried, she felt the cold like a splinter going through her bones. Henock was sleeping with his mouth agape. Careful not to wake him, Rachel gently pulled the blanket from under him and covered him so he could stay warm. Then she laid beside him, pulling his hand around her and squeezing it to bring herself closer. She ran her fingers over his chest that was covered by a smooth down of hair, counted his teeth, studied and kissed his hands. She prayed and cried a little before she finally went to sleep.

They were planning to wed in July after a number of similar scenes, but Rachel was too sick to be married then. She had tuberculosis, and she died in May.

*10:20 p.m.*

Henock stood and swayed while waiting to urinate—or was it after he was done? He could no longer trust his short-term memory. He stopped concerning himself with real people and even himself.

He suddenly remembered his friend who was fifteen or twenty years older than him and who liked to make cryptic remarks. They were friends a long time ago when he was young and foolish enough to believe that life would get better as he got older, that he would grow out of the darker days of his childhood. He had been young, arrogant, and gullible.

They had been watching a sick man who had all of the physical symptoms of disease, having lost all his hair. Their pity grew as the patient became completely engrossed with a morsel of something he was fighting to push down his throat.

"A mirror is a compassionate object reflecting false images the reflection wishes to believe," his friend said. "If that man had watched himself from our vantage point, if he saw himself dining with his present condition, he would have thrown himself off a bridge and died. You can't find out the truth about yourself until you come across your own self on the street, and then you observe yourself at a distance to decide what condition you are in."

He returned from the bathroom to his table and tried to force himself to feel sleepy.

*11:30 p.m.*

There weren't many people at the bar now, but the ones who were left made a great deal of noise. He lost count of the drinks. He didn't notice the new drink that was brought to him. He feared that everyone would leave him alone, turn off the lights, forget about him, and lock him in as he remained wide-eyed and awake. When he paid, he felt as though that was the last money he would ever earn. He tipped the waiter well, and then he got up to go. His body was tired and broken—and all of a sudden he was falling. People laughed or didn't notice as the waiter and bartender helped him up from under the table.

"Izohe! Izohe!" they said as they placed him on a chair.

He fell again outside in the darkened alley, where not a soul was about. He had no idea why his body and mind had contrived to take him through there. It was raining—first slowly, then hard. At some point he fell into a ditch, as though he had been heading straight toward it. He felt the rain on his face, and he had a memory of his niece, his distant niece.

*"You know what I enjoy doing best? I like walking through a heavy rain, and when I am soaked through I like to let go of my bladder. It doesn't make a difference then because nobody notices, and I get to enjoy that freedom."*

*12:03 a.m.*

He was uncomfortable from the fall, and the rain struck him as if it were tiny pebbles. A part of his spirit that couldn't stomach defeat, neglect, or surrender got up and fled for refuge somewhere else. What remained behind, inside of him, were a jumble of memories and a desire to sleep.

*And those solitary midnight walks . . . On that lane facing the palace were the taverns where the off-duty soldiers came to drink and fornicate. And there was that one house with singers that played music on a keyboard and drew people from the street. The people inside would start fights and then be driven out by the waiters, and there was a man who sang for drinks and when he started to sing he would sober up, and because of his voice girls working next door would come in and everybody would be dancing alone when he sang, and he always sang something sad and the girls would dance close to the ground like they were mopping the floor. And he would keep walking outside until he saw the bon voyage sign at the end of the city, then go to work without sleeping. The truck drivers who delivered milk in the morning were his friends and would always stop for him and give him a lift back to town.*

*12:05 a.m.*

He crawled out of the ditch and started walking in a new direction. There was something in his eye that made his vision blurry, and all the people, cars, and dogs he met on the street had a strange aura encompassing them like halos with multicolored lights. He vaguely sensed it was past midnight. He wore no watch, but he could tell the time by the way people around him behaved. In his eyes, people were like wound-up clocks that ticked toward destruction, and he could read them to tell the time. Usually, people tried to maintain a fake air of self-reliance early in the evenings that would wear out just before midnight. Cinderella's charms of make-believe would quickly turn back into the original pumpkins and rats. He knew it was past midnight when his own attitude turned nastier. He would start picking fights or trying to grab street girls, and sometimes punches or rocks would start flying as the hours demanded it.

*He kept a black-and-white photo hidden in his wallet. It was a shot of his parents. He was an only child. His parents met and married four years after he was born. His birth father was a scholar who'd left for India the same year his mother got pregnant and never returned. When he was five, his mother and his new stepfather were in a car accident, and neither of them survived. The photograph showed a young woman with a tall Afro and a miniskirt riding up to show shapely thighs. Beside her stood a man wearing horn-rimmed glasses and a smile. His grandmother had told him that he was also in that photo, because he was in the making, although there was nothing that indicated his mother was pregnant.*

*He grew up with his grandparents. He was quite attached to both of them—his mother's father and his stepfather's mother. They raised him and educated him, and they were not dead until after he'd left for Addis Ababa to study. He felt it was peculiar how they followed each other to the grave, only a year apart, as though they were a couple that wouldn't survive without each other's com-*

*pany, though they'd never really liked each other. He wasn't there to bury them. He never knew how it all happened, or how it turned out. The blind old man died first, and the old lady followed. He remembered how he used to come from the field after a quarrel with the neighborhood boys, crying to tell somebody of his injustice, his pain. The old man would be sitting beside a tree. When he ran to him to spill his woes, shuddering and sniveling, the old man would listen, tilting his head to one side, his smallpox-blotted eyes moving back and forth. When he was done, the old man would laugh, waving the flies away, his teeth white and strong.*

*"Aye Abush!" he would say, reducing the whole tale to a joke. Then he would begin telling the boy a story he'd made up behind the closed windows of his soul. The boy would be too angry to listen to those stories then. The stories always had the same theme: the importance of unimportance, the utility of futility.*

1:40 a.m.

He was walking on the paved road in the Bole suburbs now—a taxi had brought him there. He was wearing his soiled jacket, which he had to hold on his lap due to the driver's insistence. After the taxi had turned and sped away, he'd walked slowly into an alley and could hear the dogs barking. He chose the house with a fence he could climb.

He had no way of knowing if the house had a *zebenya* or if the owner would take him for a burglar. He didn't mind if he was caught—he was too tired to care and maybe even a little crazed enough to be fearless. He sat on the steps of the porch and waited until the neighborhood dogs stopped barking. He didn't care if the proprietor of the house was in the vicinity or not. All he wanted was a moment without being interrupted. It was quiet and no light was coming from inside the house.

He didn't want to do it in a familiar place. The alcohol

gave him the necessary courage and unreasonableness. He didn't care about anything anymore—it was time for him to sleep. He was in such a hurry to get it over with that he didn't even care about the consequences of breaking into a house. They could throw his body into a river for all he cared. All he wanted was to turn off the light and go to sleep. Besides, the light had not been great while it lasted. He wasn't grateful for the light, he was bothered by it, and if he could, he would have turned it off permanently. Had he had some respect for the light, he would have gently blown out the candle, but he didn't. He had no respect for anything at all, including himself, and he wanted to kick the switch and kill the light, in this strange midnight hour, in this strange unfamiliar neighborhood, inside somebody's home he did not care to know. He decided here is where he wanted to sleep.

His head kept on replaying the sounds from his past, but he was helpless to drive these memories away. He couldn't stand it, and he feared he might lose control over himself and start making noises.

The rain was still falling softly, but he was sweating. He searched around the house and found what he was looking for. The rope was just the right length and strength. He imagined it had been used recently for skinning sheep, but he couldn't be sure. He believed it was placed there, on the iron pole, waiting patiently for him to come and use it. He took it down and gently made it into a noose. His hands were shaking but the tumult in his soul was ebbing, the rain that had been washing over his face tasting salty.

*In the elementary school somebody referred to him as poor . . . and he broke their tooth with a rock. The next person who called him poor was a girl, and they were playing volleyball and he couldn't hit the ball hard enough. He sweated his anger out and let it go. She was a girl, he told himself, and she was his first love. Later, he was disillusioned when he first saw her naked. She had big scars inside each of her thighs, like somebody had tried to stab her and had missed. She told him a dramatic story and he pretended he wasn't interested, but in reality he was merely disillusioned because he'd thought she was immaculate and unblemished.*

*2 a.m. to 3 a.m.*

He slept at length. It took, however, a long time to fall asleep, and none of it was pleasant. He felt as if he were an engine being turned on and then shut off, his body oscillating between two dramatic states of being.

Then he felt like he was being dragged out of his body, and while he would have liked to fly to the roof and toward the sky, he stayed until his body stopped kicking and became still.

It finally occurred to him while he was floating. It all became clear then, as he saw himself hanging on the high iron gate, a rope attaching him to one of the spikes.

It occurred to him that he was finally sleeping, resting.

*There was no way of telling what might have happened if Rachel had not died so suddenly. He might have continued living even if he knew her death was caused by his neglect. Rachel had accepted her fate of loving Henock no matter what. The violent and unpleasant nights were her attempts to not accept this fact, thinking that escaping Henock meant escaping death. But something changed. Henock would have accepted her death if Rachel, after the struggles and tribulations, had finally given up on him. At last, she could stop loving him and go to the grave screaming curses and calling him names, just like she would do when they fought in the past. After she got sick, however, she had changed. Rachel had grown* exceedingly silent and unapologetically loving. She stopped hiding her private feelings for Henock and would show affection openly. If she had feared that her feelings could spoil the relationship, that fear had completely disappeared. She would kiss his hands, which she'd never dared to do before unless he was fast asleep. After her illness, she started loving him all over again, this time softly. It was like receiving the love from a mother he never had. He'd had all kinds of experiences in life except being loved. Anger and distrust were the true parents who had raised him. What he gave to Rachel was the world he had grown up in.

Henock was not ready for someone like Rachel when he met her. She had already accepted her fate of loving him when he wasn't even ready to accept himself.

Although he had spent his entire life with this trauma that had been mounting and suffocating him exponentially, he might have continued on if she were there. He would have lived alongside his multiple anguishes, drinking to oblivion, taking each day as it came. But after she died without his consent, something from the center of his soul drew the line. He had to give up, and he had no idea until his consciousness had punished him with sleeplessness. He didn't think that time would run out, but in less than sixty hours, he faced the cruelest possible psychological deterioration: haunted by neighbors, chased by his own debacle of memories; devoured by his own guilt, then to be finished off with one final, dying wish of only wanting to sleep.

*3 a.m. to 6 a.m.*

He stayed hovering above his corpse until morning. He stayed not because he wanted to, but because he was anchored by some force and could not leave. He floated above the body and felt the coldness of it below him. The dogs kept barking and howling at the moon until morning.

It was the maid who first got up and found him. She was not the screaming kind, so she fainted.

*9:50 a.m.*

The police and the coroner were called. Nobody wanted nor dared to touch the body, so they made a provincial guard and another boy from the neighborhood carry him down. When the boy cut the rope, the body fell on him and he scrambled out from under it with a muffled scream. They helped the boy up, taking the rope from the corpse's neck and throwing it away over the fence.

The moment they cut the noose he was free to go. Henock went up so quickly that he couldn't tell how his body turned out or how they fought over the rope that was priceless in the black-magic market. The owner of the house couldn't stop cursing as he turned the body over with his foot. The police officer dug into the corpse's pockets and took out a wallet. *It doesn't contain any form of identification,* the officer thought, *but there's plenty of money.* The owner of the house cursed some more when he realized he had to spend the day explaining things at the police station.

*10:06 a.m. (the end and beginning)*

Henock went to the paramount zenith, with no sky having a limit, no star looking down from above it. The top: the end, the base flat as a table and final as death. Henock could look down at all there was and is, all below, all above.

# OF THE POET AND THE CAFÉ

BY GIRMA T. FANTAYE

*Beherawi Theater*

There wasn't a single day Woubshet didn't wake up at dawn grumpy. His neighbors to the left and right of his rented room were like law-appointed alarm clocks: the loud prayers of the woman who just recently converted from Orthodox Christianity to Pente, and the ear-piercing music blasted by the banker who sang along in hopes of drowning the woman's prayers, woke Woubshet up each morning. On top of everything, the landlord's cow also contributed to the cacophony by making strange loud sounds: either it was protesting being milked or declaring a longing for its calf.

But today, he awoke to the sounds of a fire truck, the *I am coming for you* declaration passing through the area. He sat up on the edge of his bed, trying to open his eyes. He sent his legs to the floor in search of his slippers. He couldn't find them. He couldn't remember where he had thrown them the previous night.

He knew he had slept in. How could he have slept this much on this day? On this special day! Angry with himself, he made his way to his shelf in search of his watch. It read 9:30. As he had feared, he was late. He dressed quickly, and hurried his way up Africa Avenue toward Abyot Square. His rushed movements made it look like he was being chased by an angry ostrich.

His long legs felt the strains of fatigue, and couldn't satisfy his heart's desire to travel faster, but his long strides sufficed in swallowing up the road quickly enough. After passing the Flamingo restaurant, he paused briefly, looking at churchgoers dressed in white, walking up and down the stairs of St. Estifanos Church.

He bent his head in the direction of the church, crossed himself, said, "Help me spend a good day, hold back my enemies, my Father," to St. Estifanos, and then went on his way. He walked by Addis Ababa Stadium toward Churchill Avenue.

He slowed his pace. He realized that he was sweating when he got to Ras Hotel from Churchill Avenue. From the left pocket of his wide coat, he took out a blue handkerchief and smiled to himself as he dabbed the perspiration from his face. He could sense it was going to be a good day—Roha Café would be filled with excitement. He couldn't even remember the last time a poetry night was held at Roha Café. It must have been over ten years ago. Renowned and esteemed poets, homegrown critics, journalists scouting for gossip, actors whom he saw daily enjoying the morning sun at Beherawi Theater would all come.

From Ras Hotel, he started moving at an even slower pace. He put his hands on his shirt to check that his collar was placed properly under his sweater. He then glanced down at his shoes and noticed that they weren't clean. He called out to the *listero* boys sitting in the sun across the main road. A *listero* in his midteens came sprinting toward him. Without removing his eyes from Woubshet's shoes, the *listero* dropped his box on the ground, knelt, and started wiping his shoes. Woubshet, with his shoe on the *listero*'s box, drifted away in thought, thinking of the evening ahead and the short speech he'd make.

* * *

It had all started last Tuesday. A young, skinny, dark-skinned, and messy-haired boy came to Roha Café and stood by the entrance. Woubshet was preparing a cup of macchiato with hot coffee.

"What's keeping you there? Either come in or go next door!" he yelled, pointing to the lively neighboring Sheger and Arada cafés.

The young boy ignored Woubshet. He stood awhile longer at the entrance, then called out, "Woubshet the poet!"

Woubshet stopped preparing his macchiato and stared intently at the boy. No one had ever called him a "poet" before.

"You're cursed. Restart the poetry evenings. You think it's enough to simply write one book, and then spend your life burning that book?" the boy said. He left without waiting for a response.

Woubshet didn't know who the boy was or who might have sent him. After closing the café he went to Tele Bar to have a drink, then spent the evening walking aimlessly.

What had he done in the past ten years? Nothing! What had he done besides burn every copy of the one book he wrote, making a bonfire like the Meskel Demera? He wanted to pound his head against a brick wall.

Woubshet Mesfin had published a poetry book titled *The Early Bird's Decree*, which became the laughingstock of critics, and professional and amateur poets alike. He had written about a bird which, unlike the Meskel bird, did not come just once a year following the scent of the *adey abeba*. It was about a bird who, when the sky became the color of the belly of a donkey, would disturb the peace of Addis Ababa by declaring, *Allehu, allehu, I exist*. One day, all the other birds copied her voice and began to say, *Allehu, allehu,* and stole her melody. That bird was never seen again. She never came back to Addis Ababa. He wrote, "Where did the bird go?" When the book made it to the public, it was mocked mercilessly. He was accused of disrespecting literature, and it had been ten years last Tuesday since, like Arius, he'd been excommunicated from the arts.

He wrote his poems at a time when Roha Café had been seen as the hottest spot for literature. It was a wonderful time for both the café and the arts. At least twice a week, Roha would host poetry accompanied by music from the *krar* and *washint,* and once every two weeks a famous artist would be invited to lead spirited conversations.

The week his book was published, critics drew their weapons and fired shots at him. When he went to open Roha Café early in the morning five days after publication, he found a copy of his book thrown on the café's veranda. He hadn't expected to receive such negativity. Poets, critics, and journalists who once jam-packed Roha Café disappeared entirely.

He closed Roha Café and disappeared from the area for two weeks. The news of Woubshet's retreat was heard across the town. He went to Dire Dawa. Upon his return, now despising poetry, he stopped all arts programs from taking place at the café. He removed the poems from the walls. He stopped associating with any poets or critics and started purchasing all the copies of his book from publishers and distributors in order to burn them, hoping that the coming generation would know nothing of it.

Roha soon became a typical café where only coffee and macchiato were sold. The glamour of the place further deteriorated once the neighboring Sheger and Arada cafés were opened.

Woubshet wanted to manage Roha Café only until all the

copies of his book had been burned. He had printed 950 copies. Less than two months after returning from Dire Dawa, he had bought 930 of them. But finding those last twenty books took him over ten years. Since he didn't know who had bought them, he kept visiting old bookstores. He would wait until the close of business to ask: "Does anyone have a book called *The Early Bird's Decree?*" But even so, up until last Tuesday, he had only bought and burned sixteen of the remaining books. He still had four books left.

But then on Tuesday, he decided to drop his ten-year effort and instead organize a great poetry event. He plastered posters across town and sent descriptions of the event to newspapers. The only concern he had was regarding the number of people attending; despite all the promotion, he didn't want too large of a crowd to turn up.

He gave the *listero* one birr and headed calmly to the café without waiting for his change. Observing the number of people outside Beherawi Theater, drinking tea, coffee, and macchiato, it might seem that Addis Ababa had been asked to come out for battle. A sense of jealousy crept up on him when he realized that his café was not open, and that all of these people were being served at Arada and Sheger instead.

But he immediately scolded himself, *Listen, Woubshet Mesfin! You are a poet, not a merchant! Let it be gold they're paying with.*

He reached inside his pocket for the key to the café, finding instead his blue handkerchief. Then he emptied his other pockets. He must have forgotten his keys at home. He approached the other cafés, angry at his forgetfulness. It seemed like the city's coffee aficionados had been called here by proclamation. The noises of clanking cups and spoons, the restlessness of the patrons, and the back and forth of the waiters made the cafés seem like a lively market.

Soon he could see Arada Café. He could also see Sheger. But he couldn't see Roha. His confusion grew. He reached the veranda, unwilling to accept what he was seeing. All the seats were taken—some patrons were drinking while standing. Every chair on the veranda was occupied.

Roha Café had been here.

But Roha Café was not here now.

He struggled to comprehend what he was seeing. He tried to convince himself that what he was seeing was not true, that he must not be awake.

The café had disappeared.

Roha Café, until eleven o'clock last night, had been situated between Arada and Sheger cafés. In a state of shock, he stood for about twenty minutes leaning on one of the posts of Beherawi Theater, absentmindedly watching the coffee drinkers on the veranda. He registered the features of each customer.

He checked the names of the cafés posted on their entryways. Sure enough, one read: *Arada Café*. Without removing his eyes from the wall, he carefully and slowly glanced to the door of the next one: *Sheger Café*.

"*Ende!* Is this real?" he said aloud. "Are you stupid? This can't be possible." He turned his face away from the cafés and toward the buildings across from him. He saw Addis Café from afar. He was correct. He hadn't confused the neighborhood. After all, he had been coming to this place for the past fifteen years.

He tapped his forehead and said: "My eyes must be failing me." He then started walking from Beherawi Theater in the direction of Ras Hotel. When he got to the entrance, he stopped. He rubbed his eyes and told himself repeatedly that what he was seeing—people walking past him, creatures calmly making their way up and down the road—was not in his dreams but in reality. He stretched. He slapped his forehead gently with his palm.

He slowly retraced the forty meters from Ras Hotel to Beherawi Theater. "What is wrong with me?" he asked himself. "Is something wrong with my eyes? It must be old age. But what if it isn't my eyes?" He grew increasingly concerned. "Have I started losing my mind? Am I forgetting things? . . . No! I haven't gone mad." He glanced at his clothes. He appeared fine. *Though I don't look well dressed, I haven't let myself go,* he comforted himself. *If I mention that the café disappeared, they'll think I've lost my mind.* He started walking slowly again. He wished the short road would extend forever. He returned to the cafés, talking to himself. As before, Roha Café was not there. "How can a single person not ask how a café that was there yesterday does not exist today?" he asked no one in particular, glancing around at the mass of unworried people drinking coffee.

He started to think of what he should do. Should he yell, *They stole my café!* If he did, they'd definitely take him to Amanuel Hospital, convinced that he was crazy. How was he going to deal with this, and what would he do for a living? As he was stressing over this, two accountants from Medhin walked into Sheger Café without even greeting him. They saw him, but pretended not to know him. He was a little annoyed. Glancing from Sheger Café to Arada and then back again, he hoped for a miracle.

A little while later, two young women walked into Arada Café without greeting him. "What's so wrong with me that they refuse me God's greetings?" he said, thinking of confronting them. But one can't really accuse others of not saying hello. He returned his eyes back to where Roha Café had been until last night.

He stared ahead in disbelief at the cafés while leaning against Beherawi Theater. More sweat started to roll down his forehead. He took out his blue handkerchief to dry his face and returned it to his pocket, only to bring it back up to his forehead again.

The short waiter from Arada Café came toward him. She had tied her hair at the back. The blue uniform she wore fit perfectly around her hips, holding the gaze of all who passed by. Woubshet liked her smile, a beautiful bright smile that could sustain him and replace every meal. She was a good friend. He'd tried to write a poem about her smile once, but not a single verse came to his mind.

She now offered a reserved smile and said respectfully, "I'm sorry, you've been standing here for a while. What can I bring you?" That other smile of hers, the one he had tried to write a poem about, was not there.

"Don't you know who I am?"

The short waitress tried to look at him humbly and shook her head.

"Look at me."

She did.

"You still don't know me?"

"I'm not sure. Perhaps I forgot. Sorry. Our job forces us to meet quite a lot of people; we can't remember everyone," she said.

"But you knew me well!"

She looked at him again, shook her head, and said, "What should I bring you?"

"I don't want anything."

"You can't stand here. Either order or move across the street. Customers might want the place. It's house policy."

"What? How dare you prevent me from standing on the veranda of my own café?" Woubshet spoke with a raised voice. This was what he'd been afraid of. "*Eshi*, tell me, where did Roha Café go?"

"What Roha Café?"

"My café! Roha Café! It was here last night."

Customers sitting on the veranda started listening to Woubshet Mesfin's raised voice. All eyes were aimed at him, like a porcupine's thorns. He wasn't sure why they were staring at him like that. The café he had worked at for so many years . . . when it disappears all of a sudden, can he not ask why?

"Aren't you ashamed when you deny the existence of a café I walked in and out of for ten years? Let us ask the people of Addis Ababa—from Mexico Square to Ambassador, from Legehar to Piassa—where Roha Café was. There is no reason to lie!"

The short waiter left Woubshet to take another customer's order. Woubshet mumbled to himself: "How bizarre! Just how bizarre."

People's eyes were still fixed on him.

"My people, why do you stare at me? Do you think I'm crazy or do you think I'm lying? He's my witness, I am telling the truth," Woubshet said, pointing his hands at the sky.

"What café is this, my friend?" It was a tall young man not far from Woubshet who asked the question, stirring his lemon tea with a spoon.

"My café, Roha Café. It was here until eleven o'clock last night. I can't find it now."

"Maybe you confused the location? I've been coming here

for two years, and I've never seen a Roha Café," the man said politely, tapping the tip of his teacup with his spoon.

"What are you saying? I'm telling you I was working here until late last night. What kind of thing is this? This has been my job for years. How many coffee addicts have I served? How can you say you've never seen it? How can I, the owner, not be trusted? Name a single poet who doesn't know Woubshet Mesfin's Roha Café. How many playwrights sat in Roha and came up with their ideas. *Dawn in Gonder*—where do you think that play was written? Was it not at Roha Café? Was he not sitting and drinking Roha Café's hot coffee? Why do you deny it? There is no reason to lie."

The young man listened silently to Woubshet and then, without responding, put a bill in the cup holder and rushed out. The lively chatter from the two cafés had now disappeared and was replaced with silence and whispered words. Some started laughing.

The headwaiter of Arada Café approached Woubshet in his white attire. He was tall and dark-skinned and had a scar on his forehead. He held his hands politely behind his back as he drew closer.

Woubshet relaxed when he saw Moges. "Moges, *ajerew. Ere,* get me out of this puzzle; where can a café go?" he said, lowering his voice.

Moges was surprised that a man he had never seen called him "*ajerew,*" a term of endearment among friends, and said, "How can we help you, sir? You are disturbing the customers."

"Moges!" exclaimed Woubshet. He clapped his hands. "Moges! You too! Moges . . ."

"Do you know me?"

"Woubshet Mesfin of Harar! He asks if I know him!"

Moges tried futilely to remember where he might have known Woubshet.

"You're acting like you don't know me!"

"I've never seen you before today."

"Stop joking and tell me where my café went."

"Which café?"

"Roha Café."

"What Roha Café? I know all the cafés from Mexico Square to Piassa, and there is not a single one called Roha."

"Why such lies? Won't God Himself judge you for denying that Roha was between Arada and Sheger for many years?"

"If the café was in fact here, where could it have gone? It isn't like the wind, you know."

"Aren't you Moges?"

"You are correct."

"Two months and twenty days ago, did I not bring a doll for your newborn baby girl?"

"Yes, I do have a daughter now, but where do you know me from that you would come to my house with a doll as a present for my newborn?"

Woubshet was furious. "Where do I know you from? How many times did you beg me for money because payday wouldn't come soon enough? How many times did I give you all I had?"

"Sir, where did you say the café was?"

Woubshet looked up at the two cafés. The coffee-drinking customers were listening to their conversation intently. "Here, of course."

As Moges tried to contain his laughter, the owner of Sheger Café noticed the commotion and approached the two. "*Getaw*, you are disturbing the area."

"Where should I go other than my own café?" Woubshet yelled.

Million took off his glasses and scrutinized Woubshet.

"*Ato* Million, don't tell me even *you* don't know me," Woubshet said.

"Obviously not!"

"How could you forget me, the man who managed Roha Café for many years?"

"Which café?"

"He asks me which café! You've been running this pretentious place for years. I know that you sold khat! Why do you pretend to not know me?"

There was confusion on the faces of his interrogators. Though they'd never seen Woubshet before, he obviously had some information about them. Million had been involved in selling khat years ago, but not anymore. Now, he just owned a house in Haya Hulet Mazoria, where artists chewed khat. "Where did you say Roha Café was?"

"How many times do I have to I tell you? It was here between the two cafés."

"When?"

"Until last night at eleven o'clock."

"And where has it gone?"

"How should I know?"

"Well, it couldn't have gotten up and disappeared," Moges said.

Woubshet was speechless.

"If it were here, where else could it be? The café couldn't have flown away," Million said, turning back to his own café. They all left Woubshet where he was standing and returned to their jobs.

How all of them could forget him in a day, and how Roha Café disappeared, Woubshet simply couldn't understand. *Am I dreaming?* he thought to himself. Impossible, he wasn't dreaming. His café was gone. When he looked up, people's eyes were still focused on him. Some were clearly pitying him.

"What are you staring at? Why are you all acting like you don't know me?" he said loudly. No one responded. "You, you!" He pointed at a short, big-bellied man who was complaining that his macchiato had too much milk. "Don't you know me? Weren't you a regular at Roha Café?"

"Who, me?" the man asked.

"Yes, you forgot?"

"Don't start any trouble, my friend. What Roha are you talking about? Did they release you too early from the mental hospital?"

"Who are you calling crazy?" Woubshet raised his voice. "Aren't I right that you take Largactil?"

The man was shocked. "I think you must be a spy, carrying our secrets around with you. Now, stop troubling me." He grew quiet, probably wondering how a stranger could know of his mental health condition. He silently went on stirring his macchiato.

Moges heard the latest commotion on the veranda and came back outside. He saw Woubshet quarreling with a customer. "You're disturbing our business. I'll call the police. Don't assume that the station is far—"

"Let a thousand policemen come. I asked about my café! I don't want anyone's fortune. I just want my café that I— Woubshet Mesfin of Harar, a poet afraid of none—built with sweat and tears."

"Don't make me call the police."

"Call a thousand policemen. Who fears death? You say police . . . no-good policemen, who fears them?"

While some customers kept watching Woubshet, others grew tired of the scene and started paying their bills and leaving. As they did, new patrons assumed their places.

Woubshet quickly made his way past Moges and into Arada Café's restroom. People inside hadn't noticed what was going on outside, so they ignored Woubshet's hurried entrance. Their attention was drawn to him only when Moges followed him, yelling, "Get out!"

"Let me urinate in peace." Woubshet locked the toilet from the inside. He could hear Moges and the others whispering beyond the door.

Woubshet closed his eyes as he stood over the sink. He feared looking at himself in the mirror, but approached it nonetheless. Who would he go to for help if he saw someone else in the mirror? He turned the tap with his eyes still closed. He felt the running water on his hands.

He cleansed his sweaty face with his wet hands.

He slowly opened his eyes.

It was him.

Was it really the actual Woubshet Mesfin that all of this was happening to? Or was his soul resting in the body of someone he didn't know? Or had he not even woken from his sleep? He remembered the story of the Ethiopian Abimelech, friend of the prophet Ermias, who slept for sixty-six years after praying to avoid watching the destruction of Jerusalem, and he thought that perhaps he too had fallen asleep, though not for as many years. Fearing that he might have aged, he looked again at the mirror. He was the same Woubshet Mesfin. He squeezed his face between his hands.

It was the Woubshet Mesfin of yesterday. His head was covered with gray hair. The skin on his forehead had formed lines. His eyes rested on his left brow, which had more gray hair than the right one. He felt his eyebrows with his fingers. Today wasn't the day to worry about his eyebrows. The café he'd run for the past fifteen years had disappeared. Even worse, he'd

watched as people who knew him walked by pretending not
to know him, unwilling to acknowledge him.

He heard Moges from outside: "You, man. Get out! I'll call
the police. You'll regret it later when you're taken to prison!"

"Roha Café, where did Roha Café go?" he asked the man
in the mirror.

Woubshet remembered when he left his birthplace, Harar,
and came to Addis Ababa to work as an accountant at the
post office, eventually leading to the bright days of Roha Café.
He had no other dream than writing poetry, day and night. He
wished to be remembered beyond his grave as a great poet and
not just a mortal man.

"*To be or not to be, that is the question . . .*" He wanted
to write just one verse like this, and travel on it forever. He
dreamed all day of when his name would be known world-
wide, when his books would be taught in schools, when his
verses would be repeated by all kinds of people. He dreamed
of being present, forever. But he couldn't remember a single
time he'd written a verse satisfying enough for himself or his
friends.

He had sent poems to every competition he knew about.
But he never heard back from any of them, not even a confir-
mation that they had received his poems. Yet he never gave
up. He spent his days writing poems at the expense of his work
and his social life.

He left his job at the post office to be with his brother in
Dire Dawa, thinking he would have more time for his poetry.
His brother was a contraband merchant. If he earned some
today, he would lose some tomorrow. That was how he lived.

"And your job?" he asked Woubshet the moment he
arrived.

"I quit."

"You'll trade places with me. I'm glad you came."

"Contraband?"

"We'll go to Artishek in the morning. Be ready."

Woubshet was skeptical. "*Abo!* Don't piss me off. I came to live here so I can write my poems."

"You're not a *mashela tebaqi*, singing to chase birds from the sorghum harvest. What does poetry do for you?"

But Woubshet had made up his mind. He lived at his brother's place for two years and finished the first draft of his poetry collection. While in Dire Dawa, his brother opened a café called Roha in Addis Ababa. After his brother died in a train accident, Woubshet took full ownership of the café and then published his book. Roha became very popular soon after.

Woubshet opened the door of the restroom and walked out. "*Ayie* Moges, you keep acting like you don't know me."

"In the name of St. Mary, I swear, I do not know you!"

Woubshet walked out of the café and stood on the veranda, but Roha Café still wasn't there. Where had the café hidden? It was beyond comprehension.

The owner of Sheger Café, Million, standing farther away, said mockingly: "Did you find your café?"

Woubshet moved past him, defiant and unresponsive. As he walked away from the two cafés, his heart filled with sadness and his spirit became burdened with inexplicable confusion.

He decided to look for people who knew him so that he could explain his situation. In the past ten years, he'd cut contact with most people from the literary world, but some still remembered him. Even if it was only because of his attempt to burn all his books. He might find a few people sympathetic to his circumstance.

He made his way to the booksellers behind Beherawi The-ater. He had an especially strong relationship with the owner of Shawl, the used bookstore. Over fifty of his burned poetry books had been bought at Shawl. He found the owner, Bekalu, reshelving some books.

Woubshet gave Bekalu a warm greeting: "Bekalu the great, you're all grown."

Bekalu looked at Woubshet with wonder. "Good morn-ing," he said in a collected and respectful tone, the tone he used to speak to the elderly.

"Bekalu."

"Yes?"

"*Ere*, listen to what happened to me."

"What was it?" Bekalu said.

"*Ende!* Don't tell me you don't know me!"

Bekalu smiled. "I'm sorry, perhaps I have forgotten you?"

Woubshet tried to stay calm. He approached the counter. "Do you, maybe, have the book by Woubshet Mesfin, *The Early Bird's Decree?*"

Bekalu paused for a moment. "I'm sorry. I've never heard of this author or book," he said.

"Are you sure?"

"In the name of the Angel Gabriel, I swear."

"You do not know me?" Woubshet repeated.

Bekalu stared at the man standing across from him. "Did you come from the States?"

"You've never seen me?"

The young bookseller shook his head.

"You used to know me, Bekalu. *Eshi*. Do you also not know Roha Café?"

"Where is it?"

"Right near here, by Beherawi Theater, where you've had coffee many times."

Bekalu shook his head.

Woubshet walked to three other booksellers that he was convinced would know him, murmuring to himself. The same thing happened—they didn't know him. He couldn't find anyone who knew him or his Roha Café. He remained certain that he was a man who had just yesterday lived in Addis Ababa, managing a café while trying to form poetic verses on white paper. It was as if his existence had been erased overnight. He dug into his pocket and searched for his ID. He looked at it. He pulled out a card that had a picture of the fearless Woubshet Mesfin from Harar. It was him.

He headed to Tele Bar behind the College of Commerce and took a chair by the veranda. This was where he had sat before he headed home last night. He had been a customer there for several years now. The waiter he knew approached him. He'd completely forgotten him as well. He ordered coffee. As the waiter returned with his coffee, Woubshet cleared his throat and said, "Excuse me, brother, do you know where Roha Café is?" The waiter shook his head and walked away.

He left Tele Bar and rushed to Tewodros Square looking for Maru, the critic and lawyer. He walked up Churchill Avenue, staring at the area, buried deep in thought. He couldn't think of any possible reason this could happen to him—he hadn't changed a bit from yesterday. The only thing that happened was that he had been erased, both in the memory of others and in what he had dedicated his life to. But how can something physical, a café, just disappear? Where would one even say it could go? He had collected and burned his poetry collection to be forgotten as a poet, but not entirely as a human being.

He got to Maru's office. Maru had been a customer of Roha since the day it first opened. The heartbreaking review he wrote about Woubshet's book forced a wedge in their relationship. But while plenty had abandoned Roha, Maru still, from time to time, came and drank coffee in silence. He reached the office, which was near Lycée Guebre-Mariam.

He knocked on the door and walked in. The secretary asked him to wait. He was soon invited to go into Maru's office. The man got up from his seat and greeted him, but not how he would greet a dear friend, only as one might greet a potential customer.

"Maru," Woubshet said.

"*Abet*," Maru responded with a smile in his rough voice.

"Please, tell me honestly."

"What should I tell you?"

"Do you not know me?"

Maru stared at Woubshet's face. He thought. He shook his head. "I'm sorry. I think I might have forgotten you. Are you a writer?"

"Roha Café. The café by Beherawi Theater where you used to go to for years—do you remember it?"

"By Beherawi Theater? No, no! I do not remember a café with that name."

"You don't know me, either? What about a poetry collection you received, titled *The Early Bird's Decree*?"

Maru shook his head. He pointed at the shelf behind Woubshet. "All the books I ever reviewed are there. Take a look. I don't know your work. I'm sorry."

Woubshet got up. He walked out of Maru's office and went back to Beherawi Theater.

Roha Café was still not there.

He hadn't eaten all day: no breakfast, no lunch.

What was the point of eating?

The poetry event was supposed start in three hours. He stood in front of Beherawi Theater and waited for the people who would have come to Roha Café for his event. The time flew by.

*One hour left.*

*Thirty minutes.*

He looked across the street to see where Roha Café used to be until last night. Patrons of Sheger and Arada came and went.

*It was time.*

Not a single person had come to Roha, and Roha Café was not even there.

He walked toward the stadium in despair, the chants of football fans engulfing the neighborhood. He headed to Abyot Square.

A young vendor carrying a stack of books ran up to him. "Almost sold out, almost sold out!" he cried, attempting to sell his product.

"Listen there, do you have a copy of *The Early Bird's Decree?*"

The bookseller started laughing.

"Do you have the book of the great poet?" Woubshet asked. "The book of the poet Woubshet Mesfin—"

The laughter didn't stop. "Hahahahahahahahaha!"

"The book of the poet Woubshet Mesfin," he said again.

Woubshet covered his ears with his hands and hurried down the road to St. Urael's Church. He wasn't sure where he was headed, but he went past the church and down the slope, and only stopped when he got to the bridge.

He fixed his eyes on the river flowing under it, tired from the summer sun's heat. Dusk was approaching.

Darkness slowly covered the narrow stream.

*Translated by Hewan Semon*

# UNDER THE MINIBUS CEILING

BY BEWKETU SEYOUM

*Arat Kilo*

"Going to Megenagna?" asked the *weyala* with half his body sticking out of the minibus. He was looking at the people huddled on the side of the road at Arat Kilo. For the *weyala*, there were two types of people: those who go to Megenagna and those who don't go to Megenagna. Many people were crowded around the taxi stop. A few were actually waiting for taxis, but most, having nowhere to go, were pretending to wait for taxis rather than appearing to be doing nothing.

Tearing herself from the group, a young woman wearing sunglasses headed for the passenger door. Moving quickly, a student from Arat Kilo University who had been standing behind the young woman, admiring her, opened the door. She got in and looked at him sideways as he stepped in behind her and sat down. The *weyala* collected their fares.

A shoeless man wearing rags approached from the row of waiting people. "Sir," he said, bending his neck toward his left shoulder, "I am headed to Megenagna . . . but I don't have any money." The *weyala* looked toward the driver.

"Let him in," said the driver.

The ragged man got into the minibus and, avoiding the seats, squatted on top of the spare tire.

The young woman with sunglasses was seated in the front passenger seat and now saw that the guy next to her had turned to talk to her. She did not give him the opportunity; lowering her head, she began playing with her cell phone. Without meaning to, she called her aunt, who answered on the first ring. The young woman told her she had bought a new *gabi* and dreamed she was eating white injera all last night.

"You have a wonderful voice," said the student as soon as she hung up.

"Thank you," she replied, without turning to look at him.

The student tried to think of what to say next. He had to get her number by the time they reached Megenagna.

The *weyala* went to the back of the minibus to collect fares. The passengers there looked as though they'd been born attached to one another. Next to an older fat woman was a skinny man with his face hidden behind a newspaper who looked as if he could have been her left arm. Then there was an old man holding a cane under his right armpit with his young son tucked under his left one. The space was so tight that there was no place for the boy's arm, so he was forced to stick it out the window.

The backseat of a minibus was intended to seat four people. But there were now five passengers lined up on it, plus the little boy. The *weyala* began collecting the fares. When he came to the old man he was handed a tattered five-birr bill. "Take my fare and give me the change," said the old man.

"What about the kid?" asked the *weyala*.

"The kid? Why should I pay for the kid? He is only a child, isn't he?" He looked toward his son as if to confirm his age. "I do not want my son to go through the same childhood I did. I feed him well enough that he looks older than he his; he isn't ten until July 12."

"Pops, we board the kid, not his age; what can I do about his age?" said the *weyala*.

The other passengers all laughed.

On the second-to-last seat, a drunk passenger breathed *tej* fumes as he slept. He was awoken by the laughter and looked around the minibus with squinted eyes. "What's going on?" he sputtered. "The driver we had before was bald; this one has hair. What is that about? Either you moved me to another minibus when I was sleeping or the other driver has been fired! Who is going to explain this to me?" Without waiting for the explanation, he leaned into the headrest in front of him and began snoring again.

The student in the front seat regarded the young woman out of the corner of his eye. Sunglasses covered half of her face and he was eager to see her eyes. It was not difficult for him to guess where she was going, probably a date with her boyfriend.

"A lot of my friends tell me I sound like Angelina Jolie when I talk," she said without turning to look at him.

The student remembered that he had commented on her voice a little while ago. "That's right, but . . ." He was straining to recall who Angelina Jolie was. "But your voice is more original."

*Who is Angelina Jolie?* He racked his brain: a journalist, an actress, a model? To avoid further discussion on the matter, he turned to the driver. "Doesn't your radio work?" he asked.

The driver began fussing with the radio dials with his free hand.

"What do you like about Angelina Jolie?" asked the young woman.

What the student had feared was now happening. Pretending he had not heard, he studied the faded picture on the windshield. It was of a pair of wings, though it was unclear whether they belonged to an angel or an eagle.

"What do you like about her?" she repeated.

"I like the respect she has for her profession," answered the student. Not wanting to give her the chance for a follow-up question, he added, "Your sunglasses are really nice."

"Thank you. They were a present from my boyfriend."

The student went quiet.

In the meantime, the old man with the cane sitting in the backseat had turned his attention to his son. With a voice loud enough for all to hear, he said: "If you don't rank first this semester, you are not my son. How long are you going to come in second place?"

"Is he in school?" asked the fat lady. Without waiting for an answer, she went on: "There is nothing that can compare to an education; not being educated has many downfalls; among them . . ." She nodded suggestively at the man squatting next to the tire who was getting a free ride. In turn, the man in the tattered rags looked toward the drunk still sleeping against the headrest.

"Today's teachers are good; they don't beat the students," said the old man. "In our time—"

"There are still teachers that beat their students," interrupted the skinny man sitting next to him who had been shielding himself with his newspaper, hoping that his interruption would mean that the old man would stop this trek down memory lane.

"In our time . . ." the old man continued, "the teachers used to beat the students severely. There was one teacher who used to amaze me. If a student was bad, he would make them select the very stick that they would be whipped with. What a guy, Teacher Chekol! I will never forget what he did to me once. He told me to go and get the stick I was going to be whipped with. Oh, beautiful youth . . . I said okay and left the classroom."

178 // Addis Ababa Noir

The old man paused and studied the passengers, who were suddenly turned toward him in anticipation, fully engaged by his story. He was shocked. He knew that the story did not have an ending that warranted either interest or laughter. He regretted that he had even begun it, and looked for some excuse to stop. He began coughing, resting his head on his son's shoulder. But then his coughing fit would not subside.

"Pops, quiet down your hacking, we're trying to listen to the radio," said the *weyala*.

The passengers who had been saving their laughter for the old man's story released it instead at this snide comment.

The fat woman's phone rang in the backseat. She answered it and began talking in English: "Hello, yes, I am inside this taxi. Yes, inside that minibus. You are inside the minibus also? Yes, we can see each other tonight." While the fat lady was talking, she threw angry looks at the other passengers. She suspected they were judging her questionable command of English. "Stop the taxi please!" she snapped.

"Stop," said the *weyala*. "Stop for her," he repeated. The passengers watched her quietly as she got out of the taxi.

"I also had difficulty with English." It was the drunk. "I'm telling the truth; when it got too difficult for me, I hired a hopeless Indian guy to teach me for four hundred birr a month. A year later, the Indian had learned perfect Amharic and then we began to communicate really well."

The student sitting in the front passenger seat had remained quiet after the young woman's mention of her boyfriend. When he heard laughter from the people in back, he thought they were making fun of him.

The young woman was in fact on her way to visit her boyfriend, who she saw once a month. He would meet her at their usual café and then, just like the month before, treat her to a slice of cake and a macchiato; after that they would start talking. What they had to say to one another would be over in the span of a few minutes, and then they'd stare at each other. Because silence freaked him out, the boyfriend would ask for the bill. To fill in the silence while they waited, he'd pull out the newspaper he had rolled up in his back pocket and begin reading. She would pull out her organizer and mark the day of the next lottery drawings and the beginning of her next menstrual cycle. A few minutes later, they'd get a room and hurry to the bed. Another few minutes and he would turn on the television and begin watching a European football game. Lying beside him, she'd count the pimples on his back.

Sitting next to the student in the taxi, thinking about her life, it all seemed as bland as an old silent movie. "Why are you so quiet?" she asked the student.

"I was thinking about something," he answered, perking up.

"What about?"

"About your boyfriend . . . If a woman is desired and liked by many, her partner should be happy. A musician would not write a great song and then insist on being the only one to hear it. When a guy has a beautiful girlfriend and buys her huge glasses like yours to shield her eyes from onlookers, it seems a shame to me."

The young woman tried to think of some way to contradict the student but the radio was blaring, "*Last week saw the passing of St. Valentine's Day . . .*" She decided to just listen to the student talk about love.

Encouraged by her silence, the student was about to continue when one of the passengers in the back said, "There is no such thing as St. Valentine! Only Christ Jesus is blessed!" It was the short skinny man hiding behind the newspaper.

The *weyala* turned to the short skinny man and was reminded of the sermon in which he'd learned that the flesh is the dwelling of the soul. *This skinny guy's soul must be homeless,* he thought to himself.

The driver now turned around and joined the fray: "The Holy Mother has the power to plead!"

"Good point! But I prefer not to talk about things that are not written in the Bible," answered the man without meat on his bones, preparing for a good debate.

"What are you implying about the Holy Mother?" said the man in the tattered rags enjoying his free ride. All eyes turned to him; the beggar wanted to repay the driver's kindness while at the same time participate in a discussion that would allow him to be forgotten as a beggar and remembered as a spiritual debater. He saw the opportunity rolled out before him and jumped on it. "I don't think you have read what Prophet Isaiah said. He said, um . . . Isaiah said—"

"What did Isaias Afwerki say?" the *weyala* interrupted.

Most of the passengers laughed, but the beggar with the free ride was immediately forgotten.

The student sitting in the front was not happy with the turn of this spiritual debate. He was afraid religious talk would make its way to the front and hinder his attempts at getting the young woman's number. His fears quickly came true.

"You're suggesting something God wouldn't like," said the young woman with a frown.

He didn't want to have to backtrack now; he had learned from the story of the Queen of Sheba that love is the art of deception. He understood he would not be able to get rid of the religious air that had surfaced in the taxi. So he attempted to use it to his advantage. "I don't know much about the Bible," he said humbly, with a smile, "but I read that David took Absalom's wife even though he had many of his own."

"You're wrong, it wasn't Absalom's, it was Uriah's," she said.

"You're right . . . Anyway, no Bible forbids the exchange of phone numbers. Will you give me yours?"

Without hesitating, she gave it to him. He then gave her his number, which she saved on her phone under a girl's name before leaving the minibus. He turned to look at her after she stepped out and noticed that as she got farther away, she grew more beautiful. He wished the cacophony of the minibus would disappear so he could keep her voice in his head, but the debate in the backseat was heating up.

"The Lord is the driver of the universe! For example, you drive this minibus; we trust you and ride in this minibus; you take us where we want to go. In much the same way, the Lord is the driver of this earth. In the end He will come; let us make ourselves clean and wait for Him, my brothers. Let us not be faced with what the proverb says: *The wedding guests are here, begin preparing the* berbere."

The driver was flattered to be compared to the Lord by this backseat preacher and so kept quiet.

"Yes, my brothers," the preacher continued, "let us make ourselves clean and wait for Him. "

"Say what you will, the price of *berbere* has nothing to do with me," said the drunk who had been half listening. "The doctor told me to stop eating it while prices are still low."

From there, the discussion turned to *berbere*, salt, and other goods. When the student heard this, something occurred to him. Spending four years on the university's campus, he never once worried about the price of goods. He had forgotten that the market existed at all; he had even forgotten that injera came from *tef*. The institution where he was spending four years was a place of knowledge. Yet he did not even know who Angelina Jolie was.

"It's not my fault," he mumbled to himself.

He stepped out of the minibus and stood on the side of the road to wait for the bus that would take him back to Arat Kilo. The *weyala* looked at him and shrugged.

*Translated by Cheryl Moskowitz*

# OF BUNS AND HOWLS

BY ADAM RETA

*Addis Ababa West*

## The Bun

Under a wide-open window stood a square wooden table, dark with age and frequent use. At its center was an open blue cloth sack, inside of which was a dark golden bun wrapped in burned fake banana leaves. To the right of the bag was a knife, the sharp side covered with a corner of the cloth. Just beyond the sack was a sliced bun, grinning like a sandstone escarpment. A cold wind was flowing in through the window, and the room was filled with warmth and the intoxicating smell of spices. A flowered curtain shading the open window moved rhythmically.

| LEGEND | |
|--------|--|
| Relations | |
| ■————■ | visual |
| ———— | tactile |
| ———— | auditory |

Suddenly, like the sad temper of a dying day, from the deep dark throat of the Tabot Maderia neighborhood, the howl of a dog emerged. As if prompted by the sound, the bun rolled gently toward the empty plane of the table. After a suspenseful pause, the wrapping leaves crackled and the bun shot outside like some wild animal. It stopped midair, centimeters from the window.

A woman had entered the kitchen and witnessed this. Befuddled, she began shouting senselessly but eventually finding the words: "Fiqre! Fiqre!! The bun! The bun!!"

Leaves glinting, the bun lingered in midair a few seconds longer, and then propelled itself into the rainy August night.

After few minutes of navigation, it approached an open window where a couple was cuddling and kissing in the middle of a room. The bun continued its flight along a ravine. It stopped to look down on a badly lit condo, where a dreadlocked young man sat on a cot playing a saxophone, while a seminude young woman lay her head on his right shoulder. On a nearby table were two steaming glasses of tea and pieces of Buhe buns. The woman, feeling a presence, turned toward the window, but the bun had already dived into the narrow valley as if to avoid her gaze.

The bun moved gracefully over the skyline of Tabot Maderia. From the east, hundreds of migrating wheatears journeyed south. The bun ascended and, as if driven by an innate intelligence, joined the procession, at the tail end of the Oenanthe.

## Fortuna and Fiqre

On the eve of Buhe, boys ran through the streets collecting gifts of buns and money, singing in cheerful high voices to the departing winter. This was also an opportune moment for Fortuna to recall how her son Geleta used to love Buhe.

Fortuna had been working hard in the back kitchen baking Buhe buns. She was a slim woman with a small bottom and big breasts, tiny of stature and with a walk like a defeated colonel. She was sitting on a love seat as usual, her dress speckled with dough. She was wrapped in the rich smell of yeast. This seat was her throne and a pulpit from which she criticized the world with impunity, spewing strange metaphors no poet could have imagined. Her recounting of the same fables, and an expanding and complicated lamentation about their lost, most likely deceased son Geleta, made Fiqre feel guilty. Fortuna talked as if her life was purgatory. She would trace new angles of perceiving the past, discover a different layer of pain, and accuse him of negligence or forgetting. Fiqre's passive empathy for their common loss didn't seem to work.

Fiqre was a tall, handsome man with thick lips, wide shoulders, and a husky voice. He felt that he was getting old faster than he wanted or was acceptable. That day he was wearing his expensive dark overcoat, khaki pants, and white Puma sneakers. He put his plastic comb back in his shirt pocket and wanted to tell her to shut up.

"Do you remember," said Fortuna, "how Geleta loved Buhe? He would wake up early in the morning and call his friends over. He loved being the lead singer. I still remember his laughter, his beautiful dimple, and his hair that was always long and full of dandruff. Never did I think my son would leave me."

Fiqre could not take it anymore. "I am tired of listening to this! In life, things happen. How many young men died this year from AIDS? They had mothers, fathers, and sisters. Unlike you, they cried their eyes out but kept quiet. From now on could you please—"

"This is Buhe," she cut in. "Very few kids loved Buhe like he did."

"Yes, he loved Buhe. So what? All boys love Buhe. Poor people especially like it. It is a pretext to get money and free buns."

"Why do you say that? You are mad. I know you used to sing 'Hoya Hoye' when you were young too. Was that for the money?"

From where Fiqre stood, he could see her eyes glinting with anger. "So what? I am trying to forget things, please."

"He's your son, Fiqre!"

"Did I ever say he wasn't? He could have stayed home like the other kids. But he wanted to be rich, so . . ."

"Rich? Oh, Medhaniealem, no. They were going to arrest him. How can you forget that?"

"Then why was he involved in things he did not understand? He was naive. Who was he to protest?"

"Do you really mean that? Is my son stupid? He was not involved in anything. Some bad people said he was. If you really mean that, then you must hate him." To show her anger, she pretended to spit on the floor. "Even if he was demonstrating, he was just a kid running around. Running around and screaming words doesn't hurt anybody."

"He had better things to do. Just so you know that. No more talk about him. Let's remember him quietly, not by crying like a child."

"Can you tell me where he is? Eh? My intelligent husband?"

"I already feed and clothe you and your retarded daughter. I built this house. Every idiot around here is jealous of you. Let's talk about other things."

"Give me my son and I will live in a tree. He has a mother and, even if he's selfish, a father. He has a sister and friends who love him. Senait misses him. She always asks me, *Mama Fortuna, have you heard anything from Geleta?* A very polite girl."

"If you talk about Senait to people and Dr. Euyel hears about it, you'll destroy her marriage."

"I always go to Dr. Euyel when I am sick. He asks me about Geleta. It was Senait's mother, so snobbish. She hurt him by calling him names. Geleta did not tell me, but I knew. Why are you pretending that you don't know? It makes me sad. If we had money then, like we do now, maybe he wouldn't have left."

Fiqre wanted to interrupt her soliloquy, but could not.

"Maybe he'll return one day. I always pray."

Fortuna was trapped by the immensity of her loss. After Geleta left, she'd walked around the new house looking for any traces of him like she was hunting a ghost. The old house had been demolished and most of its contents were left behind. Yet there was still an empty room waiting for Geleta. His few clothes had been washed and ironed, and were hanging in the new closet. His old shoes were under the bed waiting for his feet. There was a big picture on the wall of Geleta laughing, a lone dimple on his left cheek. Fortuna was always delighted that he was the only boy in the neighborhood with a single dimple.

For more than five years, Fortuna did not turn on the radio to listen to music, news, or anything that was suffused with even a hint of pleasure. If Fiqre wanted to watch TV, he did it when Fortuna was out. He wasn't scared of her, but the language Fortuna used made him feel undignified.

Now he changed the subject: "You already baked the buns?"

Surprised, she said: "You want some?"

"I'll try it."

Fortuna got up and hurried to the back room. Fiqre walked to the window and stared out into the dying August day. He could see the top of his thirdhand Mazda RX2 parked in the compound: silvery, shining, and clean. He caressed his smooth-shaven cheeks with concern and checked his wristwatch.

Fortuna came back stooped over, grunting like an old woman. She held a white ceramic plate with a bun resting on it. "My mother made this for Geleta. She brought thirteen buns in a beautiful blue *shema* bag." She gently set the plate on the coffee table, gazing at the buns with love. She sat down on the love seat waiting for her: empty and warm. As soon as she touched the thick cushion, she exhaled deeply. "Where are you going? It is getting dark."

"I have a date with a friend to finish some business," he said.

He did not turn to face her, so she could not see the lies written over his face. She had the talent of reading him by looking at the whites of his corneas, the dilation of his pupils, and the tilt of his chin.

"Take care—the world is full of air and envious people. You have to be alive to see your son."

From their daughter's bedroom, they could hear the murmur of music.

"Is Gera in bed?"

"Maybe she's still up."

"I think she loves Awassa more than Addis Ababa," he said.

"Sit down, eat your bun, and drink your tea."

ILLUSTRATION II

"Yes, yes . . ." He sat gently on a sofa, facing Fortuna.

"Do you ask about Geleta whenever you meet people?" Her question silently carried the statement, *You promised.*

"Yes, always."

It had been a long time since he had asked travelers if they knew of a lost teenager from Tabot Maderia named Geleta. For the first couple of years he did it with fervor, only to quit due to a lack of results.

Fortuna thought that she was spiritually bound to her son. They were *wehud.* She was happy whenever she had a headache because it meant that he was also having a headache, that he was still alive. If she dreamed of Senait taking a bath or changing her clothes (even if she never saw her going through such rituals), it made her happy knowing that Geleta was dreaming of his lover through her.

"Will you please get me some tea?"

Fiqre's apathy toward Fortuna's bitterness allowed him

to create clever diversions. The weighty subject was his relationship with another woman, Woede, his wife's and son's nemesis. This unethical act was in fact a spiritual and physical compensation that introduced balance in his life. The infidelity was necessary. He felt, however, a hint of guilt toward his son rather than his wife. Woede used to look down on Geleta. She thought he was a brat begotten from the womb of stupid people with a talent for perennial destitution. Geleta's love for her daughter, Senait, was an embarrassment.

Fiqre needed to manufacture another diversion. He got up from his seat, smiled, and left for the back room to talk to his daughter, Gerawerq.

"Gera! Geryiee!"

A door opened.

"Yes?"

"You know your mother doesn't like that music! How many times do we have to tell you? Use headphones!"

The door shut with a bang. Fiqre returned to the salon, tight-lipped with shame on his face. On the coffee table was a glass of steaming tea with a thick sediment of sugar at the bottom, like beach sand. He picked up the glass.

"This is my mom's *aja* bun. It's very nice. You'll like it. She puts holy water in the dough," Fortuna said softly.

"Oh, this nun!"

"I know you don't like it, but try some. It won't kill you."

"The old woman likes exactly the things I avoid."

"Why do you say that? Bread is the gift of hope."

The old woman hated him. He remembered what she'd said immediately after the disappearance of Geleta. She was sitting next to him, resting her old bony bottom on a cushioned chair.

"You see, I was looking around the city from Entoto to

Gerji, from Sebeta to Lamberet. There were men, but no fathers there. The men are all fat, lazy, stupid, and, excuse my tongue, lecherous. Their women are all made of dust but polished to shine. In the old days, fathers would go to the ends of the earth to find their children."

Then the old woman just stared at him, indicating that what she'd said was meant for him. He had wanted to say something disrespectful that would forever lodge itself in her mind like a splinter. He refrained out of respect to Fortuna, though he regretted it now.

"I brought it so that you could taste it and maybe change your mind. Tomorrow, I'll give all but one to the 'Hoya Hoye' kids." Fortuna stared at the bread and patted it like a cat.

"The cinnamon in the tea is nice," he said with fake enthusiasm, trying to avoid the subject of grandmothers and Geleta. There was a whisper of rain coming from the roof. "I have to go before the rain gets heavy."

He put down his unfinished glass of tea and walked to the door. He opened it and the howl of a dog roared in.

"You hear that?" she said. "That must be Samrawiw. Something bad is going to happen. That dog is a prophet."

"I am standing here at the door while you sit there scared of everything. I am in a better position to know what the sound means." Fiqre hated that dog. When it howled, it felt like someone in the neighborhood would die.

"I know it's Samrawiw. Oh, Mariam!" she said tearfully.

"Nothing bad will happen. Even if that is a howl, it is because the dog is in search of a bitch."

Just then he was stopped by another round of heavy howling that wound down the street, coming from the direction of the old bridge, the quarter of misery and alienation. Fiqre believed Samrawiw to be as normal as any other canine, wailing now and then to open up lungs clogged by winter mud and summer dust. Unconcerned, Fiqre went to his car, listening to the unremitting howl that seemed to be hanging around him like a halo of polluted air. He caressed his car as if it were a lady. The light rain sank quietly into his overcoat. A dim white spotlight on the street, left over from last week's black-out, quivered on the driveway. The howling stopped.

The door to the house was still open. He saw Fortuna step from the salon into the other room. He considered yelling to her to shut the door but he did not want to be noisy. Fiqre briskly walked back to the door and closed it. Then he opened the gate and drove out of the compound. Pulling away, he heard Fortuna call out to him in a low voice, "Fiqre! The bun! The bun!" as if she were communicating a secret. Already late to his appointment, he didn't respond.

He found himself on an unusually quiet street. There was an aroma of burning wood, bean sauce, and gasoline fumes in the air. From the direction of Jimma Road, young boys were singing "Hoya Hoye." He drove on, regretting that he had ig-nored Fortuna's imploring call. But before he could convince himself to go back, he arrived at Woede's.

### Woede, et alia

Woede was a tall woman in her fifties, who carried modest weight below her waist. She had thick legs like a football player and tiny, clever eyes. Her strong disposition suggested she could break bones and men. Her cell phone screamed and vibrated across the tablecloth. A text message flashed: *Tues-day*. This was Fiqre's code for *I'm coming*. He would be there in an hour.

She opened her bedroom door and shouted to her daugh-ters: "When are you leaving to go to your party?"

"Soon!"

"What does that mean? Tomorrow? Next year?"

"Five minutes!" Tsedal said with a giggle.

"And where is Lulit? Don't tell me your sister is with that good-for-nothing *azmari!*"

Another giggle. Angry, Woede walked back to her bedroom, stood in front of the long mirror, and started fixing her hair. She regarded herself: her hair had become—to her surprise—whiter, her eyes smaller, the parabola of her mouth losing its rectilinear charm, her lips developing minuscule notches. She felt a flash of terror about her fifty-five years, then decided to employ those machines of forgetting: eating well, flirting, and acting youthful.

She changed into her pajamas and slippers and threw a large towel over her smooth, curvy hips. She walked out of her bedroom, crossed the salon, and stopped in front of the bathroom door.

"Tsedal, are you not finished?"

"Give me a minute!"

Tsedal was her second-oldest daughter. She was studying at Samara University, somewhere in the east. Woede believed her daughters had become corrupted and irresponsible. The youngest, Lulit, a graduate of Yared Music School, was currently performing in an obscure band. She was already lost in a romance with a dumb musician, together disturbing neighbors with their trumpets. Her oldest daughter, Senait, was gone for good, married to a medical doctor, Euyel.

A few weeks ago, she visited Senait and stared into her blank eyes, emitting pure ennui. She should not have married Euyel.

"How are you?" she asked her.

"You know."

That was a perfect illustration of the principle of least effort. Senait's voice was subdued, thick, cold, yet clear. Those two easy words fell on her mother's ears like granite slabs. Could she tell Senait that her snobbery was just a cheap disguise, a way to somehow absolve her of responsibility? Could a mother be jealous of her own daughter?

It happened seven years ago. She went out to the countryside to visit her father and mother, leaving Senait to take care of the house. She had returned home without a warning. The front door of the house was closed so she had to enter it from the back. She found the back door ajar and everything seemed quiet. Grumbling about the unlocked house, she pushed the door open, thought of making coffee, and walked quietly into the salon. There she saw Geleta and Senait. Senait's dress was pulled up and Geleta was kissing her, his pants down to the floor. She saw with horror his primitive thrusts and Senait whimpering like a colt. She returned to the patio and sat there, contemplating the incompetence of her husband and how she'd borne his stupid children without pleasure.

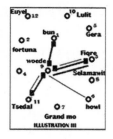

The image of this incident was burned into her memory. She understood such desires were wrong and that her current behavior was evil. But she still thought about Geleta with a desire that inflamed her loins.

Woede's daughters perceived her as uneducated (true), a woman who oozed cheap perfumed sweat (sometimes), scratched her perennially dry skin (rarely), and was a terrorist posing as a mother (often). She had overheard Tsedal and Lulit telling salacious stories, like how they moaned while being fucked. Those seeds that she had grown for nine months in her womb were injuring her.

"You only have five minutes. After that, you have to leave the bathroom!" Woede roared.

She had clout, not because she was a mother, but because she had the money. If she wanted them to commit suicide, they would perform a sweet hara-kiri. As she made her bed, she heard the howl of a dog. The noise hung in the air like it was traveling on aluminum wire. She recognized it and trembled. Six years ago, the very day she heard Samrawiw deliver the most persistent howl the neighborhood had ever heard, Senait and Euyel were wedded. A year or so ago, Samrawiw howled and then a girl, the daughter of an acquaintance of hers, was run over by a truck. Six months later she heard another howl, and someone very close to her died from unknown causes.

Tsedal came out of the bathroom with a wet smile, in a fog of perfume. Ten minutes later, when Woede left the bathroom clean and refreshed, Tsedal was already gone. Woede sat in the salon drying herself. She turned the CD player on and set the volume high so she could hear it from anywhere in the house, then walked back to her bedroom. She put on a light dress and sprayed perfume on her body and into the air around her. Then her phone started vibrating on the bedside table. She snatched it up and said softly: "Are you here?"

She rushed out of the bedroom. When she opened the door, she was hit with cold, moist air. Then she heard the howl a second time, a canine bass, sad and consistent, tearing across the air like a stone. Frightened, she glanced up at the sky as if in benediction. It took her a few seconds to sort things out, and then she walked to open the main gate. There stood Fiqre in a dark overcoat, the collar up. In a remote corner of Woede's brain, the howl scratched her with worry. Fiqre was quick to hug her. She nuzzled his neck hesitantly before delicately pushing him away.

Woede hurried back to the house and waited for Fiqre to follow, holding the door open with an outstretched hand, exaggerating the curve of her lower back. Fiqre walked in with a gentle stride and patted her where she loved to be patted. She giggled sweetly. He took off his London Fog overcoat and threw it toward the sofa, and before it landed, he was all over Woede. Hanging on each other—kissing, pushing, and pulling—they staggered to the bedroom.

With some effort, Woede managed to tell Fiqre that she must first close the window and the door. He pretended not to have heard her entreaties. His hand crawled under her dress, and she was nearly lost in his embrace.

Suddenly, she saw something bobbing languorously in the penumbra of the evening. Her mouth opened with surprise, her reflexes slowed. She cursed and nudged Fiqre out of his daze.

"Something wrong?" he asked.

"I saw something outside . . . through the window."

"It's just your eyes."

"I swear by Mariam I saw a round, floating thing covered with cloth or leaves. I do not know—"

"Maybe it's a bird."

She pushed him away and moved to the window to look outside—it was cold, quiet, and rainy. Her fear subsided. She slammed the window shut. When Fiqre approached from behind and hugged her, she was on the verge of believing that it was all in her mind.

"Oh, don't be afraid. Everything is fine," said Fiqre.

She quietly stared at him, opened her legs absentmindedly, letting his hand crawl between her thighs. But in her heart there was fear. She realized that she had never been this anxious about dying.

### Durban Dinga

Delani drove blindly, but not really blindly. He drove as if he had a purpose that he had forgotten, which made him feel a little irresponsible. The mid-August weather was pleasant. On his shirt lapel was a circular pin with the image of a laughing Mandela, framed by the colors of the South African flag. He parked at the side of Wande Cele Road in search of the victim. He knew the street as well as his own private parts. He was tired not only of this Tuesday, but of his life. The newsmen's daily rants about a changed South Africa—peace, prosperity, equality, a new age, and new times—was all baloney. He did not care about their declarations, because he was so close to the terror of everyday life.

He had been told over the police radio to go to Lotus Park, Wanda Cele Road, near M35 between Isipigo and Orient Hills. The dispatcher named Nomathemba, his classmate in Police College, told him to move his butt fast and check a dead body. It was probably a *bergie* or a *dinga*, just discovered south of the city. He asked for details. *You'll get them, fat man.*

He shook his lethargic self alert, checked his belt for the firearm he always carried, and drove slowly toward the specified location. Green foliage, dust, and the tormented hum of the old patrol car enveloped him. From the other side of the street, workers on *bakkies* unleashed loud music, thick with drums and a lot of "*ho hoy ho.*" From inside a large compound to his right, a pack of dogs yelped and howled. In the car was a half-eaten sandwich he had forgotten to throw out. He felt tired and bored despite the invigorating smell of Cape Doctor, sweetened by the aroma of ripe cantaloupes.

* * *

Some two hundred meters away, facing a line of trees and bushes, a group of people stood intently, their gazes glued ahead. His car crawled to a quiet stop behind the gathered group and he jumped out of the car, which wasn't as easy as it looked considering the extra weight he had carried into his fifties.

The crowd moved aside so he could properly investigate the crime scene. He loved such deference. In front of him, he saw a skinny young man, most probably in his early twenties, sitting on the ground with his back against a tree trunk, dead. There was not much hair on his face except a crescent-shaped goatee. His eyes were half open and directed downward. On his crotch was an oval object covered with something green and half burned. Delani could not immediately figure out what it was. To the right and left of him on a high fence, yellow clivia and black-eyed Susans shimmered. From behind the fence, he could hear loud voices boasting in Afrikaans. Delani stood in front of the man and studied him thoroughly. He had to analyze the evidence before he made any crazy assumptions. Despite the constant threat of a heart attack, he had no fear of death. To him, dead people were cool, because dead people couldn't kill you.

Delani felt he had seen the dead guy someplace before, though he was not sure where. He had known a lot of doppelgängers in his line of work, yet this one seemed somehow more real. Delani walked around the body.

He reached into his jacket pocket, pulled out a pair of gloves, and put them on carefully. *How do I know you?* He turned back to the audience and said, "Anyone touched him?"

They all shook their heads.

He checked his gloves and stepped closer to the dead

man, who wore an old Levi's jacket and khaki pants the color of soil. His belt was still in place—no indication of any fight or skirmish, and no sign of a bullet hole. In the middle of his chest was a necklace with a strange type of cross-shaped pendant. There were lumps on both his left and right chest pockets. Delani carefully lifted the flap of one of the pockets and gently took out a harmonica, its silvery plates pimpled with rust, the holes stuffed with dust and lint. Delani studied the thing for few seconds and returned it back to its place. He then fumbled in the second pocket and pulled out a few torn papers and an ID. He was relieved. When he unfurled the papers, he found that they were blank. He put them back in the pocket and started on the ID, which was old and green, made of cheap paper, and frayed on all of its corners. He had never seen this type of ID before, even though he thought he had seen every type that came and left Durban. He couldn't read the writing but could tell it was in Amharic. Since the photo matched the victim's face, he knew the dead man was Ethiopian. He stood up and took two pictures of the ID, then walked to a shady spot and called an old friend, Olmaz.

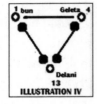

Olmaz was a woman he had met at Max's Lifestyle seven years earlier. She was a frail, quiet immigrant who had some serious ambition.

"Hello Olmaz, how are you? I was wondering if you could help me. I have a dead man from your country and I need to identify him, but his ID is in Amharic. Can you translate the card for me? I am sending you some image files. Please, beautiful woman? I'll send you a close-up. But it is not good, okay?"

He ended the call and slowly walked back, his eyes fixed

on the object resting on the dead man's lap. He pulled out a pen from his shirt pocket and used the tip of it to cautiously lift the corner of a leaf to see what was underneath.

Without realizing it, he started whistling Thandiswa Mazwai's "Nizalwa Ngobani," a song he used to love. He felt old. Suddenly, an old white man with creamy blue eyes and the build of an aged boxer called out from behind. He turned.

"Officer, I saw that thing coming in."

"What thing?"

"The thing on the man. I was heading down Citrus Drive, and I saw it coming from the north, flying. Yes, sir! Flying. I thought it was a big bird or a kite. But this thing had no tail or head or wings or string attached to it. I got closer, and it looked like a block of marble with leaves stuck to it. It turned to the right and slowly moved to the tree where the dead man was. This thing quietly hovered over the dead body. I was afraid and wanted to run away, but I was too curious. The thing landed on his lap so gently. Believe me, sir."

"What?" Delani could not believe this delusional man.

Then the phone buzzed. It was a message from Olmaz. He read: *The name is Geleta Fiqre Abdurahman*. He put the phone back into his pocket and turned to the dead man. With some certainty, he pulled a Swiss Army knife, a Soldatenmesser 08, out of his pocket and stuck it into the oval object. The blade went through it easily. He pulled out the knife and smelled the blade. He was suddenly impatient, and stuck the knife back into the thing.

He cut a slice and brought the piece close to his nose and smelled it. He could not believe it. He sniffed several more times, just to be sure. In amazement, Delani turned back to the few remaining spectators, stood up, and uttered: "It is bread. Oven fresh."

Suddenly, he saw the faces of the onlookers change. They were losing their composure. He turned to the dead man to see what was going on. To his surprise, there was red liquid dripping out from the center of the bun. An indescribable fear coursed through him. He tried to compose himself and knelt down, watching in wonder.

He was a policeman, so he had to do what he had to do. With the knife still in his hands, he dipped the tip in the oozing red liquid. Nothing supernatural or extraordinary happened. He wiped the drop on his glove and waited for some sort of surprise to occur. He then lowered his face and smelled the blob.

"What?" he whispered. Then he sniffed again. "What is blood doing inside a bun?" he asked, louder this time, staring at the group of people watching him in confusion.

## Tabot Maderia Blues

(*Seven people sit around a large table drinking beer in a bar. They listen attentively to a man by the name of Zerihun, called Zerish by his friends.*)

"You see, it was Tuesday, the middle of Pagume, a few days left before the New Year. I think it was the only morning I was ever late to work because I could not find a taxi or a bus. I was walking behind this woman wearing white clothes, so white that it was strange. She was literally glowing. Why was her *shemma* so white? (*Some shrug, disinterested.*) She turned back and saw me. She stared at me as if to say something. Why did she turn back unless she intended to say something? Her eyes were golden like a Meskel daisy. Have you seen yellow eyes before? No, I was not drunk. (*A few exchange glances, laughter caught in their throats.*) I did not drink even a glass the night before. Okay, maybe I had a couple of glasses, but I was not drunk. Suddenly, I felt like I knew her, like she was a member of my family, like she was my mother.

"When this woman turned back and saw me, I thought she planned to talk to me. I noticed, then, that her gait was quite odd. She moved very slowly, like she was trying to free herself from gravity or was made of elastic. (*A few curl their lips in mockery.*) I thought then of my lover, my Woede, my sugar mama. (*Some smile, a few chuckle.*) Please do not laugh, I need money, guys. As I told you, I used to see this same old woman in white every morning from the window of my office. It feels strange when you see at close range the woman you are used to seeing from a distance, and whiter too. There were vendors on the street shouting and selling green grass and Meskel daisies. There is something wrong with buying flowers when your life is upside down. (*Some stare at him in disbelief.*) Mine? Yes. It is upside down. I have to cajole Woede for vacation money.

"Let me get back to the more serious matter at hand. I became curious and timidly followed the lady in white. She walked hunched, like this. (*He shows them what her hunch looked like.*) You see? She looked young and yet she walked like this? I mean, she was old, but not old enough to hunch. It is like she was intending to pick something up from the street and yet picked up nothing. What was she going to pick up? Who knows—maybe she had an idea, or saw something that deserved to be picked up. Dead women tell no tales. If you're dead, you're dead. It is done. It is *fini*. Why was she so bent? Why didn't she watch where she was going? It was the end of winter and there was a glimmer of sunshine that exaggerated her presence on the street. She was a small woman and yet somehow more present than all of us. Strange, eh? I suddenly discovered that she had a shadow that was darker than mine. Mine was a sort of washed-out gray. What could that mean?

Maybe I'm wrong—maybe I was seeing things. The world thinks in black or white. If you are a fence sitter, everyone will hate you. It is better, I always say, to be hated by half of the populace, so I take sides. It does not matter whether it's for good or bad, as long as half the idiots don't hate you. I don't care what people say, but I swear I felt the heaviness of her shadow in my chest, pushing me like a hand.

"Now, there was this truck driver with a face crumpled like raisins. I saw him with his torso bent forward as if he were commanding a submarine. The fucker. He was driving slowly. Have you ever seen truck drivers drive slowly? (*Silence.*) No. This guy was driving so slowly that he could have easily turned to avoid the woman. Instead, he drove right into her. Why? Maybe he was on his phone. Maybe he was a shepherd who just got his driver's license. The truck tapped her on her left shoulder, but tapping and slamming an old woman is the same. After that, do you think the truck stopped? No! I couldn't write down his license plate number because I didn't have a pen. Why is it that on that specific day I didn't have a pen? I ran to where the woman fell and tried to help her up. She was a tiny woman, but she was as heavy as ten men. How could that be? Her arm was broken like a stick and you could see the bones. Her hips were a mess. The guy from that fruit shop came running and we carried her together, away from the center of the street to the sidewalk. But then I noticed something odd. It was rainy and muddy, yet there wasn't a speck of mud or dirt on her dress. Do you believe me? (*Silence.*)

"What's even stranger is that she had scratches, broken bones, loose teeth, and a cracked head, but no blood. Not even a drop! There was torn skin on the back of her hand (*he showed them the back of his hand*), but no bleeding. Here too! (*He showed his palm to everyone.*) No blood. Where was her blood? Where was it? Does anyone know the answer? Anybody?"

(*After a few seconds of silence, the circle of seven friends—with the exception of Zerish—grinned, chuckled, howled, roared, snorted, cackled, chortled, until some bubbles of beer foam quietly popped.*)

# PART IV

Police and Thieves

# KEBELE ID

BY LINDA YOHANNES

CMC

H elen knew the moment the new housemaid said "Meron" that it couldn't be her real name. Even without the traditional ear-to-ear tattoo that she tried to hide under a scarf, or the accent that twisted the city name, or that unmistakable odor of sheep hide, Helen could still tell the new housemaid was from the country. Later, when Meron had been with Helen and her husband Dawit for so long that domestic chores felt impossible without her, Helen would feel guilty for disdaining Meron that first day. But today, staring at Meron's Kebele ID card after she'd disappeared with the 35,000 birr from Helen's closet and finding out that Meron was really Aregash, Helen wished she hadn't stopped intuiting.

Helen and Dawit were deeply grateful when Helen found a well-paying job with a Turkish company, but Helen wished the location was nearer to her home. Commuting from their one-bedroom condominium apartment in CMC to the office in Akaky Kaliti, partly by minibus taxis and partly on the city train, was too much given the wretched public transportation of Addis Ababa. Helen sometimes shut her eyes to keep out the sight of desperate, late-for-work people in the long taxi lines. She knew that once the people were inside the taxi, the fare collector could announce he was charging up to five times the standard amount. "If you don't agree, get out right now," he would say. "No arguments." Helen took out her frustration in embittered Facebook posts, which were then liked by other passengers. As a lady in a taxi full of twelve people or more, it wasn't easy to be the one to rouse a protest. Instead, she hoped to buy a car in the near future, and Dawit wanted to help with this.

One evening, he called and told her to meet him downstairs. When he held her hand and led her through the parking lot, she thought the surprise was a person—perhaps an old friend or even a housemaid, the latter being something she had long been desperate for. But then he arrived in a yellow Hyundai Atos, went around and stepped into the passenger seat, rolled the driver's window down, and told Helen, "This is for you."

It took her some time to believe that Dawit had indeed bought her a car. Even after he repeated how he had done it—he took out a loan for 200,000 birr from work, a private construction company whose owner favored him among the civil engineers, and borrowed another 100,000 from his brother—the news still floated around her head, unable to settle. She slowly began to believe it as she ran her hand over the stereo, the heat and fan buttons, the faux leather on the small wheel, the tree-shaped air freshener hanging from the rearview mirror.

"You're too good to me." She turned to him and hugged him in the narrow cabin.

It was about a month later that their next blessing, Meron—now Aregash—came into their lives.

It had been ten years since Aregash left her childhood home in rural Gojjam for a job in the city, and Dawit and Helen were her best employers so far. They were going to pay her 1,000 birr and they wouldn't control what or how much she ate. "You are thirty-five years old," Derib, her boyfriend, always said, "a nobody counting empty years." He often told her that and reminded her of her tiny salary. "If you want to be somebody, you need to do something—maybe go to the Arab countries. That's how others make it," he said enviously, remembering his day-laborer friends and their housemaid girlfriends.

Aregash never said so to him, but she understood that and more. She knew to never steal small, meaningless amounts of money and make her employers suspicious. That was why she did what she did one Sunday shortly after New Year's Day, while Helen and Dawit were out visiting relatives. She was at home alone watching *ETV*, a show about a doctor who removed tattoos. She froze at the mention of that dreaded word that always lingered in the back of her mind: *nikisat*. As the doctor explained the technology behind it and a woman gave her testimony showing her spotless cheeks, chin, and neck, Aregash touched her own *nikisat*. She wanted to remove it so much that she had noticeably scarred her face, trying to scrape it off with her nails, to undo what her family had done to her in Gojjam when she was a little girl. For her, to be free from the tattoo was to be a presentable woman: less of an Aregash, more of a Meron. As long as she had it, she had to compensate for it.

While she was writing down the doctor's name in barely legible handwriting, there was a knock at the door. It was a visitor for Helen and Dawit. Aregash sat the guest down in the living room and went to call Helen on the phone. When Helen told her the visitor was her uncle, Aregash insisted the man have lunch and she dished up *doro wot* and the *feresegna*. After he left, Aregash spotted a shiny something on the center table. She picked it up and marveled at it up close. It was a gold Lion of Judah ring. *More than four grams*, she thought, weighing it in her palm—she could easily get two thousand for it. That evening, Helen almost flew into a rage when she couldn't find the *feresegna*, thinking that Aregash had secretly eaten it.

"I served it to your uncle today at lunch!"

Helen held her forehead. "But that was for Dawit! It is his favorite and he's always the one who eats it!"

Aregash said nothing.

"And you know that!" Helen snapped.

"What if we told Gashie Dawit this *doro* didn't have a *feresegna*?" Aregash asked.

Helen stared at her.

"Or, let me tell him that the housemaid should get the backbone sometimes."

Helen couldn't help but laugh.

Aregash slowly took out the gold ring from her apron's front pocket. "Helen, your uncle left this on the table today. I think he took it off when I came with water for his hands and forgot to put it back on."

Taking the ring, Helen forgot about the *feresegna* and thought how blessed she was to have such a trustworthy housemaid.

The Saturday Meron disappeared with the 35,000 birr from Helen's closet, Helen had returned home from the hair salon, her hair shiny and straight, to find the apartment door open. She immediately realized something was wrong. Meron was always very careful and would never even leave the windows open if she went out. Helen called out for her, searching the kitchen and even the bathroom, but Meron was nowhere in the apartment. She went into the bedroom and saw the bottom of her closet. The drawer was open all the way, and she already knew she had been robbed before looking inside.

Helen rushed to her cell phone and called Meron, hoping to hear her voice saying, *Hello, Helen, I was out shopping. I'm on my way back.* But Meron's phone rang and rang and there was no answer. Then Helen called Dawit. *Sorry, the subscriber's phone you dialed cannot be reached at this time.* It was the annoying operator again, who terribly mispronounced the word "dialed." She went to the kitchen and looked inside the big plastic bag that Meron used as her suitcase. It was crammed with useless items, some of which Helen herself had thrown in the trash: old packaging, dried pens, and a German housewares catalog. She pulled out old, cheap clothes that were flimsy and filthy. She examined the folds of the mattress and found only dirty underwear. Then, along with some papers, she came across a Kebele ID. She regarded the black-and-white image and the name written with a typewriter—*Aregash Kitaw.* She then found a passport-size photo of a man. His appearance was jarring: an awkward diamond-shaped face with the traditional cross tattoos on his temples and his broad, almost flat hairless head. She ran back to her closet and tried to sort through the thousand thoughts crowding her mind. She wondered if maybe Dawit had deposited the money in the bank because he'd found out she was going to buy him the latest iPhone as a you-deserve-it-although-we-can't-afford-it birthday gift. But she knew Dawit hadn't taken the money. Meron had grabbed it while Helen was out at the hair salon, her closet key still in the door lock.

Every birr of the 35,000 was already accounted for: 6,000 was for the iPhone, 3,500 was for church and tithe, and the rest was strictly to go to her savings account. Helen didn't know who else to call. She kept redialing Dawit's number while considering the worst. They would have no savings, Dawit would not get his iPhone, and she wondered if you had to pay tithe on stolen money. She couldn't call the police because they wouldn't be much help—she had a better chance trying to catch the thief herself. The police you go to later, to formalize things. Helen tried hard to think where Meron could be with her money.

Then her phone rang. It was Dawit.

"I got your message. What is it?"

"Dawit! You won't believe it. Meron is not Meron. Her name is Aregash and she's just robbed me!"

Long silence. Then: "What did she take?"

"She took the 35,000 birr from my drawer in the closet!"

Silence again. "When was this? Didn't you see her leave?"

She told him how it happened. "But she can't be far, it's less than a half hour since she left."

"You can't be sure of that," Dawit dismissed her.

"I am. I called right before I left the hair salon and told her to make *shiro*, and she has."

"All right, I'm coming home. Where does she go when she goes on leave?"

"I don't know."

Aregash decided to take the main road because it was safer than the shortcut Helen had suggested when Derib first said to meet him at Fantastic Hotel. She had woken up early and bathed the first day when she went on leave. She had gotten dressed in her best clothes and asked Helen where Fantastic Hotel was, because Derib had said to her when they made an appointment: "It's next to Fantastic Hotel. Ask anyone. They will show you."

That day, Helen had sensed what was going on, remembering how it was in her early days with Dawit, how much she wanted to look pretty. So she searched in her closet for something that would fit Meron. "Take these and try them," Helen had said, handing her a bag of clothes and black leather flats.

After leaving the apartment with the money, Aregash had walked rapidly out of the gated compound and crossed the city railway track, oblivious to the eyes following her with curiosity, feeling warm and full at the knowledge of all those green 100-birr notes in one place.

The distance to the pension felt far because she kept thinking about her next steps. After meeting Derib there, they would have to plan what to do next and then run away. At the pension, she checked herself into room number five and locked the metal door. Derib would arrive soon. She looked out the window and drew the curtains shut before she pulled out the four stacks of money from her underwear and sat on the bed. She was shivering a little from both excitement and nervousness. The concrete walls and cement floor of the room made her feel safe. She had to count each bill to figure out how much it was. She had never been to a bank and was disappointed when the final stack of fifties was 5,000 and not 10,000 like the others.

She called Derib. "Where are you? You're taking too long."

"I'm coming. Just wait for me!" he said. He was panting and she smiled at the thought of him running to her.

While waiting for Derib, Aregash considered her options. She could start a small business in the city. Derib would not like that idea; he always talked about buying land in Gojjam and hiring someone to farm it. She glanced down at her feet. She was wearing the black leather flats Helen had given her that first time she went on leave. When she handed her a plastic bag with clothes in it, Aregash had smiled and thanked her, but felt none of it—Helen had a closet full of nice new clothes and a tall stand full of shoes, but all she could give her were her old castoffs—and then she felt so generous about it. The black leather flats now looked beneath her. She took them off and tossed them across the floor, then lay on her back, legs folded. She could now finally afford more than cheap mass-produced clothes from China. She would buy custom pieces from boutiques and wear clothes that half the women in town weren't also wearing.

*Thirty-five thousand is a lot of money, and it is MY money,* she thought. She was the one who brought it. She suddenly got up, as if on cue, and looked around the room for a good place to hide 5,000 birr. She couldn't hide it in her underwear; Derib would probably seduce and undress her. On the other hand, he might not notice as he would be too excited by the time he got to her underwear. For her, sex felt like it was only for men, thanks to her childhood circumcision that cut away her means for pleasure. The only part she enjoyed was the restful nap that followed.

She eyed the plastic jug and bowl at the corner of the room. They never used it. They always washed up in the common toilet and shower area outside. She put the 5,000 on the cold cement floor and covered it with the plastic bowl, then placed the jug on top.

Helen was fiddling with her phone, waiting for Dawit, when she thought to call Betru, a distant relative and one of Addis Ababa's most infamous criminals. From stealing car parts and selling them in Somali Tera, to becoming a major stolen parts dealer who negotiated with car owners for their own parts stolen the previous day, Betru was now quite accomplished in the field.

"Did she have a boyfriend? A man she went to?" he asked after hearing the story.

"I think there was this man she talked to on the phone."

"Do you know anything about him? His name or where he lives?" Betru asked. "Because there's definitely a man with her on this."

Dawit left work and went to the police station before heading home to Helen.

"Your Kebele ID, so pristine! Look at what the others come in with," the police officer said as he started to write down Dawit's report. He pulled out a small stack of dog-eared IDs from his drawer.

Dawit was impatient to tell the story of what had happened, as if talking it out would give the situation some shape, so it would feel less like a tremendous assault on his household, his manhood.

"You said your maid, correct?" the officer said, then went on talking: "There was a woman here this morning. A wealthy woman! She came to report that she was robbed of all of her gold jewelry by her maid. When I asked how much they were worth, she said 300,000! And she looked like that was true. Imagine that!"

Dawit wanted to talk to the police officer at the next desk—he seemed sharper, faster. If what people said about the police working with criminals was true, he had the face.

Helen sat holding the passport-size photo of a man she found in Aregash's things and thought about what Betru had said. She remembered all of the advice she'd let fly past her ears. Her mother's friends always talked about housemaids when they gathered.

"If it's just the maid and me in the house, I lock my room," one of them once said.

"It was on the news last Sunday . . . the maid let her boyfriend in, and he killed the woman and then together they robbed her clean! You should never trust them or treat them as anything more than servants," another one said.

"I don't care if my bedroom collects so much dust that it gets into my eyes: I will never, ever let the maid in there," someone else added.

For Helen, they had been old feudal women who failed to afford all humans equal dignity and made a lifestyle out of whining. She was proud of having a greater appreciation for housemaids.

Suddenly Helen remembered—Fantastic Hotel. Meron had once asked her where Fantastic Hotel was. She rummaged for her phone and called Dawit.

"One time she asked me for directions to a hotel. And I'm sure she was going there to meet him."

"Who?"

"Her boyfriend. The man behind Aregash."

"Where?"

"Fantastic Hotel."

"That's no use. She wouldn't be so stupid to go there with the money."

"Maybe. But Betru says she's definitely doing this with a man."

Dawit arrived at the apartment and once she saw him, Helen began to cry. After all, Aregash had stolen from Dawit too. He sat her down. He could see she was still in shock.

"Let's go. We'll find the dealer who brought her and head to that hotel."

Dawit got up and grabbed the car keys. On their way, Helen sat in the passenger seat looking out the window, checking every couple on the street to see if they were Aregash and her boyfriend.

At the reception desk of Fantastic Hotel, Dawit tried to persuade the receptionist, who almost laughed at his request. "Never! I can't let you go knocking on every room to check who's inside," the man said.

Dawit then tried asking whether a person named Aregash was staying at the hotel, and again the receptionist refused. He was the irritatingly truthful type. He told Dawit he would only give such information to the police. Dawit kept repeating their story of stolen cash, but Helen understood that their progress had stalled. She felt a headache coming on, and she left the dark interior of the lobby and stepped out to the main road for some fresh air.

The strength of the sun outside was oppressive. Looking directly along the wide-open gate of the pension next door and into the compound, Helen saw a man bending over a concrete water basin. He looked like he was pretending to wash himself, glancing occasionally over his shoulder toward the rooms. Then Helen realized: it was the man in the passport-size photo she'd found in Aregash's things. She sprinted in his direction with a burst of energy. The guard, who was leaning on the gate in his ill-fitting uniform and clownish police-style hat, hurried behind her when she dashed into the pension.

Aregash jumped from the bed when she heard it. Not that it was startlingly loud, but it materialized her fear. She had dozed off and was expecting Derib to wake her when he came back from the washing area, to talk about what to do next.

"*Leba! Leba! Yazut!*" It was a woman with a familiar voice.

Aregash rushed to the window, squatting to avoid being seen. Helen was there and they had caught Derib. She saw him shield his head as Dawit grabbed him by the collar. Aregash turned the other way and rammed her knee into the edge of the old wooden chair by the window. She picked up the small jute bag even as she saw it was empty. The three 10,000-birr stacks were gone. Her heart froze for a moment. She searched among the few objects left in the room but the cash had vanished. She lurched for the plastic bowl in the corner of the room, swiped the 5,000, and ran out the door and through the back entrance of the pension.

Helen was desperate enough to shove her hand into Derib's boxers, where she found the three 10,000-birr stacks.

"It's her! She did it all!" Prone, Derib futilely tried wriggling out of the hands that held him.

People had come out of their rooms to see what was going on. They began to shout "*Leba!*" and started hitting him. When they finally stopped, his clothes were torn and his face was bleeding.

"Speak! Where is Meron—I mean Aregash? Where's the rest of the money?" Helen yelled in his ears, surprising herself.

Derib spoke through his sobs: "She's in room number five!"

Helen, Dawit, and other bystanders ran to the room. The place looked like someone had recently been there, but it was now deserted and no money was found inside. Some of the men went out through the building's back employee entrance, spilling out into the Meri *gulit* market where countless women sold countless items in stalls separated by imaginary lines. Dawit and several of the others started searching for Aregash, but they got swamped in the constant stream of people as soon as they began.

Helen was talking to the police who had taken charge of the crime scene. Still, everyone wanted to lay a hand on Derib, who by this point was shirtless and crying like a child.

"Stop! He's in police custody now! You cannot just hit him!" one of the police officers scolded.

"Let's go to the station and you'll file a report," another officer said.

"And the money?" Helen was afraid their 30,000 would be taken in for investigation—permanently.

"You caught him red-handed and he's admitting it's your money. You can take it. What remains now is the other suspect," the first officer said.

Helen offered grateful prayers for having recovered some of her money, and didn't feel guilty for condemning Meron for her deception. She believed it would follow and haunt Meron wherever she went.

# NONE OF YOUR BUSINESS

BY SOLOMON HAILEMARIAM

*French Legation*

The heat was unbearable. The afternoon sun beat down on Tadesse, causing beads of sweat to drip into his eyes. He covered his face with one of his books, but it did little to cool him down. He looked small in his over-size hand-me-down uniform, walking along the left side of the road, as was customary for pedestrians. Through squinted eyes, he saw dozens of police officers marching down the path ahead of him, many of them carrying assault rifles and batons.

Tadesse's entire primary school had heard about federal police whipping several students from a neighboring school. But they hadn't been punished for offenses committed in class. They were whipped for attempting to join an antigovernment rally and allegations of inciting violence.

The episode had prompted his teacher to hand out a week-end homework assignment: *Explain the differences between human and democratic rights in our constitution, and identify which specific articles guarantee these rights. If you have trouble, ask a grown-up.*

"Are there any questions?" the teacher had asked.

Tadesse raised his hand.

"Yes, Tadesse?"

"Which grown-ups should we ask?"

"You can ask your parents, older siblings, or teachers. Anyone you think could help."

"Thank you, Mr. Dargie," Tadesse said. A few other students had groaned.

Tadesse now realized the police had closed off the road to traffic, presumably because someone important was arriving in town. He wondered who this person could be. He wanted to ask, but he was nervous—so many of them held rifles, and there weren't other pedestrians in sight.

He approached an unarmed officer and said in a small voice, "Sir, can I ask you a question?"

The officer spun around, his eyes widening in surprise. "This area's off limits. Get out of the street!"

Startled, Tadesse ran back down the asphalt road. He was shaking. He didn't understand the officer's hostility. He decided to take a safer route home. The dust on the unpaved road was thick and awful. He tried to ignore it, but it burned and stung his eyes. He could see that some of his friends were also marching home in a similar fashion, attempting to block the wind with their books. Hungry and tired, he dreaded the rest of the walk.

Tadesse had paused to rest when a massive military truck came speeding down the road, raising a cloud of dust that covered everyone in its wake. Tadesse coughed, covered his face, and quickly turned onto another paved road that led to his home. Putrid odors emanated from an open roadside sewer. He felt nauseous and thought he might vomit from the smell.

When he arrived home, he climbed onto the bed he shared with his two brothers. The coils of the mattress almost touched the ground, as if they were as exhausted as he was. Just as he closed his eyes, he heard his father's angry voice.

"What are you doing? Getting in bed with your dusty uniform? I raised you better than this!"

Tadesse sprang up in fear but his father grabbed him by the collar of his shirt.

"I don't have the money to buy a new bed." His father's breath smelled sour. The man didn't earn much for the family as a carpenter, and what he did earn he spent on alcohol. "This one will be completely ruined if you track dirt and grime onto it. You better care for it, if you know what's good for you."

Tadesse's mother, who was soothing his infant brother, hushed her husband. Tadesse wriggled free from his father's grip and ran to his mother. He looked up at her and rubbed his belly. She frowned. Tadesse's older brother had already eaten the meal she'd prepared that day. There was leftover injera bread, which she sold to people in the neighborhood, but no stew to go with it. She made Tadesse pepper flour and oil to supplement the injera, so that he could partially satisfy his hunger.

Tadesse ate then went out to the yard to study. He didn't know what Mr. Dargie had meant by "democratic and human rights." He thought about his encounter with the officer on the road. He was nervous to try asking another grown-up. Then he remembered Private Teshale, a friendly police officer who lived in the building next door and regularly bought injera bread from his mother. He didn't think Teshale would shout at him like the other officer had.

Tadesse sat in the yard as the twilight grew deeper. When the sun had nearly set, he saw Teshale walking up the road toward the house.

"Excuse me, sir," he said before Teshale could go inside, "can you explain to me which democratic and human rights are guaranteed by our constitution?"

Teshale paused, his hand resting on the doorknob. "I'm not a teacher. Ask someone else."

Tadesse was frustrated, but he didn't want to give up quite yet. If the police weren't going to help him, he'd have to go elsewhere. He stood by the door, waiting for another of his mother's customers to stop by for injera. Everyone who passed through the door ignored him—they were tired and hungry and had no time for questions. They only wanted bread. Tadesse was imagining the excuses he would have to tell Mr. Dargie on Monday when another customer approached the door. He tried one more time: "Excuse me, sir, I'm supposed to ask a grown-up for help with my homework, but no one will do it. Can you help me?"

The man smiled at him, which gave Tadesse a glimmer of hope. The man seemed to be interested, but after listening to Tadesse explain the assignment, he sighed and said, "Oh, my son, I wish I knew." The man went inside without saying more.

Tadesse's mother had overheard her son's requests for help with his homework. She tied the birr she'd collected from her clients into a scarf and went outside to speak to him. "My son, don't worry. I'll go ask Mrs. Tewabech's daughter Gelila to help you. She's a smart girl."

Fortunately, when his mother arrived at the neighbor's home, Gelila was there. She agreed to help Tadesse and followed his mother home. Gelila patiently explained how the constitution protected both human and democratic rights, and helped him copy down relevant passages from a pocket-sized copy of the country's constitution she'd brought with her. Once he'd finished his homework, she stood and said, "I hope that helped."

"It did, thank you very much."

Gelila was touched by his humility, and by how quickly he seemed to absorb knowledge. "Of course. Don't hesitate to ask me any other questions you might have. You know where to find me."

Tadesse smiled and nodded. His mother invited her to stay for dinner, but Gelila apologized and said she needed to get home.

Tadesse immediately got lost in thought. He pictured what Monday would be like: Mr. Dargie would collect the exercise books, then ask for volunteers to explain the homework aloud. Tadesse would be the only student to raise his hand. He would explain the constitutional nuances so eloquently that Mr. Dargie would ask the class to stand and clap. At recess, all of his classmates would want to play with him. He'd be the most popular boy in school. He wished time would speed up.

Gelila, who was still standing behind him, smiled at his faraway expression and patted his head. "Don't worry, Tade. You're a smart boy," she whispered.

"Thank you, Gelila," he said, his cheeks warming.

She began asking him about his favorite subjects in school when Tadesse's nineteen-year-old brother, Anbesse, bolted into the yard, a stream of blood running down his forehead. His eyes were swollen, his cheeks bruised and pale. He looked like he'd seen a ghost.

Gelila screamed, "What happened to you?"

Their mother came running outside at the sound of the commotion. Seeing her son bruised and bloody left her speechless.

"Who did this?" asked Tadesse.

Anbesse was silent. He didn't want to explain what had happened to him. He knew something just as bad, or worse, could happen to his family.

"It was the cops," he said finally, after further prodding from Gelila. He spit a red-tinged glob of saliva into the dust. "They beat me mercilessly, for no reason at all. When they finally released me, they admitted I was innocent—they knew it all along."

"But that's illegal! The police can't go around beating people," Tadesse said. He watched the blood run down his brother's forehead. "Everyone is equal before the law until they are convicted."

Their mother remained in a state of shock. She examined the extent of Anbesse's injuries as tears flowed down her face. Gelila was furious. She paced back and forth.

Anbesse was, despite everything, a tough young man. He never gave up, especially if he believed there was an injustice to be corrected. Once, he'd had a dispute with their neighbor over a sewer pipe that had been leaking into their yard. The stench was making his family sick. He had confronted the neighbor and demanded that he fix the pipe. The neighbor had called over his security guard. Anbesse still had a scar on his forehead as a result of the encounter, but he'd convinced the neighbor that he wasn't someone to trifle with, and the pipe had eventually been repaired.

Their mother brought a jug of warm water from the house and washed the blood from Anbesse's face, attempting to soothe him as she checked to see whether his nose was broken.

Gelila was trembling uncontrollably. "I still don't understand. Why would they do this to you? What exactly happened?"

Anbesse sighed, then winced as his mother wiped dirt and blood from his nose. "It's all a blur. I saw a group of people running toward me, so I assumed something bad was happening behind them, and I took off as well. But in the chaos, I tripped and fell. The cops caught up to me and immediately started beating me with their batons, as if they were trying to smash me into the gravel. I tried to tell them I hadn't done anything, but they wouldn't listen. So I curled myself up, hoping that if I was still enough they'd leave me alone. If I'd tried to resist they would have killed me."

"How did you manage to escape?" Gelila asked.

"Luckily, another person the cops had detained admitted that I wasn't the man they were looking for. He told the policemen that the suspect they were pursuing had already escaped. The cops had no choice but to let me go, saying, *Well, you shouldn't have run.*"

"They should have taken you to the hospital. I'm going to go deal with this." Gelila started walking toward the road.

"Where are you going?" Anbesse asked.

"To the police station. They must be held accountable. You need medical attention."

"Gelila is right. They have to do something for Anbesse," Tadesse said.

Tadesse, Anbesse, and their mother decided to follow Gelila to the station. But before they had gotten far, they encountered three police officers on a nearby street.

"There they are!" said Anbesse, pointing to the men.

Gelila approached them swiftly and confidently. "What nonsense is this? You beat my friend for no reason, and now you're strolling in the street like you're peacekeepers. Shame on you!"

One of the cops frowned. Another said, "Who are you?"

She ignored his question. "You're supposed to protect and serve the public, but instead you are beating innocent people. What happened to justice? Is there no law in this country?"

"I have no idea what you're talking about, you crazy bitch."

"You nearly beat this young man to death. If he was guilty of something, you should have arrested him. You can't go around beating and humiliating innocent people."

"We did no such thing," the cop said.

"What is this blood, then? All of us have witnessed your bullshit!" Anbesse shouted.

The officer relented: "We thought you were the guy we were chasing." He kept his tone even, trying to calm everyone down.

"So what? You still ambushed him. We want justice!" Gelila said.

One of the policemen grew angry: "This is none of your business. You must be one of *them*. You are antipeace, antidemocracy, and antiorder."

"This is nonsense, you can't just go around punishing someone whenever you want." Gelila took a step closer to one of the officers.

He drew his arm back and slapped her in the face. She blinked, mouth agape. Then she screamed so loudly the neighbors came out of their homes. The three policemen realized they were outnumbered and started waving the crowd back, yelling at the gawkers to disperse.

Tadesse was frightened. He cautiously watched each movement the officers made, from behind his mother's skirt. Anbesse, emboldened by the gathering crowd, rushed toward one of the policemen. The officer quickly lifted up his baton to strike Anbesse on the head.

"Don't hurt him!" Tadesse screamed. He forgot his fear and took a step toward his brother, wanting to protect him.

The policeman swung his baton to strike Anbesse, but missed—and hit Tadesse instead. Tadesse fell to the ground, his body limp. In the weak light, Anbesse knelt down to lift up his brother. Tadesse's head flopped back like a rag doll.

An old man cried out from the crowd, "What have you done? He's only a child!"

Someone else screamed: "Please call an ambulance!"

The crowd gathered around the two brothers, and in the commotion the policemen took off.

"It's too late," Anbesse said quietly. His brother felt so light.

Their mother laid her head on her oldest son's shoulder, and wept.

# AGONY OF THE CONGESTED HEART

BY Teferi Nigussie Tafa

*Meskel Square*

I am in exile in Europe, while my friend Muze is a rich man in Ethiopia. I left behind all that is of value to me, my family, my culture; and today, while eating breakfast, I read in the newspaper that Muze is depositing what is valuable to *him* into Swiss bank accounts. The newspaper said that the Swiss banks are feeding off poor Africans and other third world countries and now it is "Ethiopia's turn." Muze and I were best friends, comrades for the revolution, and now we are worlds apart. Or maybe we are still friends, in spite of everything. Let me tell you a little bit about him and me. Let me tell you how we became friends, and how our friendship has ebbed.

My name is Waaqoo. Waaqoo Bonayaa. I am from Borana, an Oromo clan living in southern Ethiopia and northern Kenya. I am my family's first son. Since my father is *Qallu*, an Oromo spiritual leader, he used to tell the people when the *gada* election would be, when the incumbent Abba Gada in power would leave, and when the new Abba Gada would be anointed. His duty as a religious leader also included forecasting the time for religious activities like the Irreecha and other public festivals.

My father would burn fire in our yard every Friday evening, spending the night outside praying to God. He would examine the stars and prepare a calendar based on astronomical principles, calculating dates for every activity.

My father never carried weapons. He did not slay animals because he was not expected to do so. He was calm and always spoke gently. He was so religious that I never saw him get angry. Other than that, he watched after God's *safu* so that the laws would not be broken or overlooked; hence everybody could live up to his or her expectations. He taught others to act in the right way.

His other duty was to make sure the animals intended to be slaughtered for festivities had nothing wrong with them; animals that have spots, that are lame, or that have any defects cannot be killed for festivals. The animal chosen to be killed must also be uncontested, with no other claim of any sort made on it. If it is to be bought from someone, the seller shouldn't be a person accused or suspected of murder, theft, betrayal, rape, or any other crime.

I had such a good father and I was proud of him. Many people, especially my schoolmates, were envious of me. Girls of my village wanted to marry me. Some of them even fell in love with me. My father told me that the first *Qallu* descended from heaven and was found among the Matari clan; *Qallu* is said to be the son of God.

I grew up in a beautiful and high-minded society in which everything seemed good and balanced. Balance is the mercury of my society's morals. I didn't encounter any problems with others until I went to school. The world was perfect for me until then. It was in school that for the first time I saw people who not only didn't speak my language, but people who hated it. We were not allowed to speak our language in school and had to learn to speak Amharic, the national language of Ethiopia. Learning and understanding Amharic was very difficult for me. And understanding academic concepts in Amharic was another problem. I was facing two interrelated issues: not only would speaking our mother tongue, Afaan Oromo, result in severe punishment, but mispronouncing, misspelling, or misreading Amharic would as well.

I was dismissed from school many times, but thanks to my uncle who worked in the government, I managed to complete my education. Those in town who spoke Amharic despised us from the countryside; they said we were poor farmers who didn't know anything other than following our cattle. But I had even bigger problems. The Amhara used to tell me that my father is a priest for Satan. I would never speak a word in response because I knew the consequences. For this reason, I kept quiet—quiet as the dead—and now I think that is why they spoke however they wanted. They have the power to speak and I have only the right to listen. They have freedom to speak, freedom to name, and freedom to define who we are. I cannot speak for myself. I cannot name myself. I cannot name my experience and I cannot define who I am. If I tried to do so, they would laugh at me and demoralize me. But in spite of all this, thanks to my uncle, I managed to complete my secondary school and enter university.

One beautiful Friday morning, three months after I arrived at Addis Ababa University, I left my dormitory to go to class. I was a freshman and I didn't know much about the campus. A dark, thin, tall young man was speaking in front of the university president's office, which was once Haile Selassie's palace.

That day, students were gathered in large groups, shouting and clapping their hands. When I arrived, a man was saying: "Students of Addis Ababa University, I think you know

about our serious problem. It is feudalism and the petite bour-
geoisie. The majority of you are from the countryside. Do your
families have land to till? Have you ever had enough food for
dinner? How many of you had shoes when you were in school?
How many of you have extra pants? How many of you have
pocket money for tea? How many of you are proud of yourself
and proudly speak your own language? How many of you are
proud of your culture and religion?

"Only a few of you, I would guess, manage to live comfort-
ably. Why is that? Is it because our families are lazy? Is it because they do not deserve food and clothes, let alone a happy
life? Is it because they are naturally inferior and are not people
of worth? Answer me, my follow men: it is not!" he answered
himself. "It is not; it is because of this crooked old regime.

"My fellow men, is it just to make the poor weak, to make
them sell their pitiful belongings, in order to add more gold
to their masters' wealth? Is it right that the poor should be
oppressed, exploited, and made even poorer in order to make
the rich richer? Should we, my fellow men, allow this butcher
to keep slaughtering our farmers? I tell you! My countrymen
came here to the palace carrying the yoke of their oxen to
show how much they were subjugated and oppressed by the
feudal system. However, the regime didn't even consider their
request. Instead, it arrested them and put them in jail. Is this
a solution to our farmers' perennial problems? My fellow students, issues of land and nationality are our most pertinent
problems. Thus I proclaim: land for the tillers, freedom for our
nationalities!"

The students gathered shouted back: "Land for the tillers,
freedom for our nationalities!"

The mob grew tense when the campus police came and
dispersed everyone, arresting the speaker who was standing

on the steps that Mussolini had built during his five-year oc-
cupation of Ethiopia.

Angry because of the arrest, the students demonstrated
again the next day and threw stones at the police. The police
responded by firing tear gas, leading to injuries and more arrests.

For the first time, I experienced what I cannot express in
words. I felt as if I could contribute something to the future
of my people. I had read about revolution but I didn't understand what it meant. But now I realized I was at the gate of the
revolution. For the first time I'd heard someone who spoke on
behalf of poor people.

Suddenly I started thinking about freedom: freedom of
speech, freedom of thought, freedom of religion, freedom of nations and nationalities. Oh God! How many freedoms were
we struggling for? And to what extent?

I remembered the saying of Thomas Jefferson: *God who
gave us life gave us liberty*. What an inspiring thought. Rous-
seau then came to my mind: *Man is born free, and everywhere
he is in chains*. This is especially true in Ethiopia, in Oromia,
my nation—a nation that failed at the hands of black colo-
nialists while other African brothers failed under the cruel
yoke of white colonialism. My black brothers struggled against
the whites and won their battle. But for my people, everything
came too late. Too late to even understand their problems.
Too late to remember what happened to my grandfather.

That day changed my life. I was determined to bring down
Haile Selassie's regime. With others I had started a clandes-
tine movement. We began publishing political pamphlets. We
organized workers into unions. We organized youth, we organized women, we organized farmers. We organized all facets of
society and began a true social movement.

As I was coming back from a secret meeting one rainy day, I noticed that somebody was following me. I tried to change my course, but another man came straight for me. I moved to pass him but he blocked my path. I turned back and started running, but it was no use; the man easily caught me.

They threw me into a police car and took me to the station. There, they tortured me. They broke my foot. They gave me electric shocks. The most painful part was when they got tired of beating me, sat me down, and started listening to music. How could they enjoy music while I was suffering? Where was their humanity? What had happened to their compassion? How could a human being inflict such heinous pain upon his fellow man? An endless question for me.

The good thing about prison was that I made a lot of friends. I met Humnecha, an energetic Oromo nationalist. I met many ardent supporters of the revolution. Beyond that, my father came to Addis Ababa for the first time. My father seldom visited towns. Because of his position, it was not wise to leave the area where he lived. The Oromo cultural law requires that a priest must not leave the land he knows. But I was his son. And I was in prison. Even though it was difficult for him, he managed to visit me.

My father had a 600-mile journey. He had to cross a land he didn't know. When he arrived in Addis Ababa, he was amused. He was also confused. He thought everyone in the city was crazy, and when he shared his feelings I grew very sad. I regretted my education; I was his curse. Because of me, he had breached his station. But I'd had no choice.

After being held in prison for a month, I was formally accused of insulting the king and organizing a protest, but fortunately I was released on bail. Many of my friends were also let go. As soon as we were released, we called a general strike in Addis Ababa.

The day of the strike came and people stepped out of their fear and demonstrated in Meskel Square, demanding everything from wage increases to regime change. Everything was done in secret and at last we felt successful.

Then I started to read about the history of different parties and social movements, investigating and analyzing my people's problems. I also consulted with influential Oromo figures like Brigadier General Tadesse Birru and political activist Baro Tumsa.

With the help of these great men, we secretly founded a political party that struggled for the freedom of my people. My idea was to struggle peacefully. I said to them, "Look, we are all Oromo. In Oromo philosophy, things go wrong when there is an imbalance between different people or relationships. For example, if the relationship between a husband and wife is bad, then a problem arises for the whole family. Hence, corruption and social malaise are the result of an imbalanced relationship between humanity, nature, and God. At the most basic level we are tied together with *ayyana*, human spirit; we are all brothers, thus not meant to kill each other, nor oppress or exploit each other."

Humnecha paused before replying. "I believe in the necessity of war, but I don't think anybody deserves to die. I believe it is important to die for a just cause. The only thing we have to do is make sure the cause we want to die for is worthy enough to die for."

The debate continued like that. For me, as a son of *Qallu*, I am supposed to oppose war. But as the sons of Gada members, who give greater value to military and economic achievement, they deduced that war is justified when peaceful means are impossible. Ultimately, we agreed that at all times we should uphold and aspire toward peaceful means.

* * *

A week later, Humnecha introduced me to a student named Muze and invited us both to a meal. At dinner, Humnecha gestured to Muze and said, "Our people have a common problem and need a common solution. Ethiopia needs to be restructured so that it fulfills the needs of its people. Nations have to be free to rule over their own affairs. I hope this makes sense to you, so we can work together to hasten the fall of this old regime."

"I agree, but under one condition: that we don't oppress each other after the regime falls," I said.

"Don't worry," said Muze. "I promise, there will not be oppression after the fall of the oppressor. Comrades never exploit and oppress each other. That is why Karl Marx says: *Workers of the world, unite!* Oppressed people should be allies in their essence."

"I promise," Humencha said.

"I promise," Muze repeated.

We toasted our glasses of wine so that the world might cheer up with us, as if we were signing a treaty. We could have been warriors or, at another time, peacemakers. Maybe destroyers, maybe developers. Since we were young revolutionaries, no one knew what type of leaders we could become when we had a chance to lead.

Muze and I grew close. We met regularly and discussed everything together. In a short period of time he became my best friend next to Humnecha. We ate together, laughed together, and dreamed about revolution together.

Muze was from the northern part of Ethiopia and his family eked out a living as farmers. He was the son of a priest like me, but in a very different way. He said his people were oppressed because of their language.

\* \* \*

That summer, some of my friends gave up hope and took up arms against colonialism, which Muze and I were unhappy about.

While we were busy organizing people toward this goal, the army secretly staged a coup and deposed the king, snatching the revolution and its fruit from us. The soldiers were the ones who were beating and imprisoning us; in a nutshell, they were the right hand of the emperor. Yet, overnight they became "revolutionary" and took our mantle.

We were surprised to hear it when they formed the transitional military council called the Derg. Soon it became apparent that the military junta was simply another phase of oppression. But within three months they responded positively to our first demand—"land for tillers"—and many of us thought this was a great victory.

The military also promised to tackle the problem of recognizing our nationalities, and I was hopeful even though many of my friends were still saying it was simply a pipe dream. Many former revolutionaries lost hope and soon labeled both me and the new government as enemies, embarking on armed struggles against some of my friends and the new government officials.

The military government responded by killing people indiscriminately. Whoever was suspected of being their opponents were killed. Even Muze and I were accused of supporting and giving cover to antirevolutionaries, and we were arrested.

However, one of my relatives in the revolutionary army bribed the right politicians, so we escaped the harsh punishment others were facing. The day after we were released, I heard troubling news on the radio. It had been almost three years since Humnecha headed into the forest to prepare for armed struggle, and he had now become a rebel leader in the area west of Oromia where he was from.

The military government decided to take serious measures against the rebels. After sending a special task force to western Oromia, they poisoned the meals of the rebel leaders. Everyone died except for Humnecha, who hadn't eaten much. Still, he fell quite ill and was taken to a hospital, and once his health improved he was imprisoned in Finfinne. After I heard this news, I feared it was my turn to be thrown in jail, given their knowledge that Humnecha was my close friend. Muze likewise grew fearful as his friends in the north intensified their struggle.

One evening soon after that, my uncle called me and said that some policemen were looking for me and Muze, so we had to leave the city. We departed around midnight, disguised as farmers, after gathering our belongings. First we went to Awasa and from there to Yabelo, where my family lived. But we stayed in town because going to my family's house would have been too dangerous.

I managed to get a message to my father and he came and took us to the country, disguised now as shepherds. We spent the night outside our huts and in the early morning we left my home village for the broiling desert.

Three times we were detained and asked for identification. Luckily, my father had procured the necessary papers, and we continued our journey leading our cattle.

After a week we reached the Kenyan border. I told my father to turn back and promised him that I would head to a refugee camp and then eventually to Europe or America.

I kissed him and he left me crying as I called back for him.

Muze grabbed my arm and said, "Are you mad? What are you doing? If they catch you here, imagine what they will do to you. Don't be a fool!" I went quiet as my father departed, my gaze on the border. I prayed in my heart, *Please, God, if it is Your will, let me return to my home in peace.* I knelt and kissed the ground. Then I stood and walked slowly to the border. Farewell, Oromia.

We crossed the scorching Didi Galgalu Desert and after a day reached Marsabit. Then we proceeded to Nairobi. In Nairobi we met our African brothers who shared our nationalities. Muze insisted that it was useless staying in Nairobi talking about war, liberation, and the dictator Mengistu. He wanted us to join our comrades and fight to the end. After some discussion we decided to become part of the liberation front.

At that point, Muze and I separated. I saw him off to Mombasa, and from Mombasa he headed to Sahel and joined the northern liberation army. I returned to Nairobi and stayed there for a few weeks. I then went back to Borana to join the fight there. Soon we were able to liberate some territory. Our influence extended across the north, where we got remarkable support from the people. We were advancing and before long seized significant areas to the south, east, and west of Oromia.

In the fall of 1988 I was severely injured and had to leave the battle zone. I was taken to Marsabit Hospital and then to Nairobi before I was strong enough to head to Europe. As soon as I arrived in Germany I enrolled in the university, and I received my MA in philosophy in 1992.

A month after my schooling ended, I went back to bring the wisdom of the West to my "underdeveloped" homeland. I was desperate to see my family. As soon as I arrived in Addis Ababa, I tried to connect with my old friends but could not get ahold of anybody. So I traveled to Borana to visit my family.

I reached my family home just after midnight, without any neighbors seeing me. My family was happy when they found me in better health. I gave them European clothes and shoes and everybody was very excited. Then my father said, "Enough, let's go to bed and talk in the morning; you must be tired."

So tired that I developed a fever that very night. After a couple of days of recuperating, I walked around the village in my father's overcoat so that nobody would recognize me.

The village was exactly the same as it had always been. When I left, there had been no electricity, no clean water, no school, and no clinic—after all these years, there was still no basic infrastructure. For months I stayed there unnoticed.

While life went on pleasantly, one day the army suddenly swarmed down from the north, making their way through my homeland, leaving us overnight with the familiar sensation of fear. They were led by our own men. They banged on the doors. They broke into our house. In the middle of the night, three more soldiers pushed their way into our home, smashing things with their boots.

"Out, everybody, to the fields!"

Trembling, we all got up and headed out into the chilly dawn. My father and my mother, my sisters and my brothers.

"Out! Out!" the shouting continued. "Out to the field!"

"What about Waaqoo?" my mother whispered to my father.

"They do not know he is here."

"Maybe he should hide?" Mom suggested.

"No, no," said my father, "they will surely find him."

"But if we keep him hidden in the back, perhaps no one will see him. I am sure we can hide him safely."

"No, no," my father repeated. "It's dangerous. Better he goes with the rest of us."

Yet there was no time to argue. "Out! Out!" the shouting went on.

They were still there, rounding up all of the men, women, and children. I went to the empty field where my family was gathered. Many memories of the field washed over me, including a happy one: the tree in the middle was where my father used to tell me stories about the creation of earth and heaven, the split of Horo into Hora (Adem) and Hortu (Hawwe)—the formulation of Gada and how it led humanity to peace. The field where I had spent so many happy hours of my childhood playing with the village girls. But also a field where in the past regime, people from the surrounding villages had all gathered for meetings. Where we were told what to do and how we should behave. Where we were instructed to speak only in Amharic. The field where we were taught to speak, to write, and to think only in this foreign language. Where a phrase publicly spoken in our mother tongue brought a slap on the face from the lords or their Oromo collaborators. It was where I was told by my grandfather how others prostrated before the Abyssinian priest and were baptized and shown a change in heart by the will of God, by the unrestricted ministry of this priest, and we were saved from the sin of the ages, now acting in holiness and righteousness.

They came with their heavy rifles. They came dragging some men behind them. The men with rifles distributed themselves among the crowd. A soldier here, a soldier there, and everyone felt the alien presence close to his skin, everyone felt the gnawing concern digging into his soul.

Their leader climbed up on the platform and slowly turned his eyes over us, over the sea of faces all around him.

"Comrades," bellowed the leader, "behold the antipeace forces! They are here with us. They are in us. They are our enemy. They are against the peace and prosperity we have in our blood. Now take out your identity cards."

Everybody began taking out their ID cards except the young boys, girls, and women. Soon, soldiers with rifles came straight at me and shouted, "Show me your identity card!"

I showed them the ID I had brought from Germany. They were not able to read it so they took it to their leader and whispered to him. He studied it for a long time and told one of the soldiers to bring me to him.

"Comrades," he cried, "behold the antipeace elements! Here is the one we were looking for; here is a member of the antipeace forces in your midst." They brought me to the platform.

My mother shouted: "He is my son and he is not antipeace! He grew up and was educated here! He is Borana; he is an Oromo!" They didn't hear her and my brother took her away.

Then I went to the leader and said, "Look, I am from Germany and I just arrived back—that is why I don't have a local ID card. I was born and raised here."

"Why did you come from Germany? To fight us?"

"No, no, just to help my people, to serve them."

"Ah, you mean that we are not helping them. Take him away!"

They brought me to a detention camp in Yabello, where I learned that they had also arrested my father, one of my brothers, and many other people from the village.

In the morning, my mother and my sister came crying. I told them that we were safe, and to not worry too much about us. I had read in the newspaper that Muze had a good position in the new government and I thought he could help me. I asked my sister to track him down.

After four days, Muze arrived and intervened in our case, and we were released from prison. We were accused of supporting the antipeace forces, but Muze made sure we became known as propeace supporters. Muze stayed a day with us and then invited me to see him in Finfinne.

A week later, I went to visit him. He told me how he had gone to Sahel, Eritrea, and then to the free land of Tigray where he became one of TPLF's prominent leaders. Then he returned to our present case and said, "Look, you are wrong; I don't know why you want war. Things are not like yesterday. All that we were struggling for is now in the hands of the people. It is time to think about development. Let us eradicate poverty. Let our people eat three times a day. That is what we have to do."

"Muze," I said, "I know you have done a great job; I admire your commitment to creating a democratic political system after all these years of war. I must thank you and your comrades for your painful struggle for our freedom. But I am afraid that you're now stifling dissent and kicking out all of the other political parties. How is that democracy?"

"We don't have any other options."

"If we do not compromise, there won't be any political tolerance, and without political tolerance, there is no democracy. Democracy is nothing without appreciating different opinions."

"That is not the case, my friend. If there is no peace there is no democracy, but let's forget these dirty politics."

That night, Muze invited me to dinner at a five-star hotel

in Addis Ababa. We had an excellent meal complemented by very good whiskey. When I asked for the bill, he said, "Do not worry, it has been paid."

I asked him, "Who paid for it?"

"The government," Muze said with a laugh. "How was life in Europe?"

"It was not good, you know. Every time you are in somebody else's home, you feel strange. You have a home but you do not feel at home because you are not in your own culture. You are cut off from your roots. So I made up my mind to return to my homeland with the skills I learned in the West. But then I was accused of being antigovernment and detained for silly reasons, which makes me question my decisions."

"So you regret coming back?"

"When I came back here I had great hope. I wanted to invest and establish a good school and hospital in my hometown. But all of my dreams have evaporated like the morning mist."

"You better go back to Europe. I know you love your country but that doesn't matter anymore. You should leave as soon as possible."

Five days later I flew to Germany, where I soon learned that my ex-friend Muse, the new Ethiopian finance minister, had two billion dollars in Swiss bank accounts.

When I discovered this, I realized that my forty years of struggle had ended in nothing. Maybe struggle is not good. Maybe struggle is a curse! We all carry the agony of a congested heart. My agony, my people's agony.

# ABOUT THE CONTRIBUTORS

Lyse Ishimwe

**SULAIMAN ADDONIA** is an Eritrean-Ethiopian-British novelist. His novel *The Consequences of Love*, short-listed for the Commonwealth Writers' Prize, was translated into more than twenty languages. He currently lives in Brussels where he has launched a creative writing academy for refugees and asylum seekers, along with the Asmara-Addis Literary Festival (In Exile). *Silence Is My Mother Tongue*, his second novel, was long-listed for the 2019 Orwell Prize for Political Fiction.

**MIKAEL AWAKE** is a writer based in Brooklyn, New York, who was born in Boston to Ethiopian parents. His fiction has appeared in *McSweeney's*, *Witness*, and *Callaloo*. He is currently an assistant professor of creative writing at Lafayette College.

**GIRMA T. FANTAYE** is an Ethiopian writer based in Addis Ababa. In 2007, Fantaye cofounded Ethiopia's leading political weekly newspaper, the now defunct *Addis Neger*, which was shut down due to government pressure. In 2013 he published a collection poetry in Amharic, *Yetefachewun Ketema Hasesa (The Quest for the Lost City)*, and his debut novel, *Self Meda (Fields of Queue)*, was published in 2014. He is currently working on a new Amharic novel.

Chris Frampton

**REBECCA FISSEHA** is the author of the novel *Daughters of Silence* (Goose Lane Editions), which was a *Quill & Quire* magazine breakout debut of 2019, and was selected by Margaret Atwood for the 2020 gritLIT Festival Spotlight Series. Her short stories, essays, and articles have appeared in *Selamta*, *Room* magazine, *Joyland*, *Lit Hub*, and *Medium*, and her plays have been produced in Toronto, where she currently lives.

Naima Green

**HANNAH GIORGIS** is a writer who splits her time between Brooklyn, Washington, DC, and Addis Ababa. The daughter of Ethiopian immigrants, she is a staff writer at the *Atlantic*. Her work has appeared in the *New York Times Magazine*, the *New Yorker*, the *Lifted Brow*, and *Pitchfork*.

**LELISSA GIRMA** is a writer who has lived in Addis Ababa his entire life. He has worked as a columnist and contributor to several local newspapers. He has published five books in Amharic, three of which are collections of short stories.

**MERON HADERO** was born in Addis Ababa and immigrated to the United States when she was a child. Her work has appeared in *Best American Short Stories*, *McSweeney's Quarterly Concern*, the *Iowa Review*, the *New York Times Book Review*, *ZYZZYVA*, and others. She has previously been a fellow at Yaddo, the Ragdale Foundation, the MacDowell Colony, and is currently a 2019–2020 Steinbeck Fellow.

**SOLOMON HAILEMARIAM** was born and raised in Addis Ababa. He is the author of a number of works including *Love and Anxiety*, *The Search*, *The Priest and His Son*, *Once the Climax Is Over*, *None of Your Business*, and *The Young Crusader*. He is the president of PEN International's Ethiopia Centre and has taught at Addis Ababa University and New Generation University College. He was the recipient of the inaugural Burt Award for African Literature.

**MAAZA MENGISTE** is the recipient of fellowships from the Fulbright Scholar Program, the National Endowment for the Arts, and the Arts Writers Grant Program. Her debut novel, *Beneath the Lion's Gaze*, was selected by the *Guardian* as one of the ten best contemporary African books and was named one of the best books of 2010 by the *Christian Science Monitor* and the *Boston Globe*. Her second novel, *The Shadow King*, was published in September 2019.

**CHERYL MOSKOWITZ** (translator) is a US-born poet, novelist, and educator living in London. She has been producing English translations of the poems and stories of Bewketu Seyoum since 2007; they have been published in *World Literature Today*, *Prairie Schooner*, the *Manhattan Review*, and *Modern Poetry in Translation*. In the UK she runs projects for Creative Translation in the Classroom. Her own books include the poetry collection *The Girl Is Smiling* and the novel *Wyoming Trail*.

*Muluken Asrat*

**ADAM RETA** is a short story writer and novelist. He published his debut collection of short stories in the mideighties and published his second short story collection, *Mahlet*, in 1989. Since then he has authored five short story collections and four novels, including the 932-page opus *Yesenebet qelemat*. He was born in Addis Ababa West and currently resides in Canada.

**HEWAN SEMON** (translator) is a student of Ethiopian history.

**BEWKETU SEYOUM** is an Ethiopian poet, novelist, and essayist who was born in Mankusa in 1980. He attended Addis Ababa University where he studied psychology. Seyoum is the author of four volumes of poetry, two novels, two collections of short fiction, and numerous essays. He is currently a writer in residence and research scholar at Chatham University in Pittsburgh.

**MAHTEM SHIFERRAW** is a writer and visual artist from Ethiopia and Eritrea. Her work has appeared in *Callaloo*, *Prairie Schooner*, Poets.org, the *2River View*, *Luna Luna Magazine*, *Diverse Voices Quarterly*, and *Numéro Cinq*. She received the Sillerman Prize for African Poets for her poetry collection *Fuchsia*, and has written two more collections, *Behind Walls & Glass* and *Your Body Is War*. She currently teaches at Pacific University's low-residency program.

**TEFERI NIGUSSIE TAFA** is a prominent Oromo novelist, scholar, and filmmaker. He was born in Arsi, Bekoji. He is the author of the award-winning collection *The Secret Death of Abba Gada*, and has published dozens of articles in international academic journals. He has also produced films such as *Qondalticha*. He was an IIE-SRF visiting fellow at Norwich University in Vermont from 2017 to 2019. He is currently an adjunct professor at University of Northwestern in St. Paul, Minnesota.

 **LINDA YOHANNES** is an Ethiopian writer from Addis Ababa. Since discovering her love for literature and the written word as a young girl, she has written poetry, fiction, and nonfiction. Her work has appeared in *Prufrock* magazine, *Jalada Africa, Brittle Paper*, BBC Radio 4, *Ethiopia Insight*, and is forthcoming in *Transition* magazine. She is passionate about Ethiopia and intends to live the rest of her life there.